PENGUIN BOOKS
HOSTEL ROOM 131

R. Raj Rao was born in Bombay and now lives in Pune where he is professor in the Department of English, University of Pune. Two of his books, *BomGay* and *The Boyfriend* (the latter published by Penguin India, and translated into French and Italian), are regarded as cult classics. His other books include *One Day I Locked My Flat in Soul City* (short stories), *Slide Show* (poems), *The Wisest Fool on Earth and Other Plays*, *Nissim Ezekiel: The Authorized Biography*, *Ten Indian Writers in Interview* (edited), *Image of India in the Indian Novel in English* (co-edited), *Whistling in The Dark: Twenty-One Queer Interviews* (co-edited). Rao is a pioneering Indian academic who runs a course on queer literature in his department.

Hostel Room 131

by

R. RAJ RAO

PENGUIN BOOKS

PENGUIN BOOKS
Published by the Penguin Group
Penguin Books India Pvt. Ltd, 11 Community Centre, Panchsheel Park,
New Delhi 110017, India
Penguin Group (USA) Inc., 375 Hudson Street, New York, New York 10014,
USA
Penguin Group (Canada), 90 Eglinton Avenue East, Suite 700, Toronto,
Ontario, M4P2Y3, Canada (a division of Pearson Penguin Canada Inc.)
Penguin Books Ltd, 80 Strand, London WC2R 0RL, England
Penguin Ireland, 25 St Stephen's Green, Dublin 2, Ireland (a division of
Penguin Books Ltd)
Penguin Group (Australia), 250 Camberwell Road, Camberwell, Victoria
3124, Australia (a division of Pearson Australia Group Pty Ltd)
Penguin Group (NZ), 67 Apollo Drive, Rosedale, North Shore 0632,
New Zealand (a division of Pearson New Zealand Ltd)
Penguin Group (South Africa) (Pty) Ltd, 24 Sturdee Avenue, Rosebank,
Johannesburg 2196, South Africa

Penguin Books Ltd, Registered Offices: 80 Strand, London WC2R 0RL, England

First published by Penguin Books India 2010

Copyright © R. Raj Rao 2010

All rights reserved

10 9 8 7 6 5 4 3 2

ISBN 9780143064466

Typeset in Sabon by Eleven Arts, Delhi
Printed at Anubha Printers, Noida

For Thomas Waugh

PART I
18 MAY 1982

1

I am on my way to the police station in a state of high turbulence. The only transport I can find is a three-wheeled Badal—a cross between a sedan and an auto-rickshaw. There are four other men with me in the back seat, and two in the front. All strangers, thankfully, all of them middle-aged. I am seated just behind the driver and can see the back of his head. He has curly, unoiled hair specked with dust, and has tied a handkerchief around his neck to prevent his collar from getting sooty. A sweaty odour emanates from him. Each time the Badal takes a sharp turn, we fall on each other. Since we take more left turns than right, it's the others in the back seat who fall on me, squashing me with their weight. I am surprised we haven't overturned yet.

We ride for fifteen minutes and then the Badal stops abruptly. I had dozed off, trying to get away from reality, but a tap on my shoulder brings me back. It's the guy next to me. 'Your stop, sir,' he says. Sir? The fellow looks a good twenty years older than me. I ask the driver how much, pay up, and alight dangerously through the right door.

The street is chaotic. Two-wheelers, three-wheelers, four-wheelers, ten-wheelers, all jostle along territorially. It's a marvel we haven't produced a one-wheeler yet. Everyone honks, even if there is nothing to honk at. The traffic conspires with the May sun to make the heat intolerable. I accost a passer-by and ask where the police station is. He replies in Kannada, assuming I know it too. It's only from the direction he points to that I figure out where to go. But, although I keep walking, I don't find the police station.

I decide to ask someone else. However, this time I don't stop the first man who comes my way. I scrutinize faces, playing a sort of game with myself. He knows, he knows not. He loves me, he loves me not. Eventually, I zero in on a guy and try my luck. He wears a pink terry-cot bush shirt over navy-blue bell-bottoms, has buck teeth, a mole on his cheek and chapped feet. But he speaks English, and knows where the police station is.

Now I see the damn thing myself, thanks to the guy's precise directions. But it entails crossing another busy thoroughfare. It's only a small town, but the traffic gives it the look of a big city. We live in the age of hybrids. Three-wheelers masquerading as sedans. Towns masquerading as metros. Attempting to cross the road and get to the other side, I make several false starts before, finally, latching on to a group of people and crossing with them.

At last I've reached my destination. I'm not sure whether to enter the police station, but I do.

2

Inside, a radio is on at full blast, drowning my voice with a Kannada song. I wish it would go on forever, so I don't have to speak. I don't know how to begin, or where. What do I say to the men in uniform?

I move towards the inspector's desk. No one asks me who I am or what I want. The inspector on duty isn't in his seat. My eyes fall on a wooden sign on the desk, shaped like a Toblerone chocolate. It bears his name: K.H. Padukone. There are other things on the desk: a pen-stand full of cheap pens and pencils; a velvet pin cushion with paper pins stuck in it; rubber stamps of assorted sizes; red Rexine files tied with string, holding yellowing, dog-eared papers. There is an empty cup and a saucer made of dirty white china, with the remnants of the inspector's coffee still in it. A fly hovers on the cup's rim, then ventures into it.

The song on the radio is over, but is followed by another after a few squeaky commercials. One of the men sings with the radio. I can't tell if he and his friends have seen me. From their Gandhi topis, I can tell that they are havildars. Can they be so engrossed in the song? Or are they ignoring me? I see one of them drinking from a bottle wrapped in a towel. As he puts it to his mouth and guzzles, I manage to note the colour of the liquid. It looks like Coke, but is probably spiked. After a swig or two, he passes the bottle to one of his buddies who, in turn, drinks and hands it over to the singing man.

A jeep pulls up outside. The roar of its diesel engine alerts the havildars. The man holding the bottle at that moment quickly opens a steel cupboard and hides it. By the time the man who has arrived in the jeep enters, they are all at attention. Savdhan.

Suddenly, one of them becomes aware of my presence and asks me what business I have. His breath smells of booze. I don't answer him. Instead, I point to the jeep-man who has just taken his seat. The badge on his uniform proclaims him to be Mr K.H. Padukone.

But Mr Padukone is occupied with a fellow he has brought along and is holding by the scruff of the neck. The man joins his hands as if in prayer and weeps. A lemon-sized boil sits on his right eyebrow. He bends down to polish the inspector's shoes with his bare hands, then runs his fingers through his hair. The inspector isn't amused by these antics. As the man pesters him with his pleas of innocence, the inspector loses his temper and slaps him. It sounds exactly like a Diwali cracker. The first fataka is followed, a few minutes later, by a second, delivered to the other cheek. The man begins to bawl. The inspector asks one of his drunken havildars to take him away.

3

I am now seated opposite the inspector. He hasn't spoken to me yet, but is busy giving orders to his havildars. As he speaks, he sprays me with saliva. He has a big paunch, which becomes all the more obvious when he sits. It makes him look pregnant. I don't like his features. There's so much flesh on his face that the bones can't be seen. The voice is gruff and terrifying. I suppose it's because of his job. Years of yelling at people is bound to do that to the vocal cords. But the freakiest thing is the way he peppers his speech with English words. His favourite is 'scoundrel', which is faithfully present in every other sentence. But I cannot figure out whether he applies it to the bad guys lodged in the police station, or to his own havildars. He's also fond of coffee, which he pronounces 'caaffee'. And no sooner do the words form in his mouth than his men place a cup before him. As he sips, he looks at me. However, he still doesn't say a thing.

I timidly open my mouth to make my complaint. They call it an FIR. A First Information Report.

They've locked Su up in the house and are probably beating him black and blue. All because he mustered the courage to say that he wished to leave home and vamoose with me. They were outraged. They never imagined that a nice boy from their family could say such things. They attributed it to me. I had corrupted their lad, betrayed their trust. They ordered me to leave the house. But I could not leave without Su. I fell at their feet and sobbed. They had another kid. I had only him. They were unmoved. They kicked me, chucked my things out of the house, and said I had no self-respect. The neighbours gathered in the street to enjoy the tamasha. They were sniggering. Su was nowhere. They had exploded and shoved him into his room the moment he had uttered his audacious words: 'With him.' God knows what they were doing to him this very moment. They could be pulling out his eyeballs.

The inspector drinks a glass of water as soon as I finish. While I was talking, his eyebrows kept tightening and loosening. He tells me he has been in service for over twenty years, but has never had a story this weird. True. There aren't many like me who would go to any lengths for love. But I don't say that to him. The thought crossing his mind probably is: Why am I grieving so much for a friend?

Who advised me to come to the police, he asks. I tell him it was a lawyer, though it was Su's friends, with whom I had insisted on spending the night. In retrospect, it's clear that they saw it as a means of getting rid of me.

But the inspector is unwilling to take down my FIR. It's a family matter, he says. Who am I to interfere? Parents have the right to deal with their offspring in any way they want. If they punish them, it's for their own good. And what do I mean by accusing them of torturing their son? How can parents torture their kids? My allegations are baseless. Besides, I am an outsider. What locus standi does my complaint have? Am I his father or mother or brother or sister? Or uncle or aunt or cousin or nephew or niece? No! So it makes no sense that I should lodge an FIR. It's in my best interests to forget the whole matter and go about my business. I should not waste the officer's time.

I can't say to the inspector that I am willing to shelve my plans of filing an FIR, provided they let me talk to Su just once. He's insensitive and voyeuristic. He wants to know why Su told his folks he wished to go with me.

4

I haven't washed for days. Ever since they separated us, I have lost track of who I am. I hate the odour of sweat, but now it comes from my own underarms in strong whiffs. I visit the haircutting saloon every fifteen days. It's been over a month this time, but I am in no mood to get my hair and beard trimmed. My nails too have grown long. It's just as well this place has no mirrors. Although I'm a narcissist, I'm terrified to look into a mirror. I'm sure I resemble a scarecrow. Is this what love does?

To my horror, I discover that I have worn the wrong socks. It's a mismatched pair: the left one blue, the right one brown. I can't figure out how this has happened. My hair itches. I can feel things crawling in it. I don't know if it's dandruff or lice. I want to scratch my scalp till it bleeds, but I'm in a public place. Only beggars—dirty buggers—do such things in public.

My belly growls. It's like an animal that needs to be quietened from time to time. If I were at home, I would've spanked it to silence it. Even a little slap would do. But if I do that here, I'll be taken for a madman. I can't remember when I had my last full meal. It was probably in Su's house. My stomach is empty, yet I fart—it's the uncertainty of it all.

This police station is rather like a railway station. People come and go and you don't see the same faces again. I can't see any of the havildars who were there when I entered. Their transistor radio with its Kannada songs, their bottle of booze wrapped in a white towel—all gone. I don't see the hoodlum who fell at the inspector's feet either. The earlier set of people has been replaced, almost entirely, by a new set. Most of them are in civil dress, so I can't tell if they are cops or people like me who have come to lodge a complaint. Many of them have the heavy muscular build of policemen, but looks can be deceptive.

I hope Mr Padukone too hasn't vanished, like his men. It's only late afternoon, but the mosquitoes have already begun their rounds. The ceiling fan above the inspector's table has been switched off. They call this town a no-fan station, but I can't think of any place in India where we can do without fans in May.

As if to allay my fears, Mr Padukone is back. A bout of sneezing prompts him to blow his nose into a handkerchief. He then stuffs the wet hanky back into his pocket, without bothering to rid it of the stuff excreted. He tells me the house will have to be searched. This is a bombshell. I'm not sure it's what I want. I ask him if there are other ways of handling the case. Making a telephone call, say. Of course there's no telephone in Su's house, but I have the phone number of his immediate neighbour—it's where I would call him, practically every night. This irritates the inspector. He knows his job and doesn't want nincompoops like me advising him. When an FIR is lodged, the police have a duty to go to the site of the crime and investigate. He is a conscientious officer who never breaks rules.

He calls out to a havildar and asks for a register, which is soon placed before him. As he flips through its pages, I manage to catch the date on which one of the complaints was made: 10 August 1972. So the register has been in use for a good ten years! Mr Padukone starts to write out my FIR without pausing to ask me for details. Maybe his powers of comprehension are good, or maybe I'm a good narrator. Whatever it is, he has understood the case well. After he finishes writing, he reads out the report to me for my approval, which I unconditionally grant.

Then, he shocks me further by informing me that I too will have to go to the house along with the search party. For one thing, I will have to point out the house to them. For another, it is preferable that I see for myself, rather than rely on the search party's report.

When the inspector tells me this, I fart again. I let him know I'm plain scared of going to the house for fear of being lynched. To which he has a ready answer, of course. His men will be around to shield me. What can I say to him in the face of this? I am hardly reconciled to the idea, but I can't manufacture any excuse on the spur of the moment to convince him. So I keep quiet. If I open my mouth to say another word, he might honour me with a fataka slap.

5

It's an old Willys' jeep, ash grey in colour, with the word 'POLICE' painted in black on both the front and rear. The tyres of the aging jeep are bald. Their threading has smoothed out. God knows how may kilometres it has run in search of criminals. How many innocent people has it transported to jail? To the gallows? The jeep has no door, so all we do is hop in. The leather upholstery is torn in places and the cotton stuffing is sticking out. The interior smells of sweat. It is evident that no one sitting in the jeep uses deodorant or talcum powder.

Accompanying me are the driver and two havildars in khaki uniform. One of them sits next to the driver, while the other is with me in the back. We sit facing each other. I don't like his pockmarked face and have a hard time avoiding it. He watches over me as if I were a convict who might jump out of the moving vehicle, Bollywood ishtyle. Or at the next traffic light. The driver starts the jeep with a jerk and we're off.

I'm back on the streets of this hybrid town. A couple of hours ago, I was on these very roads in a Badal. Now, it's a Willys whose driver deserves to be given the Rash and Negligent Driver of the Year award. More than once, he nearly runs over a pedestrian or knocks down a cyclist. At times, I shut my eyes so as not to be witness to his manslaughter. But then, when I open my eyes again, the danger has passed. We've been lucky one more time. The entire journey is a series of hits and misses—mercifully more misses than hits. The only time he actually hits something is when the bonnet of the Willys naughtily taps a cow's posterior. The cow scampers in fright, making for a very comic sight. I suppose it's the man's job that has made him inhuman. As if driving through the narrow lanes of this town weren't bad enough, he has to drive for the police!

The driver pulls over, cuts the engine and reaches for a folded piece of paper in his pocket. I realize it's the address of the house we are going to. This is painful business. I wish I were not part of it. But it's too late now. I should have thought of the repercussions before venturing on this foolhardy act. The driver isn't sure where the house is. He addresses me in Kannada and asks me if I know. I find it strange. He's a resident of the town, while I'm a visitor. It's I who should be asking him. Besides, we are driving through streets I've never seen before. Never walked on, hand in hand, with Su. I hazard a guess and tell the driver where to go, although I really have no clue. He follows my instructions and only gets farther from the house, finally throwing his hands up in despair. The driver and the havildars stop someone to ask directions. In no time, I find my bearings. I spot the Rambo theatre where we had seen the film *Shaan*, Su and I. I remember it was a late-night show and we had walked back home in the moonlight. Then I see the Basava restaurant, famous for its Udipi fare. We would bide our time here, drinking cup after cup of south Indian coffee just so we didn't have to go home.

The trio in the jeep try to say something to me. I nod and mumble an answer to what sounds like a question. It's clear from their tone and expression that they don't like what they're doing and hold me responsible. They must think I'm crazy, to lead them to someone's house just to check if their son is fine. Since they blabber continuously, I wouldn't be surprised if it's curses and abuses they are heaping on me.

We are now on the street that directly leads to his house. My heart begins to pound. Some neighbours, whom I recognize, run out of their houses to investigate. My palms are wet with sweat, as is the nape of my neck. I'm terribly scared. I don't know if I am doing the right thing. Besides, I'm completely alone in this, while the rest of the universe is on the other side. When the jeep stops outside the house and the driver switches off the engine, my blood pressure rises even higher.

6

Wonderful communication, here in small towns. Modern means, like the telephone, are no match. Word has already gotten to his folks inside that we're visiting, and now they come to the front door to receive us as viciously as they can. Don't ask me how they found out. Did one of the neighbours' kids, who spied the jeep wending its way through the narrow alley, run up to the house ahead of us and inform them? Or did the sly Padukone send a secret messenger to prepare them? Or was it plain intuition? I don't know. What I do know is that now they're here, all the menfolk of the house who, just a short while ago, had conspired to separate me from Su and thrown me out of the house, bag and baggage.

I see them all—the slimy uncles and the slippery father. Their eyes are daggers as they look at me and refuse us permission to enter the house, screaming at the top of their voices. It is my audacity that outrages them. How dare I drag the police to their house, in their town—I, a mere outsider! The havildars try to reason it out with them, but the crocodiles do not budge. Where are the orders, they ask? The havildars are mere chaprasis of the police force. Even if the commissioner of police were to come to their doorstep and

R. Raj Rao

request that their house be searched, they wouldn't let him in. They rattle off the names of one or two local politicians to show that they're powerful people.

The havildars are cowed. They order me into the jeep and we drive back to the police station. As the jeep begins to move, the father and two uncles call me a harami, a mother-fucker, a sister-fucker.

When we arrive at the police station, they're already there, gesticulating madly as they speak to the police inspector. They probably came on their scooter and that's how they had got here before us. No sooner do they spot me than they gnash their teeth in rage and begin abusing me all over again. The inspector lifts a hand to restrain them, but they can't be tamed. They bury me in foul language. At one point, they even charge at me menacingly. Their murderous hands indicate that they're ready to throttle me. The inspector puts his foot down. Pretending to be on my side, he tells them in no uncertain terms that they can't do this. I'm as much of a citizen as they are, I'm entitled to turn to the law for help, just like them. I suspect he winks at them after saying this, so as to let them know he doesn't mean what he says, that he is only putting on an act.

We're back at the house. I struggle to hold back my tears. I can't believe that there was a time, not so long ago, when I was welcome here. When the residents of this house, his father and mother and sister, would speak to me ingratiatingly, be glad that I was eating with them, lodging with them. What is it, then, that has brought about this overnight transformation, this sudden change of heart? What is it that has brought me to this pass? Perhaps I'm at fault too. Maybe I should never have gone to the cops. I'd never dreamt, not even in my ugliest nightmares, that a day would come when I would be here with policemen.

The havildars prod me with their batons as we go from room to room looking for Su. The uncles and the father are quieter now. The dose administered by the inspector has apparently worked. This is a large haveli-style house. I am discovering for the first time just how many rooms and anterooms there are. He could be hidden in any one of them. I'm pining for a glimpse of him, but I'm tongue-tied. The law is in the picture now and I am the plaintiff. The havildars and the uncles keep talking to each other in Kannada. I have no idea what they are saying.

But where on earth is Su? It's clear he's nowhere in the house.

We reach the kitchen. His mother and sister, Sneha, stand by a wall, next to the red Burshane gas cylinder, dazed. They can't believe what's happening. Tears trickle down the mother's cheeks as she stuffs one end of her sari's pallu into her mouth. The havildars act like circus clowns. They open an iron kitchen cabinet to see if he's concealed there.

The fragrance of tea tickles my nostrils. I turn to check out the gas burner. Sure enough, the mother is brewing her special Lipton's tea. Real Mysore tea, unlike the CTC tea we drink elsewhere. The tea ready, she pours it out into four steel cups. Three of them are for the cops in the house and their driver. This is true Indian hospitality. The cops may be there to ransack the house and insinuate that the occupants have kidnapped their own son, but they will not be allowed to leave without a glass of water or a cup of tea. Where else in the world does one encounter such subversion of propriety?

The havildars accept the tea as their prerogative. There's no expression of gratitude on their faces. They're accustomed to receiving gratuitously. One of the havildars runs out to call the driver, while the other pours his tea into a saucer and slurps. Soon, the other havildar and the driver join him. As they guzzle the tea, they make loud, appreciative, guttural sounds.

But what about the fourth teacup? It's for me. And as the mother hands it to me, I dither. 'Take it,' she admonishes me, almost pushing it into my hands. Her moist eyes speak:

R. Raj Rao

'You've been here, under our roof, so often and we always looked after you as if you were our own child. And today, this is how you repay us? You bring policemen to our door, as if we were common criminals? Does a son treat his ageing parents so spitefully?'

The teacup in my trembling hands and the mother's wounded expressions unnerve me. As I sip, I realize how right the lady is and how wrong I am. They're human, like me. And here I am, trying my best to prove that they're monsters. Perhaps, if I were a father, I would have done exactly the same. Is the enmity, then, only a veneer, while deep inside there's an abiding love?

Our next destination is Su's room on the first floor. The moment we enter, I see the two beds, each covered with a mosquito net. It's my turn to cry, if only I were allowed to. One bed is his. The other, until yesterday, was mine.

But right now Su isn't in his room either. I had the impression they'd house-arrested him here or in one of the haveli's other rooms, like the heroines' fathers in Rajesh Khanna films. I'm wrong. All the rooms have been thrown open to us, and he's conspicuous by his absence.

This causes both the family and the havildars to turn against me: the family, for making a false allegation and screwing up their reputation; the havildars, for wasting their time. Victory provokes his uncles into yelling at me in their baritone voices. Nothing can stop them from assaulting me with a grinding stone or a kitchen knife, should they choose to. Inspector Padukone isn't here and his havildars are good-for-nothing buffoons. They prod me with their batons again and lead me towards the jeep outside. 'Chalo,' they manage to say in Hindi. This house is so large it seems to take forever to get to the front door.

During our long journey, the uncles and the havildars, as usual, converse in Kannada. I try to guess what they're saying, but give up. Kannada isn't the world's easiest language.

Suddenly, the father, only five feet tall, takes out a wad of notes from his pocket and coaxes it into the palms of the havildars. I'm stunned. Is this a bribe? Does it mean that Su was indeed in the house when we arrived? That they had bought time by blocking our entry and sending us back to the police station?

7

The havildars are pleased. My FIR has proved lucrative for them. My presence notwithstanding, they count their booty. The driver observes them and demands his share. Reluctantly, they part with a few rupees. That doesn't quite satisfy him. He refuses to drive until they pay him exactly a third. They have no option but to comply, but with the currency notes also come abuses for holding us to ransom.

The havildars having been bought by my foes, I expect them to turn hostile towards me. Instead, they are friendlier. They stop at a wayside kiosk for vada pav and I'm nonplussed when they offer me a plate. With the vada pav, comes free advice. 'Why taking so much tension, sir?' they ask in their brand of English. 'Go home, go home.' I feel like asking them for my share of the booty too.

I have a splitting headache, so the vada pav is welcome even though it's clammy. Somewhere amid the squalor of the town, I unexpectedly catch a glimpse of the setting sun. The evening peak-hour traffic on the streets suffocates us all. One of the havildars has a coughing fit. I instinctively reach for the window behind me, then realise my folly—the damn thing is a jeep with a tarpaulin top and polythene windows.

I think of him, my soulmate. Where is he at this moment? Will I ever have him in my grasp again, as I did throughout this past year? Intense emotional pain has a way of becoming physical. I feel an ache in my heart as if it were being sliced into two with a penknife. I shut my eyes and doze off within seconds. There is no anaesthetic as effective as sleep. For the rest of the journey, I slumber and dream. Su beckons to me. I bring my face close to his and we kiss.

My reverie breaks when the jeep screeches to a halt. I'm disoriented. It takes me a few seconds to recall where we are and why. We're at the police station again. Before long, I see Inspector Padukone, and things come back to me, hitting me in the face like a sledgehammer. We're lucky he's in his seat for once. The havildars go up to him directly and give him their report. The inspector looks at me as a schoolteacher would at an erring child. I'm about to soil my trousers. Drops of sweat form on my moustache.

What saves me from his wrath is the telephone. It rings, he picks it up and sprinkles his conversation with sumptuous helpings of English words: 'Oh yes . . . Why not, why not . . . The boy . . . We will see what to do with him . . . Come here with the boy . . . Sorry for the unnecessary inconvenience . . . We will open a separate file . . .'

It's obvious the call is from them, my hosts. But I can't ask the inspector. 'None of your business,' he might retort. I have a new worry now. Will they turn vindictive? Inform my folks, who don't have a clue as to where I am? I gather the courage to open my mouth and mumble something to the inspector: 'What now?' I expect him to scream, slap me even, but he doesn't. 'They will bring the boy to the police station and we will record his statement,' he says, lighting a cigarette.

My heart skips a beat. I'll be seeing Su again. I'm sure when he sees me, we'll hug each other tight. That's all I want—to hold him in my arms.

8

I am taken to a sort of waiting room and made to wait. An overpowering stench of hooch greets me. The smell takes me back to adolescence, when I would roam the red-light areas of Bombay in an exploratory mood. Prostitutes would call out to me from their cluttered cages on both sides of the street. I'd see movies at the Alfred and the Super, off Foras Road.

A burly havildar leads me to this room now, on the express instructions of Inspector Padukone. He's not one of the chaps who had travelled with me to the house. There is no dearth of men in this police station. There are a dozen or so fellows in the room. Among them, I spot the man with the lemon-sized boil on his eyebrow. He's quiet now, unlike earlier, but there is another drunk who goes on babbling. He thumps his chest and says he's king of the world. The havildar silences him. It's easy—all he has to do is give him one of those fataka slaps.

When the havildar leaves, I feel uneasy. Luckily, the door is left open. I half-expected to be locked up in this room with the others, like a fully-fledged criminal. I am the newest entrant here, open to being ragged by my seniors. They do not actually rag me, but one of them, with an unwashed stubble on his chin, stares at me so hard he gives me colic. I try to return his gaze, but give up halfway. As for the others, I can't bear to look at them. They are an unsightly lot, and almost all of them stink.

Sitting cooped up in this room isn't flattering. The men here are the scum of the earth, the dregs of society. If not pickpockets, they're bootleggers; if not beggars, drunkards. What am I doing in their midst? I—with a master's degree and a lecturer's job in a college. It does my morale no good to be brought down to their level. Couldn't they have seated me in the inspector's cabin? I have a good mind to get up and run away. To hell with my complaint!

It's dark now. The tube-light comes on. Several small insects hover around it. A mammoth lizard tries to capture them. Its hunger isn't quelled, no matter how many insects it gobbles. I am grateful to the lizard for helping me kill time with its antics.

What's my crime? For me, love is a full-time job. One is a lover exactly the way one is a scientist or a doctor or a lawyer. Or an engineer. Love is a calling, a vocation—and I am not the first man to discover it. Besides, who on earth will love Su like that? No mother or father or sisters or brothers or uncles. No wives. Forty thousand wives can't make up my sum.

And yet, here I am in this hellhole, at the end of my tether, inhaling germs from the creep next to me who coughs like a TB patient.

9

Time doesn't pass easily in this room. The lizard has disappeared behind the tube-light. I gaze at my wristwatch. The seconds tick away, each seeming like an age.

I am restless. I stand up and begin pacing the room. The man with the stubble still looks at me, but my colic has subsided. 'Sit down,' one of the inmates says to me. It's the guy with the lemon-sized boil. I want to tell him to mind his own business, but I keep quiet. I walk diagonally across the room, skirting the rotting wooden table in the centre. On reaching the far end, I turn back. I make more than a dozen such rounds and then, on impulse, stroll out of the room.

There are the usual havildars, but no one challenges me. I walk towards the inspector's cabin, and suddenly stop in my tracks. My heart starts beating so loudly I can actually hear it, the din of the surroundings notwithstanding. My tongue goes dry. Sweat gathers on my eyebrows.

There he is—Su—in the striped blue shirt I had bought him, flanked by his two carnivorous uncles who are hungry for my flesh. They are in audience with the inspector. I try to catch his attention, but he refuses to yield. I can't tell if he really hasn't seen me or is pretending. He looks tense. I feel like running up to him, grabbing him. The carnivores speak animatedly to Inspector Padukone. He, on the other hand, is quiet except for the occasional monosyllabic reply to the inspector's questions.

None of them knows I'm watching them. If they find out, all hell will break loose again. What poison are they pumping into the inspector's ears? Why can't they call me and let me expose their lies? This is patently unfair. I am made to sit with outlaws, while they are comfortably perched in the inspector's cabin, cups of tea before them. I feel like a fish out of water. All of them speak the same language and are from the same town.

He, my heart-throb, looks devastating, even in his devastation. Those are the very lips I had kissed till yesterday. I want them again, as I do his whole body. Desire engulfs me as I observe him from an unbridgeable distance.

I keep massaging my fingers out of nervousness. The sound of cracking knuckles reassures me. I return to my prison cell and make an attempt to sit still among my fellow captives. We are the wretched of the earth. My stomach continues to make growling noises. What does it expect me to do? Order a masala dosa from the police canteen?

Idly, I look at my watch again and follow the movements of the second hand. It provides me with concrete proof that time is actually passing. Sad songs keep buzzing in my head. *Kya se kya ho gaya bewafa tere pyaar mein*. Look what's become of me because of my love for you, you unfaithful bastard.

I hear a havildar call out and imagine it's me he wants. It isn't, but I stand up and walk out of the room all the same. I return to Panorama Point, from where I can spy on my opponents. The old sods are still there, but my yaar has been whisked away. Having gotten him to say his lines, they have sent him offstage.

One of the uncles writes something on a sheet of foolscap paper supplied by the inspector. He struggles with his pen, pausing every now and then as words fail him. He seems to have trouble with his grammar, knowing not a thing about clauses and verbs. I am tempted to run up to him, snatch the sheet of paper from his hands and tear it into a thousand bits. That's a fit way to deal with his falsehoods. That he's lying is clear from the fact that he looks up to the inspector for help and makes him dictate virtually every sentence. I'm deeply pained by Inspector Padukone's treachery. He pretended to be on my side, but is now wholly on theirs. Do I see them slipping currency notes into his hands as well?

10

I don't know when my feet take me back to the room. Nor when I lean my head against the wall and doze off. But now I am tapped on the shoulder by a havildar who is here with summons from the inspector. I stand up, yawn, flex my arms and comb my hair. I am desperate for another cup of tea. I see a chai-wallah with an aluminium kettle in one hand and a dozen dirty china cups in the other. It's amazing how he manages to balance them. I have half a mind to accost him and snatch a cup, but decide against it at the last minute. The guy is obviously here to serve the cops, not nuts like myself. It may be against protocol for me to hail him and pay him a few coins in exchange for his syrupy tea.

I see Inspector Padukone at his desk and forget all about the chai-wallah. Having wreaked havoc, the carnivores seem to have left. The inspector looks up from his desk, sees me approaching, and motions me to come over quickly.

My heart palpitates and I quicken my pace. I am offered a seat and asked to sign a bunch of papers. I start reading each one of them, but this infuriates him. I'm wasting his time, he scolds me. They're routine papers that I have to sign anyway because I have lodged a complaint. I don't believe him, but I quickly put pen to paper.

The thought that's uppermost in my mind is: What now? I came here in order to be united with Su. But he's nowhere to be seen. Where is he? Did he bear me out? Admit that his folks had locked him up all night?

But these are not questions I can ask the inspector, given his present demeanour. He frowns and looks at me as if I were a meddlesome intruder. All because of the machinations of those carnivores. I finish signing and return the sheaf of papers to him.

Then, somehow, I gather the courage to ask him my question after all: What did Su say? The inspector looks me in the eye and seems ready to strike. My heart races like a bullet train. I'm almost certain I'll be slapped. I'd never imagined one of those Diwali firecrackers would be coming my way too. However, something comes over the fellow, and he restrains himself in the nick of time. A fuski fataka.

That he desists from slapping me doesn't mean that he's eager to answer my question, of course. He fiddles with the papers on his desk so he can avoid giving me a reply. But when his eyes momentarily meet mine and he sees me looking askance at him, he is trapped. He knows that my question cannot be evaded any longer.

'The boy denied he was locked up in his room or tortured by his parents, as you claim in your complaint,' he grudgingly says. 'I have his written statement.'

The answer doesn't satisfy me. What written statement is he talking about? I saw only the carnivores putting pen to paper, not him. But even if he did, I want to know the circumstances in which he wrote it. Was it under duress? Did the carnivores tutor him? Besides, if he did give them something in writing, why can't I read it? But to expect Inspector Padukone to answer another question, or to show me the written statement, is to wish for a rocket ride to the

R. Raj Rao

moon. Expecting another bothersome question, he gets up and leaves.

11

I know that the matter has come to an end, and that I must leave. But I continue to hang around for goodness knows how long. It's as if, all other strategies having come to naught, I want to evoke the inspector's sympathy. Throw a tantrum, as a child would when it has been denied its favourite toy. I'm a dying man and Inspector Padukone is my piece of straw. But that's how I see it, not he. Who am I to him? The very sight of me angers him as he returns to his desk after yet another break. He had all but forgotten me, but here am I again.

'You there,' he contemptuously addresses me. 'I will protect your interest if you leave the town immediately. Or else I can get you into trouble for lodging a false complaint. I can detain you under various sections of the IPC.'

'I was only waiting for you, sir,' I nervously begin, swallowing the lump in my parched throat, 'to ask if there are any other formalities to be completed before I go.'

'No other formalities,' he snaps. 'Just make straight for the bus stand with your baggage and take the first bus out of town. As I said, if you obey my orders, I will protect your interest.'

That seems to be one of his favourite phrases. Protect your interest. He probably picked it up from the police books, together with all the other jargon printed there. Does he really know what 'protecting my interests' means? It means rescuing my darling from his tyrannical folks and uniting him with me. But that clearly is not something that he, or anyone of his ilk, is capable of doing.

'I can't leave the town right away, sir,' I lie. The prospect of going away without Su seems unbearable. It's like returning from the burning ghats after cremating a loved one. 'I have a reserved ticket for the Mahalaxmi Express, the day after tomorrow.'

'Then cancel it,' he harshly retorts.

'I . . . I don't like bus journeys,' I stammer. 'They give me a headache. I prefer to travel by train.'

'Shut up and don't argue with me,' the inspector thunders. 'I have already warned you. If you get out of the city at once, I will protect your interests. Otherwise, I will inform your parents.'

This is a new threat. First, it was the threat of jail. Now, it's my parents. How would the inspector know whether or not my parents are alive even? But I must admit that the mention of my folks unsettles me. All the guy has to do is pick up the telephone and make an STD call to Bombay and I'll never be able to face them again. For all I know, the carnivores have already parted with the number which they must have extracted from their son. I decide it's time to quit.

'Thank you, sir,' I mumble as I walk out.

Just then, something comes over the inspector, the protector of my interests. The prick's conscience pricks. 'Listen, son,' he calls out to me. 'We are not your enemies. We are your well-wishers. It is not right on your part to interfere in other people's family affairs. This is a small town and people here are conservative. Do you realize how much shame you have brought upon the family by taking the police to their home? They have to live in that very locality, with those very neighbours, for the rest of their lives. You are a boy from a good family. Go back to your parents and concentrate on your studies.'

The inspector's compassionate words stimulate my tear duct. 'I will do as you say, sir,' I mutter through tears and mucus, and walk out into the open.

12

The streets, as usual, are full of traffic. People seem to be on the roads for no apparent reason, walking in all directions just because there are roads to be walked upon. There is utter chaos at street corners, with everyone coming in everyone else's way. The silence zone signboards on the pavements seem like a practical joke the municipality is playing on its citizens.

I go wherever my legs carry me. I spot an Udipi restaurant and stop for a plate of idli-sambar, only so I might stay alive. As I emerge from the restaurant, a group of bejewelled, sari-clad hijras arrives and pesters the manager for money. Strange they should be here after dark—like me, they must have had a bad day. There are four of them in the group, one very tall and evidently the leader, the others shorter. Though dressed like women, they have rugged manly faces with traces of stubble. The shorter ones are flat-chested, but the leader has boobs. Are they falsies? I realize I know so little about hijras.

Their presence proves to be such a diversion that I decide to follow them as they go from shop to shop, begging. Everywhere, they announce their presence by a series of fataka claps, reminding me of Inspector Padukone's fataka slaps. Most shopkeepers oblige the hijras by parting with small change. Not out of charity but, I suspect, to avoid a scene. A few niggardly ones, however, shoo them away and are appropriately taught a lesson. The leader, the tall one with the nose-ring whom I think of as Begum Sahiba, lifts her sari and vehemently thrusts her pelvis in their faces. The others follow suit. This makes the traders go red with embarrassment and, before long, they fall in line, opening their treasuries to dig out a few coins.

The hijras abandon their begging when the cluster of shops ends. The bustling trading street gives way to a dimmer, sleazier one. Here, the hijras squat on the ground to light beedis and count their booty. Begum Sahiba tucks away the currency notes in her blouse for safekeeping. The shorter hijras trust her blindly. There's much bonhomie among them—the bonhomie of the dispossessed. Their silver anklets jingle in the darkness.

I'm strategically stationed several feet away from the hijras. There are soliciting women too in the vicinity, and there are their male clients, furtively negotiating. I expect the hijras to have a hard time procuring customers, since they have to compete with the women. Why should straight men patronize them when there are real cunts available? However, I'm wrong. A young man wearing dark shades approaches them and sneaks into the darkness with Begum Sahiba, who swings her buttocks as she walks with greater exaggeration than Su. A while later, another hijra is picked up, leaving the other two to fend for themselves.

The amorous hive of queen bee Begum Sahiba and the other hijras and prostitutes is destroyed when a havildar arrives on the scene and blows his whistle. Everyone scampers in fright. If the cops lay their coarse hands on these dispensers of pleasure, they'll eat the forbidden fruit to their hearts' content before confining them to dingy prison cells with no one to bail them out. In the blackness of the night, I lose sight of Begum Sahiba and her troupe.

I amble along to the cycle shop, where I'm parked for the night.

13

I dream.

Su and I are in the Vrindavan Gardens. It's late evening. Fountains spring up all around us. Electric bulbs light them up, painting the water. Like Holi. Then, of course, there are flowers. They bloom in abundant varieties. Roses and marigolds, jasmines and chrysanthemums, lilies and daffodils—they're all there. Their colours and fragrances intoxicate us and fill our hearts with joy, as balloons are filled with air. Fireflies dance. We are happy.

We locate a little temple at the far end of the garden and offer homage to the deity, although we don't know who it is. But god is god, no matter what. He accepts our prayers and promises to keep us together in life and in death. I pluck a rose and give it to my sweetheart. He does the same. Our love is solemnized. We have realized the meaning of paradise.

PART II
DECEMBER 1978 TO
MAY 1982

---

9 December 1978

1

Siddharth, tall yet small, as if on stilts, wouldn't have been on that excursion to Pune had his parents, both Bombay-based medicos, not invited him to join the group. They were journeying to Khandala on a jaunt with other medicos. Someone dropped out at the last minute, there was an extra ticket and Siddharth's father persuaded him to go with them. 'You don't have to stick with us throughout,' he said. 'When you're bored, you can always buy another ticket and return to Bombay or proceed to Pune to meet your friends. You will save more than half the fare.'

The argument convinced Siddharth who rarely saw eye to eye with his folks. Any talk of saving money always appealed to him. Although he'd finished his MA over a year ago, he was still jobless. However, when, amid all the singing and frolicking of his parents and their buddies (which embarrassed him a good deal), their train reached Khandala, he refused to alight. 'I'll continue to Pune,' he told his dad matter-of-factly. 'Idiot, your ticket is only up to Khandala. At least get off and buy another ticket for the rest of the journey,' his father chided him.

Siddharth did as he was advised, but the train that had brought them to Khandala had left by then. He had no choice but to wait for the next train, that came an hour or so later.

He had a hard time turning down the pleas of the group to spend the day with them, and bid his parents adieu. 'I'll join you next time,' he said lackadaisically.

An hour later, Siddharth was on his way to Pune. Two hours later, at two o'clock in the afternoon, he was at his destination, and he trekked from Shivajinagar station to the Engineering College Hostel nearby, where Farouq lived. Farouq was an Iraqi friend of Ram's who had come to Pune to study engineering. When they'd bumped into him at an ice-cream parlour on Bombay's Marine Drive a couple of weeks ago, he'd assured Siddharth that he could stay with him in his hostel room whenever he was in town. 'My room partner is a cool guy from Belgaum,' he had said. 'I'm sure he won't mind a pal visiting for a day or two.'

Even then, Siddharth recalled, the words 'Belgaum' and 'cool guy' had caused his heart to flutter. He had a preference for small-towners. Now, as he plodded on towards the hostel, he wondered if it would be Farouq or his room partner who would be there to receive him.

A few minutes later, Siddharth found himself knocking on the door to Farouq's room. Room 131, E Block. It wasn't locked from the outside, which meant that at least one of them was inside, if not both. The door did not open instantly, making Siddharth suspect that the lazy buggers were having their siesta. But then, he heard the latch click from within and the door was flung open.

Subhan Allah, Siddharth exclaimed to himself as he set eyes on Sudhir for the first time. He had never seen a guy so slender and youthful in all his twenty-three years. It was as if his fantasies had suddenly come true.

Sudhir was inelegantly dressed in a banian and striped pyjamas. He had a textbook in his hand, with his index finger serving as a bookmark. Siddharth observed him closely. His skin was the colour of wheat. He had straight hair and a silken, hairless face with no signs of a beard. His eyes were

R. Raj Rao

deep set, and on his left cheek was a beauty spot. He did not speak but merely blushed as Siddharth introduced himself as a friend of Farouq's, and held the door open as Siddharth entered with his rucksack, considering it is his duty to be courteous to his room partner's guest.

2

Siddharth did not hold his horses. Even as he initiated a conversation with the chap, he initiated sex. His method was to slip his hand into the other's while they talked—a hand could work wonders.

What's your name? Where are you from? Belgaum, isn't it? Farouq told me about you. I met him in Bombay. He's a good friend of Ram's and Ram's a good friend of mine. Ram too studied at the Engineering College and did Metallurgical Engineering like Farouq—that's how they know each other. Farouq praised you a lot, said you have a wonderful nature. How old are you? Twenty? You don't look a day older than sixteen! What do your parents do? Oh, your dad is a doctor? So is mine. They're in Khandala right now, on a picnic with their doctor-friends. I was supposed to go too, but I came to Pune instead. My destiny brought me here. I was destined to meet you. We've known each other for barely half an hour but it seems like I've known you all my life. I think, in our previous birth, we must have been Laila and Majnu. You agree? How many brothers and sisters do you have? Only one sister? What does she do? Do you like Pune or do you miss Belgaum? I've never been to Belgaum. Would love to go there. Will you take me along in the summer holidays? Belgaum has a nice climate, no? What are you reading? There was a textbook in your hand when you opened the door. Oh, come on, don't be so studious! You want to top the exam or what? Me? I did my MA in English and secured a first class by fluke. You want to improve your English? Oh, sure, I'll devote as much time teaching you how to speak English as you want. I'm your yaar, I'm fida on you! Count on me as you would on someone you consider yours.

All along, as he spoke, Siddharth let his hand sit in Sudhir's. His heart palpitated. Sudhir didn't disengage himself from Siddharth's grip, making the latter confident. It was likely he relished it too. Siddharth kneaded the hand as an Indian housewife kneads dough. This caused both their hands to perspire a little, the perspiration serving as glue. Occasionally, he rubbed his index finger against Sudhir's palm. This was an obscene gesture that meant, 'I want to screw you.' This too Sudhir did not object to, allowing his room partner's odd guest to do whatever he pleased with his hand.

The coupling of hands made Siddharth hard. As his shirt was tucked in, the bulge was there for the world to see. Siddharth glanced at it from time to time and hoped that Sudhir would observe it too. He did not catch him spying it though. Throughout the conversation, not once did Sudhir lower his eyes. Yet it was unlikely that he hadn't noticed. Siddharth would have given anything to figure out the state of Sudhir's dick. But, as his striped pyjamas were very loose (they seemed to be his grandfather's), this wasn't knowledge that would come his way easily. Once or twice, Siddharth got bolder and brought their conjoined hands to rest on Sudhir's crotch. At such times, however, the latter was scrupulous enough to move them away slightly, to rest on his thigh.

Other than that, Sudhir managed to make tea for Siddharth on an electric stove.

Siddharth freshened up in the hostel bathroom and convinced Sudhir that they should go for a Bollywood film.

R. Raj Rao

3

No sooner had Sudhir locked the room and deposited the key on the ventilator for Farouq, than Siddharth grabbed his hand again. No one saw it as a transgression. On a campus that was predominantly male, where most boys came from India's smaller towns, it was a common sight. That they were no longer boys but young men wasn't a thought that vexed them. None of them viewed what they did as sexual— it was merely masti. If anyone interpreted their actions as proof of their gayness, they would accuse him of possessing a sinful mind. Siddharth loved that, because he could use it as an alibi. While he maximized his thrill, wasting not a single moment as he clung to his yaar while they walked, it conveniently passed for dosti. That was the beauty of living in India.

They reached the main gate of the hostel and stood at the crossroads, trying to find their bearings. Pune was neither Sudhir's city nor Siddharth's. But Sudhir had a better sense of direction, and it took him just a few seconds to determine which road led to Deccan Gymkhana. He pointed out a few landmarks to his yaar, such as the Pataleshwar Caves and the Jangli Maharaj Temple. Siddharth tried to make small talk, but he was running out of ideas. He had already exhausted all he could say to Sudhir at the hostel itself. In any case, conversation wasn't his real aim. But the mouth had to keep working in partnership with the hands, as long as they were in public.

People there were aplenty on this arterial road (Junglee Maharaj Road) of the city built by the Peshwas, especially since it was dusk. Their presence notwithstanding, Siddharth put an arm around Sudhir's shoulders, while Sudhir put his around Siddharth's waist. At first, it was just half the arm, up to his elbow. But, gradually, Siddharth had his whole arm, up to his shoulder, around Sudhir's neck as if it were a python.

This automatically brought their cheeks very close and, from time to time, taking advantage of the crowd on the street, Siddharth let them touch. Following Sudhir's example, who wore only bush shirts, Siddharth quickly un-tucked his shirt to conceal his hard-on. Sudhir noticed it but refrained from commenting. However, he put his foot down when his obscene friend tried to use his python-like hand to unbutton his shirt and squeeze his nipples. 'Log dekhenge,' he whispered. People will see.

They reached Deccan Gymkhana and checked out the movie that was playing at the city's most trendy theatre, the Natraj. It was *Amar, Akbar, Anthony*—a jubilee hit, now almost in its hundredth week. Sudhir wanted to see the film simply because he hadn't seen it. But Siddharth vetoed it on the grounds that the auditorium was full and that the film dealt with threesomes. How could he carry on his nefarious activities if there were people to their left and right? Walking past the PMT bus terminus, they came to the ramshackle Deccan Talkies and bought tickets for *Satyam, Shivam, Sundaram* for which there were no takers as it was a rerun—the hall was more than half empty.

'I prefer romance to comedy,' Siddharth told Sudhir in a bid to justify his actions as, torch in hand, an usher led them to their seats.

4

Only the last four rows of the auditorium were full. A few men lay evenly scattered on the other seats, but the seats hadn't been allotted to them. They moved upfront of their own accord, preferring privacy to comfortable viewing. Taking his cue from them, Siddharth nudged Sudhir and suggested they occupy two aisle seats in the K row, which was devoid of patrons. At first, Sudhir was reluctant to shift.

More so, as the light had already gone out and the commercials had begun. But once again, Siddharth's persistence forced him to relent.

The conditions were now right. It was dark and there was no one in close proximity. Siddharth undid Sudhir's fly and shoved his hand into his trousers. For the first time since they'd met, exactly four hours ago, he was sure that Sudhir was stiff. This gladdened him. He continued to fondle his sweetheart, in no hurry yet to get past the underpants. But then, to his astonishment, it was Sudhir who took charge of his hand and guided it, stopping only when his dick popped out of his trousers. Even in the dark, Siddharth could see that it was beautiful. It was coffee-coloured, on the larger side, and the foreskin had rolled back. Siddharth bent down to kiss the moist dick-head. He ran it along his lips, the way ladies apply lipstick, smacking them every now and then.

Truth to tell, both men were so absorbed in the business at hand that they did not know when the movie began. All they saw was that Zeenat Aman hid one side of her face in her sari because it was brutally charred. As long as the hero, Shashi Kapoor, did not see the disfigured side, he was fine, but the moment his eyes caught sight of it, he was repelled. Siddharth thought it was an excellent metaphor for man's latent schizophrenia. And then, of course, there were the ubiquitous songs. One was about Krishna asking Yashoda why he was coffee-coloured, while Radha was white as milk. Another was the title song.

Much to Sudhir's discomfiture, the lights suddenly came on at the interval, even as Siddharth played with his equipment as if it were a car's gearshift. He hurriedly shoved it into his trousers, uncertain whether anyone had seen. But it continued to shamelessly protrude, making it impossible for him to go out to pee or drink a cup of tea. Siddharth left him in his seat while he went out to buy a packet of popcorn from which they jointly ate.

During the second half of the film, which seemed to go on forever, Siddharth was surprisingly still. Sudhir wondered what had come over him. He gave him surreptitious glances, but could not figure out why his yaar had suddenly lost interest. Even the love scenes in the film failed to stimulate him.

If there was one thing that Siddharth did not want to do, it was to wank Sudhir in the auditorium. It amounted to pre-empting his plans for the night—their honeymoon night—as they slept in Sudhir's single bed, despite Farouq's presence. He was seized by an intense desire to fuck. He was the husband, Sudhir the wife. He would screw him through the night, entangle himself in him as a dog entangles itself in a bitch and, in the morning, it was possible that his seed would travel and lead to the flowering of a child in Sudhir's womb. They would go to the Jangli Maharaj temple and get married.

While these stupidities preoccupied Siddharth, *Satyam Shivam Sundaram* came to an end and they got up with everyone else to leave.

5

They went to the Poona Coffee House for dinner, where they ordered palak paneer and six tandoori rotis. Siddharth may have been able to live on love and fresh air, but the meal was insufficient for Sudhir who was used to consuming regular thali meals—comprising chapattis, rice, vegetables, curd and the Maharashtrian amti or varan—at a mess nearby. However, he cherished the experience of eating at the famed PCH. Besides, palak paneer and tandoori rotis were dishes he had hardly ever eaten before, and they tasted extra nice in the company of his lurid friend. Not that the friend wasn't concerned about his going to bed hungry. When, after the movie, he'd asked Sudhir where he ate his dinner and learnt about the mess, he had given him the choice, even

R . Raj Rao

volunteering to eat at the mess himself although he hated rice plates which he found spicy and oily. But Sudhir did not want the others at the mess, many of whom were from his hometown, to see Siddharth. Their affair was a felony and he wouldn't be able to face the boys if they asked him who Siddharth was. Hence, he opted to eat at the restaurant, in spite of Siddharth's warning that it would only be a mini-meal because he was broke.

After the meal, Siddharth ordered two cups of tea. Tea was an excellent appetite killer. A cup of steaming hot tea after lunch or dinner filled the extra space in the belly that the food itself had been unable to. Later, they nibbled the saunf that the waiter left at their table along with the bill, preferring to pay up at the counter so that they could skip giving him a tip.

As they got out of the restaurant, Siddharth belched. When Sudhir told him they could walk back to the hostel instead of taking a bus, he said he couldn't agree more. 'Even our thoughts are starting to be the same,' he exclaimed. He observed that Sudhir, while walking, swung his hips exactly like Zeenat Aman in *Satyam Shivam Sundaram*.

In order to make his yaar happy, Sudhir took a detour and they headed for Fergusson College Road that ran parallel to Jangli Maharaj Road. Although he did not spell out his motives, Siddharth thought he understood why Sudhir did that. Fergusson College Road was much quieter at this late hour than Jangli Maharaj Road. Here, they could fearlessly resume their pornographic acts as they trekked back home. As was his wont, Siddharth did not waste a single minute. His arm became the python again, coiled around Sudhir's neck. In turn, Sudhir involuntarily put his arm around Siddharth's waist. The popular saying *Jab miya biwi razi toh kya karega kazi* came to Siddharth's mind.

The tranquil road became deserted when they walked past Café Ramsar and came to the police grounds. Siddharth paused and looked around. They were under a huge banyan tree. He brought his lips to Sudhir's and they began to smooch. It was a full-blooded kiss, Siddharth inserting his tongue into Sudhir's mouth and allowing it to reach his throat. Sudhir felt stifled. His tongue had no place in his own mouth! Soon it started to wrestle territorially with the invader, who was stronger. The two tongues played judo with each other for a long time, giving their owners a taste of the food they had just eaten. At last, the marauding tongue withdrew and the two men started to walk. They were as hard as Cuddapah stone, but Pune slept early and almost no one came face to face with them as they ambled towards the hostel.

6

Farouq was already in bed, snoring, when they entered. Sudhir switched on the light, but he did not open his eyes. Instead, he drew the blanket over his face and continued to sleep soundly. Siddharth was ready with the pleasantries he would have had to exchange with Farouq. He had no interest in him beyond that—Middle Eastern men not being his scene—so it came as a relief that conversation with Farouq could be deferred till morning.

Siddharth followed Sudhir to the washroom at the far end of the corridor. Taking advantage of the darkness in which it was plunged, he hugged Sudhir tight and turned their mouths into boxing rings once again. But then, suddenly, they heard students approaching and Sudhir quickly shoved Siddharth aside. He frantically motioned him to get out of the washroom, not wanting his hostel mates to see the two of them in it simultaneously. Siddharth got out in the nick of time, just as the boys entered in a group. They looked at him, then saw Sudhir in the washroom, and said in Marathi, 'Kai re, kai karto?' What man, what are you doing? It puzzled both Sudhir and Siddharth. Was their remark general—the sort boys like to make—or had they actually got wind of what the two of them were up to?

The episode temporarily put Sudhir off. This guy, Siddharth, whom he would not have known from Adam until a few hours ago, was shaming him before boys with whom he lived and studied. What right had he to do that? To make matters worse, he had to leave the washroom without completing the tasks that had taken him there in the first place—brushing his teeth and emptying his bladder.

But then, all was forgotten when they switched off the lights and cuddled up in bed. Certain that Farouq was secure in the land of Nod, Siddharth pulled Sudhir's pyjamas down and lubricated his backside with vanaspati oil. He felt the pink flesh at the borders of his arsehole throb. Rubbing his own dick-head with oil, he turned Sudhir on his stomach and mounted him. His dick became a piston fitted closely inside the shaft that was Sudhir's arse and moved up and down, forwards and backwards. Chuk chuk gaadi, chuk chuk gaadi. It was excruciating. The only thing that stopped Sudhir from howling was the fear of waking Farouq. Even in his agony, he raised his head periodically, like a lizard, to ensure Farouq wasn't looking. And then the meek Sudhir inherited Siddharth's semen, which he pleasantly felt spilling into his inmost recesses in short squirts. What he did not realize was that his own semen had discharged too. It lay there on the bed-sheet in a little pool of white, like spilt milk, slowly seeping into the mattress. He wanted to clean up, but if he opened the door to get to the bathroom, Farouq would surely wake up and be witness to their misdemeanours. Nor did the Engineering College provide washbasins in hostel rooms. So there was no option but for Sudhir and Siddharth to lie on the cum. All night they were sticky, but Siddharth loved it. At dawn, he screwed Sudhir again, before dropping off into a slumber.

When Farouq's timepiece buzzed at six, he was surprised to see two guys in the adjoining bed. And when he discovered that one of them was Siddharth, whom he'd met in Bombay, he almost fainted from shock.

10 December 1978

7

Sudhir wasn't by his side when Siddharth's eyes opened. He looked at his watch—it was half past nine. The radio was on, broadcasting the news in English. Sitting up in bed, he saw Farouq with his ears glued to the radio. He was short, with bushy eyebrows, and looked much fairer than he had in Bombay.

'Morning, Farouq,' Siddharth greeted him.

'Oh, good morning, good morning,' said Farouq warmly, turning around. 'So glad to see you. I had no idea you were coming to Pune. I was surprised to see you fast asleep in Sudhir's bed when I woke up this morning.'

A shudder passed through Siddharth's spine. He remembered how they had . . . Did Farouq see that? Luckily, it was winter and they had been under their blankets.

'Well, Sudhir has left for college,' continued Farouq. 'I'll get you some breakfast.'

Siddharth thanked him and went to brush his teeth. Last night's bathroom adventures suddenly came back to him. He was engulfed by a wave of sadness. Why had Sudhir left so abruptly? Couldn't he have woken him up?

Returning to the room, towel in hand, he saw Farouq applying butter and jam to slices of toast.

'Hey, how's Ram?' he inquired.

'He's fine,' Siddharth replied. 'Has a well-paying job with Larsen and Toubro. He sends you his regards.'

As Siddharth munched the toast and sipped the tea that

Farouq had prepared, he chatted him up, asking him all the questions he had ready in his armoury. Farouq answered but was distracted from time to time by something on the radio. It was news, apparently, of hostilities between Iran and Iraq.

Soon after breakfast, Farouq too left for college, handing over the key to Siddharth and instructing him to leave it on the ventilator when he went out.

'I know,' Siddharth affirmed. He was about to ask Farouq if he knew when Sudhir would return but refrained, remembering, before it was too late, that discretion was the better part of valour.

Scarcely had Farouq left the room when there was a knock on the door. Siddharth's heart raced. Was it his yaar? It wasn't.

Instead, it was one of his classmates. 'Sudhir ahe ka?' he asked in Marathi. And when he discovered that Siddharth wasn't a Maharashtrian, quickly switched over to English. 'Myself, Ravi. Ravi Humbe,' the stocky, curly-haired chap said. 'I'm a classmate of Sudhir's. Me coming from same place as Sudhir. Belgaum city. Sudhir not in room?'

When Siddharth told Ravi Humbe that Sudhir was in college, he made himself comfortable and continued his tête-à-tête.

'Who are you?' he inquired, not intending to be rude. 'How you knowing Sudhir?'

Siddharth realized that this was a question that would come his way again and again in the Engineering College Hostel. He had to manufacture a stock reply that would satisfy the inquisitive.

'Mr Ravi Humbe,' he confidently began. 'What gives you the impression that I'm Sudhir's friend? I don't know Sudhir. I'm a friend of his Iraqi roommate, Farouq. You know Farouq?'

The trick worked. Ravi Humbe was confused. How could an Indian have an Iraqi friend? He apologized and took his leave, scribbling a note for Sudhir. 'Keep off my boyfriend, you bastard,' Siddharth jealously felt like telling him.

8

They went for a long walk to Sambhaji Park, a hot cruising spot in the city. Then they went elsewhere. Their limbs took their usual positions. Either their hands mated or their arms became pythons. As their legs exercised, so did their mouths. Sudhir told Siddharth a little about himself.

I come from a small town, Belgaum. It's actually in Karnataka, but there are a large number of Maharashtrians there. We speak Marathi at home but we also know Kannada. We are just one brother and one sister. My father is an Ayurvedic doctor. He has two clinics—one in the house and another in town. My mother, she's just a housewife. In our community, women don't work, you see. We're Marathas—it's considered below our dignity to send our women to work. Although my sister is doing her BA, that's only to pass time. My parents will soon get her married and that will be the end of her studies. We live in a large wada house in the Shahapur area of Belgaum. My father constructed the house on a plot given to him by his father. The house has two storeys. I have my own room on the first floor. I'm not very good in studies. True, I got into the Engineering College, but that was on a reserved seat. No, no, I don't mean the backward category. I told you, we're Marathas. But there are special seats reserved for students from Belgaum, because Belgaum is a disputed area. It's actually in Karnataka but the Maharashtrians in the city, who are in the majority, want it to be in Maharashtra. When we were small, the Shiv Sena fought for our cause. There were riots in Bombay—you have probably heard of them. How old were you then? Ten? I was about seven. It was because of them that the government kept some seats in engineering and medical colleges reserved for us. There are six boys from Belgaum in my batch. Ravi Humbe, who met you, is one of them. In our house, there are two big portraits in the prayer room—one of Shivaji Maharaj, and the other of Balasaheb Thackeray.

They had reached the Chaturshrungi temple and began ascending the hill. Siddharth thought he heard someone in a passing auto-rickshaw shout, 'Homo!' Ignoring the remark, he asked Sudhir to continue. But Sudhir suddenly lost interest. Acceding to his request, they decided to skip the temple of the goddess Chaturshrungi and climb to the top of the hill. Here, settling down on a stone bench, they viewed the city like a pair of birds in flight. They stayed there until sunset descended on the hill. Then they walked back, their feet dusty and aching.

The door of E 131 was locked when they arrived. But the lock was swinging on the door, indicating that Farouq had closed up and left barely a moment ago. Stepping inside the room, Siddharth lay on the bed and passed out. Sudhir, meanwhile, busied himself with the myriad chores that characterize a hosteller's life: cooking, cleaning, attending to his books.

When Siddharth woke several hours later, it was already past midnight. His stomach growled, for he had gone to bed hungry. Sitting up in bed to take stock, he saw that the lights had been switched off and that Sudhir lay by his side, asleep. On the other bed was Farouq, who snored like a generator-car. Dismissing the thought of waking Sudhir to ask for a biscuit or a slice of bread, he mounted him instead—to fulfil his other hunger on the last night of his stay. But this time, he exhaled loudly as he pumped so that Sudhir, who was a light sleeper, rose and stuffed cotton into his nostrils to silence him. Neither man enjoyed the sex as much as they had the previous night. Repetition is known to breed monotony. But Sudhir was also tense because Siddharth had gone to bed without setting the alarm. If they did not keep an eye on the clock, he was sure to miss the train. Nor could he remember by which train Siddharth was travelling. He knew that the morning trains to Bombay, like the double-decker Sinhagad Express and the Deccan Queen, left pretty early. But when he tried to ask Siddharth in the midst of all their lovemaking, his question was brushed aside with the flick of a hand. Sudhir's last memory, before they fell asleep again, was of Siddharth pressing his mouth against his and wanting it to stay that way.

11 December 1978

9

As if to torment his lover, Sudhir tuned in to Vividh Bharati at 7 o'clock in the morning. A couple of years ago, he had seen the film *Aandhi* where the hero, Sanjeev Kumar, tells the heroine, Suchitra Sen, that the best way to wake him up is to switch on the radio. This is because she chooses a particularly bizarre way to get him out of bed— she takes his finger and dips it into a cup of hot tea! Sudhir suddenly remembered the scene now, as he saw the clock, and realized that both the Sinhagad Express and the Deccan Queen would have left.

At this hour, only old, sad songs played on Vividh Bharati. And while switching on the radio bore fruit, causing Siddharth to open his eyes and blink, the songs themselves made him wistful. Tears trickled down his face, which he wiped on the pillow. Separation from Sudhir was imminent—in a couple of hours, he would be on his way to Bombay, while Sudhir would remain in Pune, biding his time at the Engineering

College Hostel with the likes of Farouq and Ravi Humbe. He would be leaving his heart behind, and it hurt already— as if his heart had been severed from the rest of his body with a knife. As one sad song followed another on the radio, Siddharth indulged in his emotions. Why did he have to leave? Why couldn't he stay on at the hostel forever? His trance was broken only when, returning from the bathroom, Sudhir saw that he had still not risen from bed and tickled the soles of his feet with his fingernails.

Siddharth sat up in bed, guffawing. 'Stop it,' he playfully reprimanded his sweetheart.

'Your train has already left, Mr Bombay Boy,' replied Sudhir.

'I'm going on the Hyderabad–Bombay Express. It leaves at 9.50 a.m. What time is it now?'

Sudhir shoved the clock in Siddharth's face and he saw that it was already a quarter to eight. He jumped out of bed and hurried through his ablutions, getting dressed in fifteen minutes flat. After that, he stuffed his things into his rucksack, even as he sipped his tea. All at once, a new anxiety took possession of him. Where he was grief-stricken, not sure when they would meet again, Sudhir seemed to go about his business perfectly calmly. Did that mean he wasn't involved with Siddharth the way our hero was with him? Studying Sudhir, he was horrified to discover that he was readying himself not for the railway station, but for college. Didn't he want to be with him till the train pulled out of the station?

'I have an important Thermodynamics lecture at 9.30,' Sudhir confessed when Siddharth interrogated him. 'I can't miss it.'

However, seeing how unhappy his reply made his yaar, he changed his mind and decided to accompany him to the railway station.

'You are the romantic type, whereas I am practical,' he said, as their lips touched.

10

They walked part of the way to the station, cutting across through the Pune Municipal Corporation's imposing edifice. It being the office hour on a working day, they were unable to find an auto. The streets were full of unruly two-wheelers that hampered movement. Siddharth cast glances at his wristwatch every few minutes. They had dawdled away in the room, exchanging addresses and so forth, expecting the Hyderabad–Bombay Express to be late, as it usually was. But when Siddharth called the station from a public phone just outside the hostel, a voice on the line told him that the train was 'running right time'. Neither of them had anticipated that finding an auto-rickshaw would be so difficult.

Sudhir found his mate exceptionally sullen. He couldn't believe this was the same guy who yesterday and the day before had almost given him a headache with his incessant chatter. At the same time, it flattered him to think that he was capable of making someone so crazy that, as parting loomed, he sank into despair.

'Auto,' Siddharth broke the silence, as he spotted an empty one near Juna Bazaar. They hopped in and, when they settled down in their seats, Siddharth began to cry, much to Sudhir's embarrassment.

'Pune and Bombay are not that far,' Sudhir consoled him. 'You can come here whenever you are free. And I will also come to Bombay sometimes.'

But Siddharth wasn't the sort who could be lulled with promises. For him, seeing alone meant believing. Only when they were actually together again would he be convinced that it was really happening. In the meantime, the only thing he could do to ensure that his beloved stayed in touch was to make him co-dependent in some small way. With this in mind, he asked Sudhir if he needed anything from Bombay. Their

R. Raj Rao

auto was caught in a traffic jam near the State Transport bus terminus and, though the station was barely a couple of minutes away, Siddharth panicked. The Hyderabad–Bombay Express had probably already arrived.

'I need a textbook called *Engineering Thermodynamics* by A.R. Roychoudhury,' Sudhir replied. 'I couldn't find it in the bookshops in Appa Balwant Chowk. Can you look for it in Bombay? I'll pay you later.'

'My darling, you don't have to bother about payment,' Siddharth said, jotting down the title. He resolved to look for it that very evening in the bookshops that dotted Kalbadevi Road. It was bound to be available. Once he got it, he would neatly parcel it to his sweetheart. Or, if he had the money, maybe he would even travel to Pune to give him the book himself. There couldn't be a more wonderful excuse for them to get together again.

Siddharth's spirits soared. They paid the auto driver and hurried towards the footbridge. They got to the platform just in time. The guard had already blown his whistle and the train was pulling out. Siddharth hugged Sudhir and kissed him on both cheeks, his eyes full of tears again. He ran alongside a sleeper coach, ready to jump in. Just then, Sudhir grasped his head and kissed it.

'Don't forget me. Write to me,' Siddharth said, his voice choked with suffering.

11

The train was full, as all trains to Bombay inevitably are. Siddharth had a self-contained window seat by the gangway but he couldn't shield his wet face from the curious glances of fellow passengers. He tried putting on his sunglasses and looking out the window. But suddenly, he burst into tears and had to rush to the toilet where he sobbed and wailed like a professional mourner for a full twenty minutes. The noise of the wheels playing tabla on the tracks was so loud that Siddharth's cries were drowned in it. When he was done, he dried his face and emerged from the bathroom in a state of catharsis.

Upon reaching home, he repeated the exercise, causing his parents to suspect that he had upset his stomach by eating trash. There were no sounds in the bathroom to mask his sobs, though, so he kept the tap running at full force while he cried. That Bombay was experiencing a water crisis was not one of his concerns at the moment. Crying always made Siddharth feel better and so he cried, unperturbed by the thought that it was a womanly activity.

Afterwards, he got dressed and left the house to look for Sudhir's book. Kalbadevi Road, in Bombay's Dhobi Talao, may be lined with bookshops on both sides of the road, but none of them stocked the thermodynamics book that Sudhir wanted. Siddharth was tired of going from shop to shop and repeating the tongue-twisting words, 'engineering thermodynamics', every few minutes. Nor was the author's last name, Roychoudhury, any less taxing. He did it, of course, for love's sake. But even that couldn't stop him from, finally, scribbling out the words on a piece of paper to show to booksellers—at least his mouth would not ache.

An hour later, Siddharth was still roaming the streets in search of the book. Some booksellers offered him substitutes, while others promised to order it for him within a week. But neither of those alternatives satisfied him. If he had to win a place in Sudhir's heart, it was imperative that he got him the Roychoudhury book—nothing less, nothing more. This motivated him to board a BEST bus and go to Dadar, where, like Kalbadevi Road, there was a large number of bookshops dealing in school and college texts.

Here, Siddharth got the book Sudhir wanted.

R. Raj Rao

He felt triumphant as he paid the money and collected the brown paper bag that contained his treasure, double-checking that the title and the author were correct: *Engineering Thermodynamics* by A.R. Roychoudhury.

Siddharth's next destination was the General Post Office. He decided that, the traffic being chaotic, it would take him aeons to get there by bus. So he trudged to Dadar station and stood in a serpentine queue to get himself a local train ticket. Less than an hour later, he was outside the GPO at VT, getting the book wrapped in sackcloth to parcel to Pune. Then he wrote out Sudhir's name and address on the parcel in as calligraphic a hand as he could, got the book weighed and stamped, then had it dispatched.

Siddharth spent the night imagining Sudhir's expression when the postman knocked on his door and delivered the parcel. He was in love.

28 December 1978

12

Siddharth boarded a train with two of his friends from the university—Anthony, a Keralite who dreamed of becoming a Jesuit priest and considered Stephen Daedalus a clown, and Dhananjay, an Indian from Mauritius—for Khajuraho and Varanasi. The trip had been set up long ago and, although he now felt disinclined to undertake the dusty journey to central India (Sudhir being the only thing on his mind), he couldn't back out without incurring the displeasure of his classmates. Reluctantly, he fished out his rucksack again, put his personal effects together and got ready to catch the Calcutta Mail via Allahabad, which left at 9 p.m. His parents went to VT to see him off and gave him and his two companions a host of instructions pertaining to food, water, and safety. Do this, don't do that.

When the train left, both Anthony and Dhananjay couldn't help remarking that Siddharth wasn't the usual, jubilant fellow that he was on campus. He knew they were right, but no matter how hard he tried to disguise his feelings, they somehow showed. One of the things that had cast him into a state of despair was that no letter from Sudhir had arrived since his return from Pune. Why, this guy, whom he was absolutely nuts about, hadn't even bothered to acknowledge the receipt of his parcel. Siddharth had no idea whether he had received the book—for which he'd paid a good 150 rupees—or whether it was lost in the post. These past few days he had constantly been chasing postmen, hoping in vain that a letter from his yaar would finally arrive. The hours immediately after the day's post had arrived were the hardest. He would have to wait twenty-four long hours for a possible change in his fortunes. And now they were going away for a whole week. Which meant that he couldn't even live in the sanguine expectation of receiving a letter in the next day's mail.

Anthony and Dhananjay tried their best to humour Siddharth. They discussed their classmates and professors, bitching about them audaciously. They engaged in banter and tomfoolery. But the smiles and laughter they evoked in Siddharth were only cosmetic. As the train left Kalyan Junction and took the north line that led to central India, he longingly looked at the south line that led to Pune, where his heart was. He wished he could jump off the Calcutta Mail and hop into the south-bound Madras Mail that followed. That would take him to his cherished destination and bring him peace. But Siddharth knew he would have to stick it out with Anthony and Dhananjay for the next seven days, no matter how much he suddenly detested their company.

R. Raj Rao

At Khajuraho, stronghold of the Chandelas, the orgiastic lesbian sculpture on the temple walls, depicting cunnilingus, fellatio and rimming, led to a rancorous debate among the classmates. While Siddharth defended the sculpture and said he was all for free sex, Anthony and Dhananjay called it prurient and decadent. Their tour guide, a Rajneesh disciple in orange, agreed with Siddharth about free sex, but said that his master was opposed to sexual perversions such as homosexuality, lesbianism, incest and bestiality. These, said the Master, occurred when we repressed sex in the name of morality—as most god-men preached, but did not practise. At this, Siddharth pounced on him too, calling his views baloney. Tempers soared so high that not even the chilled Khajuraho beer was able to cool them.

17 March 1979

13

Siddharth had a penchant for counting days. It was ninety-six days today since he'd last had a glimpse of Sudhir.

On the thirty-first day of the separation, just a week after he returned from his central Indian tour, a postcard from Sudhir did, in fact, arrive. It was in response to another that Siddharth had written on the twenty-fourth day, as soon as he landed home. The text of the letter did not amuse him. Sudhir wrote that he had received the thermodynamics book and was grateful. However, to Siddharth's complaint that the absence of a letter all these days meant that he had forgotten him, his reply was that he wrote to his mother only once in a while but that did not mean he forgot her? How can a lover be compared to a mother, thought Siddharth. Is he Hamlet? But the handwriting sort of made up for the letter's contents.

Siddharth was struck by the tiny, effeminate letters in purple ink on the cream-coloured postcard. He brought the postcard to his nose to inhale the fragrance of ink and paper, but thought that it smelt of semen instead. It required his utmost willpower not to succumb to the temptation of rushing off to the Engineering College Hostel that very instant.

But now, as the days were nearing their century, he was at his wits' end. He felt that if he did not see Sudhir soon, he would have to see a shrink.

Opportunity came knocking on his door in the form of an injunction from his father to check out a property in Khandala. His father was in two minds—should he go himself or send Siddharth who was whiling away his days without remorse? Siddharth heard his father thinking aloud and decided it for him. He wholeheartedly volunteered to perform the task, causing his father to wonder if the sun had risen in the west that morning.

He left on the early-morning Deccan Express—the very train by which they had travelled ninety-nine days ago. And after dutifully completing all the work assigned to him by his father, he arrived at the station just in time to board the Koyna Express—again, the very train that had taken him to Sudhir. Siddharth wasn't superstitious but trains, like gods, could be propitiated.

The slow Koyna Express sickened him, halting at every wayside station—Talegaon, Dehu Road, Chinchwad, Pimpri, and Khadki—before it finally rolled into Shivajinagar, the stop for the Engineering College Hostel.

14

Siddharth may have retraced his steps to Room 131 in the hope that the events of 9 December 1978 would repeat themselves. When something exhilarates us, we want it to happen again, we say, 'Once more!' But can things ever be the same again?

Thus, it wasn't Sudhir but Farouq who opened the door this time, when Siddharth knocked. And last time's civility was supplanted by a slight annoyance at the intrusion.

'Hi, hi,' he said, obviously in a hurry. 'Your yaar is not here. I'll tell him you have come.'

Siddharth wondered where Farouq had picked up the word 'yaar'. Moreover, why did he call Sudhir his yaar? Did he smell a rat?

'I am taking your yaar out to a movie this afternoon,' Farouq continued after Siddharth had thrown a nostalgic glance towards Sudhir's bed and set his rucksack down. Farouq was all spruced up, smelling of Old Spice and about to leave. 'Why don't you join us?'

'Okay,' Siddharth said. Although it elated him, he wished Farouq would stop using the word yaar. It did not suit him.

'Come to the Mangala theatre at 3 o'clock. It's just five minutes from here on foot.'

At 3 o'clock, Siddharth found himself outside the Mangala, waiting for his friends. There was a mob of people outside the theatre: some of them patrons; others, blokes without tickets; still others, ruffians selling tickets in black. Many were waiting for extra tickets—young men who constantly sidled up to him and asked, 'Extra?' The movie showing in the theatre explained the crowds. It was Prakash Mehra's blockbuster, *Muqqaddar Ka Sikandar*, staring matinee idol Amitabh Bachchan, sex symbols Raakhee and Rekha, and he-man Vinod Khanna.

It was hard to spot anyone in that crowd and Siddharth was certain he would fail to notice Sudhir and Farouq. He did not even know if they already had tickets or intended to join the jokers looking for extras, or buy them in black. But then, suddenly, he saw them coming and they saw him too. Farouq waved out to him and was instantly gheraoed by throngs of hopefuls hanging around for extras. This, because he thoughtlessly extracted three tickets from his shirt-pocket in full view of the public, and almost had them snatched out of his hands.

'Hi, Sudhir,' said Siddharth to his heart-throb, but the heart-throb was cold. 'Hello,' he returned the greeting.

The momentum of the mob pushed them into the foyer, and here Siddharth learnt that the third ticket was actually meant for Ravi Humbe who'd backed out at the last minute because of a toothache.

He waited for Sudhir to say something. Anything.

The auditorium was packed. They had seats in the upper stalls—not aisle seats, but seats in the middle of a row, surrounded by guys. Siddharth was tense about the seating arrangements and was relieved when Sudhir ensconced himself in the centre, with Farouq to his left and Siddharth to his right.

No sooner did the lights go out than Siddharth made his move, first attempting to slide his fingers into Sudhir's and then going directly for his crotch. But each time he was rebuffed. Sudhir took the wandering hand and returned it to its rightful owner. Hey mister, keep your hands to yourself, he seemed to say.

In the end, Siddharth gave up. He had seen *Muqqaddar Ka Sikandar* earlier and didn't particularly care for it, though his take on it was that Amitabh Bachchan was in love, not with Raakhee or Rekha, but with macho-man Vinod Khanna. Even so, it was going to be three hours of unrelieved tedium. This volte-face on his yaar's part was unexpected. Did a full house and the presence of Farouq in the seat next to him bother him so much?

But things remained more or less the same after the movie ended and they returned to the hostel. To Siddharth's questions, Sudhir replied mostly in monosyllables. He refused to go out for a walk or for dinner, saying he had a class test the next day. And he wasn't especially curious to know what had brought Siddharth to the Engineering College Hostel again though, more than once, the latter spelt it out for him, hoping to make him see reason. 'My dear, I've come here just for you.'

The night was the cruellest of all. It was Farouq and Sudhir who slept in one bed, as they surrendered the other to Siddharth, their esteemed guest. Siddharth helplessly watched them frustrate his plans. He even began to suspect that the Iraqi had stolen his boyfriend. First, they had gone out to a movie together, and now they were sharing a bed. Such things happened with impunity in hostels. More than once, he sat up in bed to check on the two. Were they up to mischief? Why couldn't Farouq go back to Baghdad, or Basra or wherever he had come from, and leave his yaar alone?

Siddharth collected his things and left the Engineering College Hostel while it was dark. In the other bed, the two still slept adulterously. He wanted to ask for a refund. Of the tears he had shed, the energy he had expended, the anxiety he had suffered. He scribbled out a note for Sudhir and left it on his study table: 'It was good knowing you.'

15

That summer, Siddharth got addicted to the appointments page of newspapers. Differences of opinion between him and his father were growing, the father beginning to see his son as a good-for-nothing. A job was the only answer. Once he was on his own, he wouldn't have to kowtow to his father.

The newspapers were full of ads for teaching jobs. This was the time colleges advertised for vacancies and conducted interviews, readying themselves for the new academic year in June. Siddharth responded to scores of ads, some of them from godforsaken places. Rural India seemed prelapsarian to him and he wasn't averse to spending the rest of his life in a small town or a village, though the thought of teaching

Shakespeare or Shaw to peasants' sons sounded absurd. He made daily trips to the post office, stuffing his biodata into thin rectangular envelopes and affixing stamps. In the end, he got a job in India's unique college, located in the heart of Bombay's red-light district. Azad College, as it was grandiosely called, insisted on a maximum—not a minimum—percentage from aspiring students. In order to be admitted here, one had to have scored no more than forty per cent in higher secondary. Even forty-one per cent wouldn't do. Such was the concern of the trustees, freedom fighters all, for India's down and out.

Siddharth's parents weren't flattered by the news of their son's first job when they saw the address of the college on his appointment letter. Not only was his salary ridiculously low—750 rupees a month in those hard times—but the college was situated in a lane known as 12th Lane. 'How can we tell our friends that our son works in a college situated in a lane?' Siddharth's mother asked.

Though Siddharth's subject was English, the students who went to Azad College knew not a word of the language. They grinned and smirked as he taught, wondering why he was wasting his breath on them. 'Sir, couldn't you find a job in any other college?' some of the two-plaited girls asked him in Marathi, and then burst into laughter.

A few weeks later, Siddharth stopped 'teaching' his class. All he did was to write down on the blackboard the meaning of almost every word in the lesson—omitting not even prepositions and articles. Forty-five minutes, thus, smoothly passed without his having to look at his wristwatch even once as he waited eagerly for the bell. Moreover, he had his back to the students for the greater part of the 'lecture', and was spared the ordeal of looking at their sneering faces.

During the lunch break or free periods, some of the giggling girls sang for him. '*Aane wala pal, jaane wala hai,*' they hummed, from Amol Palekar's *Golmaal*, for his entertainment. Two of them, Savita and Pramila, took singular interest in him, frequently asking him his bus-stop as if they planned to visit him at home. The thought mortally scared him. Maybe they're looking for a husband, he said to himself. A suitable boy. He decided to do everything in his power to make himself ineligible.

16

As was his wont, the postman slipped the letters in through the ventilator. Amidst all the official mail addressed to his father, Siddharth spotted a bluish-grey inland letter bearing his name. The girlish handwriting was unmistakable. Yet Siddharth did not lift the letter off the floor at once. He let it lie there, unwilling to tear it open and read its contents that, doubtless, would put an end to his joy. Somewhere deep down perhaps, he harboured the irrational belief that the letter wasn't real, that touching it would cause it to disappear. But then, impetuous as he was, he couldn't stay long without opening it.

The letter was there. He saw it every time he went past the hallway towards the front door. And he finally picked it up and prised it open so clumsily, the letter tore into two. With some irritation, he held the bits together and hastily read.

Engineering College Hostel
3rd October 1979

My dear Siddharth,

Do you remember me still, or have you wiped me from your memory? Actually, even if you have forgotten me, I cannot forget you. That means my love for you is greater than your love for me . . . But seriously, I think of you every day. I think of how rottenly I treated you when you were here last time, about six months ago. But now I want to say sorry. I want you to forgive this humble friend of yours. I will be very happy if you come to Pune for a few days. The Diwali holidays are coming soon. But I am not going home to Belgaum this time because I am busy with my project work. My room partner Farouq has gone to Iraq. So we both will be alone in the room, ek bar phir. I am anxiously waiting for your arrival, and if you tell me by which train you will be travelling, I'll come to Shivajinagar station to meet you.

Your yaar
Sudhir

Euphoria gripped Siddharth the moment he finished reading the letter. His actions became maniacal as he took the Air India calendar off its peg on the bedroom wall and checked the dates. Next, he dashed off to VT station to book his ticket and got it by a hair's breadth—being the last customer the booking clerk served before he shut his window at the stroke of five. For the rest of the evening, Siddharth's parents noticed that he was more talkative than usual and kept pacing the flat as he read Sudhir's letter over and over again.

Siddharth's ecstasy continued in college the next day. He led Savita and Pramila to an empty classroom after classes were over and got them to sing a whole bevy of romantic numbers, imagining Sudhir and not them to be before him. As a reward for their singing, and also to celebrate his love letter, he invited them to the best Udipi restaurant in the area and treated them to masala dosas. They wondered why their professor had suddenly grown so generous, but they did not know how to ask. Nor was he going to tell.

17

It surprised him that both his parents came to see him off at VT. The Deccan Queen to Pune left at 5.10 in the evening, which was roughly the time they opened their clinics. But today they didn't mind keeping their patients waiting and grumbling while they drove their only son to the station to be united with this small-town guy with whom he wished to have an affair (about which, of course, they were in the dark). 'Be careful,' they told him several times as he deposited his bag on the rack above the window seat and returned to the platform to be with them. They were referring only to his impending journey, not to his love affair, but it irritated him to be still thought of as a small boy. 'Please guys, I'm twenty-four. Old enough to look after myself,' he said to them, wishing that the guard would blow his whistle soon.

Eventually he did, and Siddharth bid his parents adieu, only for formality. 'Come back soon,' his mother said to him, walking alongside the moving train, annoying him further. 'Yes, mom,' he replied without attempting to hide his wrath.

Fascinated by train journeys normally (who said he wasn't a small boy?), Siddharth didn't enjoy this one because the three hours that the Deccan Queen took to reach Pune felt like eternity to him. He drank cup after cup of railway tea to bide his time, feeling okay as long as the train ran at its assigned speed and awful when it slowed down or came to a dead halt. Is this the Deccan Queen or a freight train, he asked himself at such times. A couple of hours later, the sun set. The train was on the Western Ghats. From here it ripped through the night at top speed, not stopping even once. As the breeze lashed his face, Siddharth remembered Boney M's *Night Flight to Venus*.

Then came the moment when the train slowed down—Shivajinagar was approaching. And Sudhir was tangibly on the platform, waiting for his yaar who couldn't believe his eyes.

They hugged, kissed even, since it was dark and Shivajinagar was poorly lit. But when it came to conversing, both of them were tongue-tied. Sudhir was reticent as always and Siddharth hated hackneyed questions. Still, a few of these escaped their mouths. The thing really on Siddharth's mind, however, remained unsaid—which was that Sudhir looked even more bed-worthy than before, that his camp walk had already given him a hard-on! He led him to the swanky Bamboo House Restaurant opposite the Engineering College Hostel, where everything was made of bamboo—floor, walls and ceiling. And coincidence of coincidences, the song that played as they entered was *Ra-Ra-Rasputin, Russia's Greatest Love Machine* that immediately followed *Night Flight to Venus* on the Boney M LP. So it was Boney M who celebrated their reunion, with Siddharth fancying himself a modern-day Rasputin.

Money flowed freely out of his purse at Bamboo House, what with the sumptuous à la carte dishes that he ordered. To Sudhir's comment that it was immoral on their part to spend so much money, Siddharth's reply was that, unlike last time, he had a job now, even if it wasn't a well-paying one. Whom was he earning for, if not his yaar? Sudhir was flattered by this, but took care not to blush. As if to prove his point, after their meal (and the generous twenty-rupee tip that he gave the waiter), Siddharth held Sudhir by the shoulders and led him towards Deccan Gym. When Sudhir looked at him askance, saying, 'Mister, have you forgotten the way to my hostel?' Siddharth surprised him by announcing that they were going for a late-night show at the Natraj, no matter which film was showing. It turned out to be another Amitabh Bachchan starrer, *Mr Natwarlal*.

Siddharth's intention in taking his boyfriend to the movie was, of course, not the movie itself. But the packed house at the Natraj, as usual, frustrated his plans and, to top it all, he found *Mr Natwarlal* to be the silliest film ever made.

Walking back to the Engineering College Hostel after the show, cigarettes in hand, they were like the proverbial hare and tortoise. Siddharth was in such a hurry to make out that he walked twice as fast as Sudhir and had to wait, every few

R. Raj Rao

yards, for the latter to catch up. As for Sudhir, he ambled along on purpose, noting with much amusement his friend's disquietude. 'Intezar aur abhi,' he shouted to Siddharth from a distance, confident that it was late at night and no one would hear.

When they reached the hostel, Siddharth dragged Sudhir into bed without changing. It was all right as long as they were making love but, after they were done, Sudhir wondered why they had to sleep on the same narrow bed all night when the other one was vacant. Siddharth responded to that by copulating with him again, causing the other to exclaim, 'What stamina!' Sudhir climbed on top of his lover immediately afterwards, feeling Siddharth's backside with his long fingers before inserting his own penis into it. 'Didn't know you could also be active,' Siddharth remarked as he was being fucked. 'Shh,' Sudhir said. 'No talkingduring sex.'

They would have gone on all night, taking turns, if Sudhir hadn't said, 'Will you fuck Farouq when he returns?' and Siddharth hadn't lost his libido forever.

18

Siddharth's students, all with aggregates of forty per cent or less, couldn't figure out what had come over their teacher. He taught them with renewed vigour and, what was more, no longer viewed them with condescension. This, in spite of the fact that there was a difference of day and night in their backgrounds. While he had grown up in south Bombay, India's most westernized locality, they were mostly from Bombay's mill areas. While he had gone first to St. Xavier's School and then to St. Xavier's College, many of them had passed out from schools and colleges run by the Bombay Municipal Corporation. Siddharth wasn't a snob, no, but to be fair to him, no one could help feeling superior to the students of

Azad College. If he now came across as more amiable than before, sincerely attempting to empathize with them and see things from their point of view, the credit for that surely had to be given to Sudhir.

In many ways, Sudhir was no different from Siddharth's students. He had studied in the Marathi medium and was hardly cosmopolitan in his outlook. On the contrary, provincial was the word that described him best. But what he made his lover see was that people couldn't be compared and judged when they had not been born with the same privileges. And privilege, or the lack thereof, was not something that human beings could choose before coming into this world. It just happened. Either you were born privileged or you weren't. It was morally incorrect, then, for some human beings to look down upon others.

Siddharth was so grateful to Sudhir for the insight that, shortly after his return from Pune, he used it as a pretext to invite him to Bombay. He knew his parents would never approve of their son's artless friend. Why, he could already hear his father damning Sudhir with words like 'simpleton' (which happened to be his favourite). But, what the hell, he couldn't live in fear of his folks all his life. He was independent now and had a right to live his life the way he wanted. If it didn't suit his parents, he was prepared to walk out on them and set up house elsewhere.

Sudhir, who had never been to Bombay, was pleased to accept his yaar's invitation. Yet, Bombay scared him. It conjured up visions of conmen and pickpockets and people toppling out of local trains. Not only was he not on the train he said he would travel by, but he didn't bother to phone. Siddharth—who had asked Deepak, one of his childhood chums, to accompany him to VT—was frantic. There were scores of upcountry Indians who got lost in Bombay. What if Sudhir turned out to be one of them, and his face was flashed on TV? But Deepak advised Siddharth to be calm, smoke a joint

R. Raj Rao

and check the next train from Pune. Lo and behold, Sudhir was there.

'You fool, I nearly died from the anxiety,' Siddharth said to Sudhir as he stepped out of the train. Sudhir merely grinned and said, 'Sorry, I missed the first train.' (This was a lie. Fact was, he had had second thoughts.)

Had it not been for Deepak's presence, Siddharth might have smooched his boyfriend, VT's multitudes notwithstanding. But Deepak was conservative, as all men of contacts tend to be. Siddharth had solicited his help in getting Sudhir a room at bargain price. Deepak knew the owners of several lodges in the vicinity and had assured Siddharth that he would find them a room that was 'cheapest and best.' This was easier said than done, considering that Christmas was around the corner. But, true to his word, as they drove to the Liberty Guest House, straight from VT in a taxi, he got Sudhir a room for as little as seventy-five rupees a day.

Not that Deepak was comfortable doing any of this. He did it merely for old time's sake. He may have known that Siddharth was queer but now, as he witnessed his fiery passion for this girlish boy, he was disgusted. He was exasperated when Siddharth paternally asked Sudhir if he'd eaten on the train. 'Is he a kid or what?' thought Deepak.

As for Sudhir, he felt deeply offended when he found out that Siddharth was putting him up in a lodge. His traditional sense of hospitality was violated. Was this any way to treat a guest? He was much better off in his room at the Engineering College Hostel than in this rathole that passed for a lodge. Only a thin partition divided his room from the reception desk outside, where people continually blabbered. But then, Siddharth wasn't at fault either. What could Sudhir, who had grown up in a large wada house, know of the dilemmas of a south Bombayite, whose flat was so small that he didn't even have a room of his own?

Sudhir refused to yield when Siddharth approached him

with a lovemaking proposal, soon after Deepak had left. 'How indecent,' he said, certain that, if he agreed, everyone on the other side of the partition would have a dekko, a free show. He remained cross with Siddharth for the rest of the evening and Siddharth left in a huff.

Early next morning, however, Siddharth returned to the Liberty Guest House to patch up with his mate. Sex was not the topmost thing on his mind any longer. 'So, how would you like to spend your day?' he asked his yaar in all earnestness. The yaar's reply—'I would like to see Bombay. It's my first visit here, remember?'

And so they saw Bombay, in Siddharth's own unique way. Not for him the exotic Bombay Darshan buses run by the Maharashtra Tourism Department that burned a hole in everyone's pocket. Instead, they went to Churchgate Station and bundled themselves into a jam-packed local train, managing to find window seats in spite of the rush. 'For the flavour of it,' Siddharth told Sudhir, noticing his unease. Upon reaching Andheri forty-five minutes later (it was a bada fast train) they immediately boarded a double-decker bus back to town, occupying the front seats on the upper deck, which Siddharth called 'the cockpit'. As the bus wended its way through traffic, Siddharth gave Sudhir an 'aerial view' of his city, with a running commentary. He pointed out everything— churches, temples, malls and art galleries. On seeing the Victoria Jubilee Technical Institute at Matunga from the bus, Sudhir remembered that a schoolmate of his studied there. He made Siddharth promise to bring him back to the institute another day (for he was to be in Bombay for a whole week). But Siddharth couldn't help feel a twinge in his jealous heart— which he wore on his sleeve for everyone to see.

'You nutcase, he's not that kind of a friend,' said Sudhir.

However, as it turned out, the trip to VJTI did not materialize. Our duo spent the rest of the week gallivanting in south Bombay, alternating between the Gateway of India,

R. Raj Rao

Marine Drive, Chowpatty, Malabar Hill and the Prince of Wales Museum. It was only on the penultimate day, as they waited for New Year's Eve, that they went for a sky theatre show to Worli's Nehru Planetarium where, with Sudhir by his side in the darkened auditorium and the stars above, Siddharth was in seventh heaven.

On the night of 31st December, the promenades around Apollo Bunder were full of people. On the stroke of midnight, all the ships in the harbour tooted and flashed colourful beams into the starless sky. As if this wasn't enough, the gathered mass of humanity insisted on blowing their own bugles, bought from the scores of vendors who hovered about, raising the decibel level so high that Sudhir was forced to plug his ears with his fingers. 'Why do Bombayites make such a fuss about the New Year?' he remarked. 'In my town, people go to sleep quietly and realize only the next day that it's a new year.'

This isn't to suggest that he didn't enjoy himself to the hilt. It was an open-air pageant, free of cost and something he was not used to witnessing. But the highlight, surely, was that more than a couple of times someone in the crowd pinched his bottom and, once, even squeezed his dick. 'Don't be a slut,' Siddharth reprimanded him when he reported the matter, but Sudhir was flattered. That he, a small-towner, was desirable to Bombayites boosted his self-esteem.

'Happy New Year, Happy New Year,' everyone said to one another even though they were strangers. Many openly drank on public thoroughfares, for this was one wanton night when they would be forgiven. 'Hooligans,' Sudhir teasingly called them, aware that his host took any criticism of his city and its people personally.

It was close to dawn when, strolling back amid the ribaldry on the streets, they reached the Liberty Guest House and Siddharth insisted on kissing Sudhir full on the mouth. 'New year,' he explained. If he didn't stay with Sudhir in the lodge, it was only because of his folks who, doubtless, would nag him throughout the first of January, and that was not how he intended to begin his new year.

His parents notwithstanding, the day did not augur well for Siddharth who had to perform the unpleasant task of seeing his love off at the station. College was reopening and Sudhir had to return. 'Bunk,' Siddharth advised him but Sudhir knew better. He had scored abysmally low marks in his internals and was afraid he would have to repeat the year. As the guard waved his flag and the train began to crawl, Siddharth made a New Year's resolution—he would spend all his weekends in Pune. A second-class season ticket didn't cost much. What was to stop him, then, from going there on Saturday afternoons and returning on Monday mornings? There were trains to Pune throughout the day.

Sudhir craned his neck and waved to Siddharth till the train left the platform. He was woebegone too, for never in his life had anyone bestowed so much attention on him. On reaching his hostel, he wrote a postcard to Siddharth, thanking him for the gala time. Then came the carefully worded, if somewhat clichéd ending. 'You stole my heart. I think you are a thief.'

The postman gave the postcard to Siddharth's father, who promptly read it before passing it on to his son. 'Wish he would use sealed inlands,' Siddharth swore, elated anyway at receiving the letter. He made the Punjabi-dressed Savita and Pramila sing him the old Johnny Walker song in college the next day.

Jaane kahan mera jigar gaya ji
Abhi abhi yahin tha kidhar gaya ji.

19

The principal of Azad College sent Siddharth a strictly worded memo for 'dereliction of duty'. He observed that Siddharth hardly spent the mandatory four hours in the staffroom. There were complaints from students who never found him in college to attend to their queries. The memo rankled in Siddharth's mind, for this was the same principal who, only a couple of months ago, had openly proclaimed him to be one of the best teachers in the college.

The principal wasn't capricious. Earnestly implementing his New Year's resolution, Siddharth virtually lived in the Engineering College Hostel now, coming to Bombay only for his classes. He would step off the train at Dadar, cross over to Western Railway to board a local to Grant Road and walk to college just in time for his lectures. On finishing, he would adopt the same procedure in reverse to get back to Pune as quickly as possible. But Pune and Bombay were discrete cities, separated by a distance of 192 kilometres, and this was tropical India not temperate America. The express trains took four and a half hours to reach and there were frequent delays, especially on the ghats, with freight trains forever derailing. Siddharth often entered class more than fifteen minutes after the bell had rung, only to find half of his students gone. The arduous journeys made him look dishevelled and weather-beaten (he usually found sitting space only on the footboard of coaches) and his travel fatigue prevented him from giving his best to the students.

In Pune, he restricted his romancing and lovemaking to the night. By day, Siddharth was a male bird preoccupied with building his nest. He fancied himself a householder with responsibilities, intent on setting up a home where he could live blissfully with his beloved. The first step was to relocate to the city and find a job. He hired a bicycle and pedalled to every college to ask if there were vacancies. Everywhere, it was the same story—sorry, no vacancy. Some principals advised him to leave his biodata with them, for a vacancy was likely to arise in the 'near future'. Others asked why he wished to leave Bombay and settle down in Pune. Siddharth could hardly tell them the reason. He dutifully gave them all his biodata but was sure they would never write back. Why should they, when they headed prestigious institutions of higher learning, some of them set up by the British in the nineteenth century, in this city that was described as the 'Oxford of the East'?

Siddharth's dedication, his single-mindedness of purpose, touched Sudhir. He had never imagined that a man could put himself to so much trouble just for love. Love ke liye kucch bhi karega? While he cruised about in a car in Bombay, he had actually stooped to a cycle here. 'Even Shah Jehan and Mumtaz Mahal wouldn't do it,' he said, making Siddharth instantly blush. He felt his brief was to reward his yaar for his efforts by giving him top-quality sex. There wasn't a night when they didn't copulate, spending a warm two hours in each other's arms, before turning in. The lack of sufficient sleep began to tell on both of them. Sudhir obtained very low marks in his next internals too. As for Siddharth, he was no longer enthusiastic about his work. His classes were a bore and a chore.

20

It was Sudhir who suggested that instead of Siddharth always coming to Pune, he could sometimes get on a train to Bombay. 'To make life a little less mushkil for you,' he said with concern in his voice. 'But you must promise to keep me with you at home. I refuse to stay at the Liberty Guest House.'

Initially sceptical, Siddharth reflected on it and came to the conclusion that it wasn't such a bad idea. He might be the son of his parents, but he had a right to have friends and, moreover, his parents had a duty to be hospitable towards them.

The parents, who were silent spectators to their son's absences, were appalled on meeting Sudhir. As they saw him eat with his fingers or grope for the right English words during a conversation, they felt that their son had let them down. 'Where did we go wrong?' his mother sobbed. They also saw that Sudhir came from a family that, by their standards at least, wasn't urbane. His clothes looked worn and, whenever he passed by, a sweaty odour emanated from them. Yet, outwardly, they tried to be civil towards him. They asked him about his parents and had long chats with him about the career prospects for engineers.

Observing his gait, Siddharth's father found it odd that he should be pursuing a manly course like engineering. 'He should have done Arts like you,' he told his son in jest, offending him no end.

'Dad, you're prejudiced,' Siddharth jovially hit back.

'What prejudiced? Why does he toss his hips like a girl while walking?'

'That's just his natural style.'

A few days later, they had a more rancorous duel when his father found Siddharth closing the door of his room at night. Siddharth, who slept in the carpeted sitting room of their two-room flat, always complained about Bombay's heat—more so after he had started going to salubrious Pune. He dealt with his discomfort by keeping the fan on at full speed and sleeping with all the windows and doors open. (If permitted, he would have liked to switch on the air conditioner too, but here the father put his foot down, saying he wouldn't pay for the electricity.) So the father wondered why he now closed the door.

'For privacy,' Siddharth replied.

'Are you two up to some dirty business?'

'No.'

'Then don't close the door as long as you are living in my house.'

'Yes, sir.'

Sudhir, who overheard this exchange between father and son, felt so snubbed he refused to let Siddharth touch him again in his parents' flat. 'But they're fast asleep,' Siddharth often pleaded with him in the dead of the night, but to no avail.

Gradually, his visits to Bombay stopped. It was a city that didn't give its lovers space.

21

Ravi Humbe, who had lived in a private room so far, was finally allotted a room in the Engineering College Hostel. He spent much of his free time with Sudhir now, using studies as a pretext. Fact was, he detested his room partner Ashwin, a diasporic Gujarati from Kenya, who was something of a nerd. He envied Sudhir who had his hostel room all to himself—Farouq still being in Iraq. However, it didn't take him long to figure out that Sudhir wasn't, in effect, the only boarder in his room. This stranger from Bombay, whom he had once met and who claimed to be a friend of Farouq, had resurfaced and was spotted in the room every other day. When Ravi Humbe interrogated Sudhir, he merely shrugged. Taking this as a sign that his classmate wasn't bold enough to tell the intruder that his presence was preventing him from concentrating on his studies, Ravi Humbe lectured Sudhir on filial duty. His father worked hard and sent him to a professional college in order to give him a good life. It was incumbent on him to study well, graduate and get a nice job as quickly as possible. His parents had expectations and he was obliged to fulfil them. How wounded they would be to learn that he had scored such poor marks in his internals! And the low marks were solely attributable to the fact that he didn't spend as much time with his books as he ought to. If he, Ravi Humbe, could do well, why not Sudhir? Both came from the same town.

'Fuck his ass,' Siddharth said, when Sudhir reported Ravi Humbe's speech. 'Don't you see he's plain jealous? He would have liked to have a friend like me. But it's you who have me, while I don't give a damn about him.'

Siddharth's offhand way of dealing with the issue didn't

R. Raj Rao

amuse Sudhir, who saw trouble ahead if corrective measures weren't taken in time.

'My dear man,' he began—

'Man is right,' Siddharth interrupted.

'Will you please shut up and listen? The matter is serious. Ravi Humbe is from my place, I know him well. Cook up some excuse, some reason that will convince him that you come here on business, not for time-pass.'

They thought and thought till Siddharth got it.

'Idea!' he exclaimed. 'Tell the bugger I come here to teach you spoken English. Engineers need it, don't they?'

Sudhir shrugged, but that's the explanation he gave Ravi Humbe the next time he came to his room. However, it backfired. Ravi Humbe declared that he would be present for the sessions too for, if anything, his English was worse than Sudhir's. So Siddharth actually had to frame a course and give them lessons in spoken English after a hard day's lecturing at Azad College and a cumbersome train journey to Pune. In no time, word spread among all the Belgaum-ites in the Engineering College Hostel. Less than a month later, Siddharth found himself conducting a fully-fledged class for over twenty, for which he received not a paisa by way of remuneration.

'See what love has done to me,' he whispered into Sudhir's ears one night. 'It's made me a bloody slave.'

22

Ravi Humbe was in Sudhir's room again. He was persuading him to let two of his friends, both students in Siddharth's spoken English class, 'parasite' with him for a while. They hadn't been lucky enough to get hostel rooms, he said, and they found private accommodation expensive because their parents were poor farmers. It was Sudhir's duty to help guys from his own town. It must be said that, for once, Sudhir didn't allow himself to be used as a doormat. He turned down Ravi Humbe's request, pointing out that, before leaving, Farouq had given him express instructions to let only Siddharth and no one else stay in the room. They were 'fast friends', he lied, who had known each other long before Farouq joined the Engineering College. That he could manufacture a lie on the spur of the moment, just to ensure that his nefarious activities continued, meant much. Anyone who has tasted hostel life knows how risky it is to be a spoilsport—one is ostracized by the entire clan.

Ravi Humbe, of course, did not believe a word of what Sudhir said (he wasn't a good liar), but he didn't wish to wage war. He begged Sudhir to let the guys sponge off him for just three days, during which he would scour the city for alternatives. If Siddharth showed up unexpectedly, he could always sleep in Sudhir's bed, while the two homeless guys used Farouq's. Farouq wouldn't have a clue. He, Ravi Humbe, would personally launder his bedclothes before he arrived. The reference to Siddharth staggered Sudhir, coming as it did from Ravi Humbe and, that too, in the context of sleeping arrangements. Did the fellow have a whiff of what was going on?

As it happened, Siddharth arrived from Bombay that very afternoon and was pissed off with Sudhir for letting Ravi Humbe manipulate him. 'You are jeopardizing our privacy,' he yelled. 'Those two guys are now my students. How can I screw you when they are in the other bed, voyeuristically looking on?'

Sudhir consoled his yaar. 'Only three days,' he pleaded. 'After that, Ravi is getting them another place.'

That evening, after their Spoken English class, Siddharth was reintroduced to Kishore and Gajanan, the two boys who would be staying with them. Both had smooth chests. Kishore, whose build and crew cut made him look like a policeman, had an almost feminine chest with pink, full-

R. Raj Rao

blooded nipples. Gajanan, by contrast, was skinny with curly hair resembling Ravi Humbe's. But his equipment always tilted to one side when he sat, making it tough for Siddharth to keep his eyes off.

Happy with their class, his students all decided to go for a late-night show. Sudhir declined, Siddharth being his excuse. He had to cook for him, carouse with him. Or else he would die of boredom in their spartan hostel room. Siddharth's role as their English teacher provided the alibi here, for which Indian student doesn't instantly recognize the need to be of service to his guru?

Afterwards, as they lay in bed, Sudhir confessed that, had it not been for his humdum, he surely would have gone with the boys for the flick. 'Don't waste time now. Let's get down to business,' he said. 'We don't have the full night to ourselves. They'll be back at midnight.'

'All because of you,' grumbled Siddharth, still upset. Sudhir fondled him and couldn't help remarking that these days he didn't stiffen as easily as before.

At this, Siddharth sprang on him. 'Mister, who said I'm not a good performer?' he asked. 'Without applying Fevicol, I can stick myself in you. You won't be able to disengage.'

This really happened. And they fell asleep that way.

When Ravi Humbe and party opened the door with the spare key and switched on the light, they saw. 'Hush,' said Ravi Humbe to the others, putting a finger to his lips. He didn't want them to be woken up. He stealthily tiptoed to his room to fetch his camera, and clicked. Even the ribald laughter of Kishore and Gajanan, while Ravi Humbe was away, didn't wake them.

But the question was—where in India could Ravi Humbe give this roll for developing? He would have to send it to Castro Street.

Ravi Humbe returned to his room. Kishore and Gajanan retired for the night on the other bed. However, unable to sleep,

Kishore sat up in bed several times at night to surreptitiously check out what Sudhir and Siddharth were up to. More masti? He was possessed by an intense desire to try out the stuff on Gajanan who snored by his side.

23

Ravi Humbe was in a quandary. To write, or not to write. One half of him told him it was his duty to faithfully report what he'd seen to Sudhir's father before Sudhir went completely astray. The other half wasn't so sure. They weren't kids any more. Who was he to mind Sudhir's business, even if they were from the same town?

After much deliberation, he decided in favour of writing. But this was easier said than done. For one, he wasn't good at composing letters. For another, he didn't know where to begin. What could he say? My dear uncle. I must inform you that your son has a homosexual friend from Bombay who regularly comes to his hostel room to fuck him? I actually caught them red-handed? No, no, he didn't have the guts. It was too embarrassing. How could he write words like that to his classmate's father, who was as good as his own?

Strewn on the floor beside his desk were several crumpled balls of paper. These were drafts of the letter he had destroyed because they were no good. If only he could solicit help. But whose? Siddharth would have been perfect, but he couldn't seek his help to draft a letter about him!

24

The guy was shadowing Siddharth. Of this he had no doubt. He had just emerged from Shivajinagar station and was footing it towards the Engineering College Hostel,

R. Raj Rao

when their eyes met. There was something in that countenance that made Siddharth look back as he walked. He knew he was being stalked. He was annoyed, not least because the fair stocky fellow wasn't his scene. Besides, he was Sudhir's—hook, line and sinker. What irked him was that the guy marched along as if in a walking race and was bound to catch up, sooner or later. Then came the crossroads where Siddharth hoped to give him the slip. But this was Pune, not Bombay, and there were too few people on the roads to facilitate his escape. The upshot? The guy was still in hot pursuit. Siddharth was now in a dilemma. Should he enter the Engineering College Hostel or mislead the chap by going past the hostel and walking towards Deccan Gym? He chose the latter course, afraid that if the fellow, whoever he was, saw him step into the hostel, he would know where he was staying, and hassle him for the rest of his life.

'Excuse me,' he heard the guy call out. He quickened his pace, but it didn't help. The stranger was a brisk walker, and he was now tapping Siddharth's shoulder and extending his hand for a handshake.

'My name is Gaurav,' he panted. 'And yours?'

'May I ask why you are stalking me?' Siddharth snapped, not concealing his anger.

'Oh, no, no,' replied Gaurav. 'Don't get me wrong. I've heard so much about you, about your Spoken English class, that I just wanted to have a word. Can we have a chai?'

Of course, Siddharth would have declined the invitation had Gaurav's words not been so flattering. 'Okay,' he found himself saying. 'But please make it quick.'

What did Gaurav say to Siddharth over chai at a nearby kiosk? That he was from Bombay and was, in fact, a student of the Engineering College and lived in the hostel. That he wished to introduced him to his room-mate who was gay.

Siddharth's ears cocked at the word 'gay' like a cat's or a dog's. 'Excuse me,' he said. 'I thought we were going to discuss my Spoken English class. You don't need it, though. Your English is excellent.'

But Gaurav urged him to end the farce. 'You can trust me,' he said. 'I live in Room 83, C Block. Please come to my room whenever you have the time. I have so much to show you.'

The tea arrived and they sipped it. Siddharth confronted Gaurav with the question that nagged him the most, namely, who'd outed him. But Gaurav refused to divulge anything. 'I just know,' he said.

As they parted a few minutes later, Gaurav renewed his invitation to Siddharth with such fervour that Siddharth grew suspicious again. But wait a minute, his inner voice said. Could it be that blighted Ravi Humbe who'd spilled the beans? He must ask Sudhir.

Recollecting his encounter with Gaurav in tranquillity, however, Siddharth decided to keep Sudhir out of it, at least for the time being. This much he knew—he would go to C Block. But the actual visit took place only a week or so later, during his next expedition to the city.

Gaurav welcomed Siddharth effusively and introduced him to his room partner, Vivek. Their room was full of gay porn, all of it imported from the US. Most of the magazines had semi-naked hunks on their covers, white as cream, conventionally handsome but incapable of turning Siddharth on. Hence, he took only a cursory look at the magazines before putting them down, astounding Gaurav and Vivek by rejecting their offer to lend him the stuff.

'Not my scene,' he said, intriguing them further.

From the corner of his eye he gave Vivek the once-over and discovered that he found him much more cock-teasing in his shorts and T-shirt, complete with hairy legs, than the guys in the magazines. Unlike Gaurav, Vivek was tall and on the darker side, with a sharp aquiline nose. Not a patch on Sudhir, of course, and not half as maidenly, but certainly okay for emergencies. Be that as it may, he was totally unprepared for their next question.

'Are you gay?' Gaurav asked him point-blank. He answered by throwing the question back at him. Gaurav stumped him even more with his answer. 'Yes,' he said. 'And so is Vivek. I've already told you so.' Siddharth couldn't imagine anyone being that audacious.

As they got busy making tea on their little electric stove, Siddharth glanced at the walls of their hostel room, which were covered with pin-ups of shirtless Hollywood stars, none of whom he recognized. Meanwhile, Vivek offered him a cigarette (a 555), which he accepted only so as not to appear rude. He managed to successfully brush his fingers against Vivek's while taking the cigarette. This surely was a bonus.

Talk shifted to Siddharth's 'yaar' and suddenly he grew circumspect. He wasn't going to say a word about Sudhir to these street-smart blokes who lived just two blocks away. He presumed that they didn't know who he was—at least not that he was a student of their own college. But he could be wrong.

Having smoked the cigarette and drunk the tea, Siddharth got up to leave. Both Gaurav and Vivek shook hands with him, informing him that, approximately a month later, they planned to host a party—a gay party—in their room, which he and his yaar had to attend. 'No excuses,' Gaurav raised a hand, just as Siddharth was about to open his mouth. 'We want to see you at the party, and that's it.'

25

So they went to the party. Siddharth felt jealous when Sudhir reported that he knew all about the C Block guys. Did it mean that he too . . .? However, he couldn't decide if Sudhir was telling the truth or shamming, just to appear with-it. Probably the latter, he consoled himself.

The music was so loud it could be heard miles away from C Block. When they got to Room 83 and found that the door was locked from inside, they knocked. But there was no response for a long time. It was only when they furiously banged on the door with their fists that someone opened it— someone other than Gaurav or Vivek. Suspicion was writ large on his face.

'Yes?' he asked, as he stepped out, fastening the door behind him. Siddharth introduced himself, but it wasn't until Gaurav was summoned to verify their identity that they were allowed to enter. 'Why don't they give everyone a secret password?' Siddharth whispered into Sudhir's ear.

The room was full of cigarette smoke. All the furniture had been moved out. Elvis sang on the cassette player (and, afterwards, it would be Abba, The Beatles and Boney M). Guys danced in pairs, but the absence of even a single girl did not seem strange in this men's hostel. This was how events like New Year's Eve were celebrated. Then their eyes got accustomed to the dim psychedelic lighting and they were able to see that this was no run-of-the-mill stag party. For here, guests drank not only beer, but also champagne, Scotch and rum. Here, they smooched as they danced, in full view of others. Here, most of them wore not shirts, but shorts. That is to say, they were topless.

Emboldened by what they saw around them (man, after all, is influenced by his environment), Siddharth and Sudhir joined the dancers. Siddharth's eyes wandered. He found many of the hunks appetizing and wondered who they were. Surely, all of them did not belong to the Engineering College Hostel. Were they from other colleges and other hostels in the city? How did Gaurav and Vivek know them? Their networking skills were remarkable.

R. Raj Rao

As their eyes further adjusted to the dark, they found there was an orgy in progress by the window at the far end of the room. (The window of course was shut.) A guy screwed another, who sucked a third's dick, who milked a fourth's tits, who had his tongue rolled in a fifth's mouth, whom a sixth masturbated, even as a seventh attempted to fuck him. No one could not have a hard-on seeing this. Siddharth noticed that Sudhir had one, and vice versa. Anyone could join and enlarge this Frankensteinian entity, but Siddharth and Sudhir abstained. They were spectators at the party, rather than performers.

Noticing that he and his companion felt like fish out of water, Gaurav approached Siddharth. 'Mate, I hope you are enjoying yourself,' he said.

'Sure.'

'You don't seem to be in your element. Care to dance?'

'Why not?'

Now, Siddharth and Gaurav danced while Sudhir watched. Siddharth, of course, didn't have his heart in it. It would have been different if it were Vivek. But no, this was Gaurav. He saw that Gaurav perspired a lot as he danced and this made him smell foul.

Meanwhile, Sudhir was approached by another set of guys who did not belong to his college. There were three of them and, spying him as he stood by himself, they invited him to be the fourth. The four of them danced together, Sudhir the most awkward of the lot. The word 'disco' wasn't even known in his town! As they swung their hips, one of them, who introduced himself as Rajan, brought his face very close to Sudhir's. A kiss was inevitable, and Sudhir let Rajan kiss him—more out of politeness than out of passion. Luckily, Siddharth did not see.

'Are you alone?' Rajan asked him.

'No. I have my friend Siddharth with me.'

'Same here—I have my partner Mahendra. But swapping is normal at such dos.'

Sudhir didn't take the hint. He was the only one among the four who didn't guzzle beer as he danced. When he was reunited with Siddharth half an hour later, Rajan and company having given up on him, he found that Siddharth too was tipsy.

26

Sudhir's father sent him a letter by Express Delivery. Needless to say, it was in response to Ravi Humbe's letter. Ravi Humbe's letter had disconcerted him, but he decided to keep his cool. Husband and wife discussed the letter and came to the conclusion that the matter wasn't as serious as Ravi Humbe made it sound. That it wasn't necessary, at this stage, for the father to bus it to Pune to find out what was going on in his son's life. Accordingly, all he advised him in his letter was to devote his time to books and keep his non-academic activities to a minimum. Ravi Humbe wasn't referred to at all, nor was Siddharth.

However, it was child's play for Sudhir to put two and two together and figure out who had filled his father's ears with poison. He wanted to confront Ravi Humbe, but Siddharth advised him against it. 'Why make it an issue?' he asked.

Instead, he made Sudhir reply to his dad's letter post-haste, to 'set the record straight'. Sudhir wrote the letter under Siddharth's supervision, as if it were a doctoral thesis introducing him to his family as a scholar and lecturer in English, whose company was helping him improve his own English. 'Don't believe a word of what Ravi Humbe says,' he wrote as a postscript.

When his parents received the letter, their fears were allayed. Why, they would like to meet this man who had made their son his pupil.

R. Raj Rao

27

Towards the end of May 1980, Farouq, absent for a whole semester with special leave, returned from Iraq with alarming news. Young men were being conscripted into the Iraqi army. Making capital of the fact that Iran was weakened by its revolution, Iraq planned to invade it when the latter could do little to defend itself. However, the need of the hour was for Iraq to consolidate its early victories and, with this in view, President Saddam Hussein had decreed that all men below thirty would be required to serve in the army for a minimum of three years.

Farouq had managed to escape by the skin of his teeth. Airport officials had tried to prevent him from boarding the Delhi flight, but relented when he fibbed about studying for a degree in Military Engineering. 'Return as soon as you finish writing your exams,' they commanded him, as they stamped his passport.

'Imagine being a soldier for three long years,' he grumbled. 'My studies will be further interrupted. I won't be able to complete even my graduation, let alone my postgraduation. Do you think the college is going to readmit me after a gap of three years?'

Siddharth and Sudhir consoled Farouq. Siddharth stroked his back while Sudhir made tea. They observed that he had become more stylish in appearance, with a *Jewel Thief* style cap and a French beard.

'I'll have to stay put in India till the war is over,' Farouq continued, lighting a cigar. 'Won't be able to go home even to see my mother. You guys will now have to consider me your permanent guest. Your country will have to provide me shelter.'

'Farouq,' Siddharth spoke suddenly, startling Sudhir. 'There is a saying in Sanskrit, the language of our sages— Atithi devo bhava. The guest is god. Every Indian believes in it to this day. You needn't worry. You can stay in Pune as our guest for as long as you want. Or you can come with me to Bombay. Ram and I will look after you.'

'Thank you, friend,' cried Farouq. He presented his hosts with small tokens that he had remembered to pick up on his way to the airport. A photo-frame for Sudhir. A carved pen-stand for Siddharth. He had also brought them a bagful of pistachios.

'So kind of you,' said Siddharth, as they all sipped tea.

28

The train was at 1 a.m. Auto-rickshaws being exorbitant at this late hour, they decided to bus it to the station. But there was a catch—the last bus left at 10 or thereabouts. What would they do, hanging out at the station?

It was Sudhir whose grey cells worked. 'Why not see the late show at the Alankar?' he asked. Alankar was a movie theatre close to the railway station.

'Brilliant,' said Siddharth. 'The movie will end around midnight and give us enough time to have a chai together before I board my train.'

They then stumbled upon another hurdle. How would Sudhir return to the hostel?

'No problem,' he said resourcefully. 'You go to the station by bus, and I'll follow on my bicycle.'

The bicycle had its own history. It wasn't brand new, but it served its purpose. It was actually one of the several cycles that sat in the courtyard of Sudhir's house in Belgaum. No one quite remembered when or how it had got there. Sudhir's father helped him load it onto the roof of a State Transport bus to Pune and, lo, he was suddenly mobile. Siddharth used it too—it saved him the bus fare, which was rather steep in Pune.

Siddharth realized Sudhir's suggestion was the best course,

R. Raj Rao

yet his mind was uneasy. The newspapers carried stories every day of cyclists being crushed to pulp by buses and lorries. God forbid, if that ever happened . . .

Kala Patthar was based on the real-life story of coal miners in Chasnala, suffocated to death in the bowels of the earth. It had two heroes, Bachchan and Shotgun Sinha, who, once again, Siddharth proclaimed were the real romantic pair.

Bachchan starrers being marathons, it was past 12.30 by the time the film ended and they crawled out of the theatre to the honking of cars and auto-rickshaws. The station was just a stone's throw away, so there was no danger of Siddharth missing his train. They had steaming hot masala chai at one of the several pavement stalls that dotted the area around the station, and walked over to platform number one from where the Sahyadri Express left. The train was being announced when Siddharth realized he had forgotten to buy Sudhir a platform ticket. He scrambled to the ticket window, with visions of Sudhir being caught by black-jacketed ticket collectors and thrown into the lock-up, only because he couldn't afford the fine. I won't even be there to bail him out, Siddharth said to himself.

By the time he was back, the train was already at the platform. Sudhir was lost in the crush of alighting and boarding passengers. Siddharth grew frantic, letting out a fart or two. This was unnecessary, for his head stuck out of the crowd and Sudhir spotted him easily. 'I told you to stay where I left you,' Siddharth said. 'Now let's go find my compartment.'

The compartment was the very first one, adjacent to the engine. A chai-wallah approached them and Siddharth bought himself another cup of tea. Sudhir hated tea, firmly believing that it led to acidity, as his father had told him. Siddharth finished his tea, yet the train showed no signs of moving. He looked up and found that the engine was missing. Pune was a major junction, where express trains switched from electric to diesel traction. So it would be another fifteen minutes, at least, before the green light flashed.

'Why don't you push off?' Siddharth advised Sudhir when he found him yawning. 'It's half past one already.'

'I'm a boy not a girl,' replied Sudhir. 'Boys can stay out all night without any problem.'

'Are you sure? That you are a boy, I mean?'

'Bastard.'

It was good-humoured teasing. Siddharth was upbeat because he was going to Belgaum, Sudhir's hometown, on a three-day trip. This was his first visit there though, a couple of years ago, he had passed through it on his way to Goa. Though late, he had sat up on his berth to view the houses and streets in sparkling blue neon lighting. Had he known, then, that he would find happiness in that very town? That he'd travel to Belgaum one day to meet his prospective in-laws and ask for their son's hand in marriage? For that's how he thought of them. Sudhir might have come with him, had it not been for his semester-end exams. But, Siddharth continued to fantasize—it was better that he would not be around when talk of his marriage took place. It would make him so shy.

Sudhir's yawns brought him back to the here and now. The lights changed from red to amber and, all at once, the Sahyadri Express whistled. Within minutes, they were out of each other's sight.

29

Five auto-drivers at the station refused to ferry Siddharth to the area where Sudhir's family lived before a sixth agreed. 'Too much far,' said one of them. 'Too many narrow gullies and too much people on the road,' added another. Some of them were ready to go, provided he was willing to pay them fifty per cent of the return fare. 'Why should I?' retorted Siddharth. 'It's not night-time now.' Finally, one of them relented, motioning him to enter.

R. Raj Rao

Siddharth discovered that the town wasn't half as idyllic as it had appeared that night from the train window. It was humid and dusty, polluted by decrepit vehicles.

After a rollercoaster ride through main roads, side roads, and bylanes, the auto-driver announced that they had reached the Shahapur area where Sudhir's house was located. 'Congratulations,' Siddharth felt tempted to say to him. He knew the house number by heart, but the houses didn't seem to be arranged numerically here. There was no pattern. House number 1546 followed house number 1325, he noticed with dismay, as he peered out of the three-wheeler. The auto-driver asked him if his hosts had mentioned any landmarks. 'Yes,' said Siddharth, his frown giving way to a smile as he suddenly remembered. 'Basava Tea House.'

Soon, the vehicle was outside the Basava Tea House and a few inquiries led him to Sudhir's place. But the driver would not free Siddharth till he had parted with fifty per cent of the return fare, although he'd promised to charge by the meter. 'One hour it is taking to come here,' he said.

'You cheat,' Siddharth wanted to scream, but restrained himself because the Raikar family (Sudhir's folks) had already assembled at the door to greet him and he didn't wish to create a scene.

'Welcome, welcome,' said Sudhir's father, shaking his hand and continuing to shake it for a couple of minutes. Siddharth observed that his voice cracked, like an adolescent's. Some people continued to remain adolescent throughout their adult life, he thought, charmed by the Ayurvedic doctor's boyish ways. He seemed to laugh for no apparent reason.

Immediately, Siddharth was taken on a labyrinthine tour of the haveli which left him utterly confused, even as the womenfolk (to whom he was not directly introduced)—Sudhir's mother who covered her head with her sari's pallu the moment he arrived, and his younger sister, Sneha, who merely bit her nails and smiled—disappeared into the kitchen. Used, as he was, to the dinky 500 square feet flat in which he grew up, the house seemed to him as large as Buckingham Palace.

Sudhir's father sat him down, offered him water and tea—in his letter to his parents, Sudhir had described his yaar as a tea addict—and tried to make conversation although he wasn't very fluent in English. While he wanted his guest to feel free in their house, what he actually said was 'feel freely'. I will, thought Siddharth, but unfortunately Su isn't here.

In the evening, Dr Raikar turned away the motley group of patients who had gathered at the front of his house, where his clinic was located, asking them to return the next day. He explained that they had a distinguished guest from Bombay who had to be entertained. The patients nodded and left without a murmur. Soon after, the doctor started his Bajaj Chetak scooter, and he and his guest were off on a tour of the town.

Siddharth formed a different impression now, for they rode to the outskirts surrounded by hills and brooks, where they had a magnificent view of the crimson sunset. His host told him of the resplendent Gokak waterfalls nearby, to which the citizens of Belgaum invariably took their visitors. Good place for our honeymoon, where we can shower together, Siddharth was thinking when the doctor spoilt it all. 'I and you will go there one day,' he declared.

The outing over, the family sat down to their evening meal, offering Siddharth a seat at the head of the table. The father recited a short Sanskrit prayer before they ate. It was satvic food, served in steel thalis. No one conversed as they ate, for Sudhir's father believed that the food on the plate felt belittled if undivided attention wasn't given to it. And when dinner was over and the mother and sister had finished cleaning up, the lights were switched off for the night without much ceremony, making Siddharth wonder if he was in a monastery.

A bed had been laid out for him in a room on the first floor, to get to which he had to ascend a narrow flight of stairs. This was Sudhir's room, the father informed him, giving him

R. Raj Rao

an alarm clock. (He pronounced the word as 'allah-ram'—in the interests of religious harmony, Siddharth thought.) But the room was totally without character. Nothing in the room bore the father out. No books, posters, cassettes, shirts, pants, shoes or underwear anywhere, that mark a young man's room. Siddharth's fatigue and the insipid room to which he was consigned cast him into a dreamless sleep from which he arose at sunrise to the singing of the Gayatri mantra. At first he thought it was Sudhir's mom and sister who were singing, but soon discovered it was actually the cassette player.

Siddharth dressed and went down and the good doctor engaged him in conversation again. He was pleased, he said, that his son had a friend who was a scholar with such a strong command over English. His good karma, nothing else. When, to impress him further, Siddharth told his host that he planned to do his PhD, and that the abbreviation stood for Doctor of Philosophy, he was immediately asked to write philosophical articles for *Pathway to God*, a Belgaum journal on whose editorial board the doctor was.

'I will, I will,' said Siddharth, who suddenly saw himself as Krishna and Sudhir as Arjuna. He said as much to his host, who replied, 'And you must prepare him for the Battle of Kurukshetra which, so far as he is concerned, is BE (Civil).'

'Certainly,' replied Siddharth, who now thought of all the times he had screwed the doctor's son.

30

By the end of the second day, Siddharth was bored with his stay in the Raikar household and wished he could advance his ticket. Even twenty-four hours, which was the time left for him to leave, seemed impossible to pass. True, he was experiencing traditional Indian hospitality. Sudhir's folks, especially the patriarch of the household, fussed over him constantly. He even went after him to the bathroom to check if there were clean towels. Not once did he have to ask for something to eat, or that his bed be made—his needs were anticipated before he could open his mouth. How different all this was from the attitude of Bombay parents who had no time for their own kids, let alone their friends' kids or kids' friends.

And yet, though they seemed to subscribe to the view that their guest was dearer to them than their own lives (*Mehmaan jo hamara hota hai, wo jaan se pyara hota hai*—the lyrics of an old Raj Kapoor song buzzed in Siddharth's head throughout his stay in the Raikar home), they were regimental to the core. Things followed a set pattern. There was no room for flexibility. Perhaps it would've been different if Sudhir had been around but, without him, three days were seventy-two hours too long.

Thus, when the hour of his departure finally arrived, he was glad to be leaving. His one regret was that he couldn't actually live out his fantasy of asking for Sudhir's hand in marriage. The Raikars were too prosaic to make any sense of this, even as a joke.

31

Anarkali, whom Siddharth called Begum Sahiba, was born in one of Belgaum district's diminutive hamlets as a male child with five siblings. When she attained puberty, her body language traumatized her. Her voice was high-pitched. When she sat, she involuntarily brought her legs close together, like a woman. Her walk was no different from that of Dream Girl Hema Malini, whom she adored. And she loved to dress in a sari.

Anarkali's father was an impoverished farm labourer, with four daughters and a five-figure debt on his head. His first wife was dead, but he had not been able to find a second. His health was failing. His two sons, who'd dropped out of school early, had no choice but to lend him a helping hand, tilling the soil. But this wasn't something that Anarkali could imagine doing. She was no bull who would plough the fields. She was a milch cow whose job it was to raise her calves.

Anarkali's drunkard father wanted her to bring him a daughter-in-law to do the household chores. Being the elder of the two sons, the family looked to her to fill the vacuum caused by her mother's death. The daughters of the house were here today, but tomorrow they would leave for their husbands' homes. Only a daughter-in-law would permanently slave away for the family. But women didn't turn Anarkali on. She couldn't visualize a sex life with women. Her fantasies centred on he-man Dharmendra, the moustached Kamal Haasan, the lanky Amitabh, and the smooth-faced Mithun. There were men in the hamlet too, with whom she was in love. But the love was unrequited, frustrating her. For Anarkali, a life without sex was no different from death. Her future was a blank slate. She often wondered why God had done this to her—given her an outer shell that made the world see her as a man while, inside, she was all feminine. Maybe God was distracted while making me, she thought, and so I arrived with a manufacturing defect.

One day, Anarkali left home to join a hijra clan in Belgaum city. Her family did nothing to trace her, viewing it as one mouth less to feed. Anarkali too felt much more at ease with her fellow hijras, most of them with personal histories similar to hers, than she did with her own family. Though many young hijras in the clan weren't castrated, and so continued to be men, Anarkali felt this was fraudulent. She undertook her castration rite soon, in the temple of the goddess Yellamma at Saundatti, very close to Belgaum, and acquired her new name, Anarkali, shortly thereafter.

The rite itself was gruesome, with her penis, testicles and scrotum all felled at one go sans anaesthesia. Anarkali howled as the surgery was being performed, but members of the clan beat their drums so hard while they demonically danced that she didn't hear her own cries. Afterwards, the pain lasted for days and the wound took weeks to heal but Anarkali insisted, stoically, like the Zoroastrians, that the severed pieces of her flesh be fed to the stray cats and dogs that hovered about the place.

Charismatic as she was, Anarkali soon assumed leadership of the clan. She acquired skills such as dancing and massaging. The hijras begged, whored, sang, danced, ate, prayed and slept together. And rarely, if ever, did disputes arise among them. Anarkali managed their finances with greater élan than many a chartered accountant. What the hijras wouldn't trade off for all the gold in the goldfields of Karnataka was the sense of community that their new identities provided. They may not have degrees, diplomas, well-paying jobs, bank balances, flats, cars and colour TV sets. But they had found happiness.

32

The term being on, Siddharth had taken the train all the way to Bombay, but he very nearly alighted when, opening his eyes, he saw that it had reached Pune. Cries of 'chai garam' rent the air. He would have a cup of tea, two maybe, and trek to the Engineering College Hostel, he thought. Night walks were fun. The air was cool and the streets were free of traffic. The only annoyance were the stray dogs that became fiendish at night, barking ferociously and chasing anyone who ventured into their territory. But even they could be fended off with stones.

Back in college, he indulged Savita and Pramila. They were yoked, in his mind, to his recent hosts whom he now deified, having compared and contrasted them with his own parents. Both girls came from families very similar with the Raikars and seemed to be Bombayites only by default. In spirit, they were closer to the people of Belgaum or Kolhapur or Satara—towns he had passed on his way. After college, he would spend a whole hour with them in an empty classroom, gossiping and listening to Hindi film songs from every Bollywood movie released in 1980.

The coming days saw him resume his tri-weekly trips to Pune, ostensibly to hold his Spoken English classes. While the others in the group had to be content with spelling, vocabulary and syntax, for Sudhir Siddharth devised an advanced course.

'Let's translate Bollywood film songs into English,' he said. 'There's no better way to master the language. Let's begin with *Sholay*.'

Before executing their task, they embarked on a preliminary discussion of the film. '*Yeh dosti*,' Siddharth pointed out, 'is a love song sung by two homoerotic men who shun the company of women. A woman appears in the song and is summarily dismissed by the toss of a coin. She's, all said and done, a kebab mein haddi. The lovers speak of eating and drinking together, living and dying together, for life. *Khana peena saath hai, marna jeena saath hai, sari zindagi.* Isn't this the kind of domestic arrangement we call marriage? Moreover, "sari" also indicates their desire to dress in saris.'

However, the status quoist in Sudhir was unwilling to accept the interpretation.

Siddharth continued. 'The lyrics get progressively lewder. The world sees us as two, but we're actually one. *Logon ko aate hai do nazar hum, magar dekho do nahin.* This is accompanied by a visual where Dharmendra, riding pillion on a motorbike with Amitabh, is made to look as if he's sodomizing him! What do we mean when we say two people have become one? We mean they're fucking. As if this isn't enough, there's a run-on line that says, *Tere liye le lenge sabse dushmani.* If you ignore the enjambment, *le lenge* implies Amitabh's willing to get fucked by Dharmendra. For that is what *le lenge*, as everyone knows, means. The song ends with Amitabh astride Dharmendra's shoulders, the back of Dharmendra's head massaging Amitabh's crotch.'

Sudhir was still unconvinced. 'They're just buddies,' he said to Siddharth. 'You have a one-track mind.'

Siddharth clinched the issue by asking him a question. 'If Dharmendra sang the same song with, say, Hema Malini, would you then say they were buddies? No, you'd say they were lovers. That's because you have been brainwashed into believing that only a man and a woman can be lovers. Gaurav has a word for it—heterosexism.'

Sudhir was confused.

They began to translate the whole song, Sudhir in charge of the source language (Hindi) and Siddharth in charge of the target (English). After many disagreements over the choice of a word, or the meaning of a sentence, they succeeded in their task, avoiding a literal rendering.

We won't end this friendship,
We shall be together even in death.

Listen my friend:
Your victory is mine
My loss is yours.
Your sorrow is my sorrow
My life is your life.

For you I will risk this life,
For you I will play with fire,
Make enemies of the whole world.

People see us as two,
But actually we are one.
O God, bless us
So we never separate,
Never wound one another.

We shall eat and drink together,
Live and die together,
Till life lasts.

33

Returning to Bombay one day, Siddharth found a letter waiting for him. The handwriting looked like Sudhir's but, on scrutiny, he saw that it wasn't. In any case, why would Sudhir write to him when they were together every Monday, Wednesday, Friday, Saturday and Sunday?

Ripping open the letter, he discovered it was from Sudhir's father. This is how it went.

Belgaum
30 November 1980

My dear son Siddharth,
Re: Your recent visit to Belgaum

We were very happy to have you with us this month. We hope we could do everything in our capacity to make your stay in Belgaum comfortable. If we committed any errors, kindly forgive us as you would forgive your own parents. After you left, we were depressed for many days.

Sudhir is very lucky to have a friend like you. Please teach him how to study and pass in First Class, just like your good self. I have spent much money to send him to Pune for engineering course, and would one day like him to go to America. Kindly help him to improve English, which is very important these days in order to get good job.

You must visit us in Belgaum again. Please come whenever you feel to, our door will always be open to you. My Mrs and daughter Sneha were also very glad that you graced our house.

Kindly send me your article on Bhagavad Gita for Pathway to God by return of post. We will publish in

next issue only which is already in press. Please
remember that it is not only Sudhir who loves you, but
all of us too. We think of you as family member.
    I will end letter now with kind regards to you and
your kith and kine.

                                                    Yours,
                                        Dr Madhav Raikar

A funny feeling came over Siddharth as he finished reading the letter. The man could do with some English lessons himself, he thought. Kith and kine! Why, 'kine' was the plural of cow in old English! Then, the thought: is he his son's rival for a place in my heart, in love with me himself?

As the days went by and the year drew to a close, Siddharth found himself thinking more and more, not just of Sudhir, but of his father, mother and sister, his recent visit to their sprawling wada home, and of the city of Belgaum itself.

His own parents continued to harangue him for absconding from home for over half the week, for not contributing to household expenses though he was employed, and for not attempting to find a job in a decent college that wouldn't shame them before their colleagues. 'How can you get a job in a good college if you don't read the classifieds in the *Times of India* and respond to advertisements?' his father asked him.

Siddharth didn't answer the question, partly because he had no answer and partly because he did not wish to have another argument with his father, with mother dear soon joining in. What did they know of the unemployment that was rampant in the country? They talked as if jobs were available on a platter, waiting to be grabbed. Just because it had been all hunky-dory in their time, did not mean it was the same now. Moreover, he wasn't sure if he wanted to switch over from Azad College just yet. Would he be able to take the train to Pune three times a week if he were employed in

St. Xavier's or Jai Hind or Elphinstone—colleges his parents thought of as the next best thing to Oxford and Cambridge? Students in those colleges were reputed to be snooty, poles apart from the likes of Savita and Pramila. They would scoff at the idea of singing Hindi film songs to him in empty classrooms after college. Bombay, he was convinced, was a city without a heart. His parents, though not born in Bombay, had grown to be thorough Bombayites over the years. They were deracinated to the core. It was environments like Azad College, and girls like Savita and Pramila, who, though a part of the mercenary city, had retained something of the real India that he had briefly tasted in Sudhir's home.

How affable Sudhir's father was—not just to him, who was their guest, but to all and sundry, his wife, his kids, his patients. He may not have possessed the latest Premier Padmini Deluxe, the way his own father did, changing cars every couple of years, but his Bajaj Chetak scooter was good enough for him to take his son's yaar on a tour of the town, taking time off from work. Learning that Siddharth aspired to publish articles and see his name in print, the man had offered to get his writings published in *Pathway to God*. What had his own father done for him by contrast? Only ridiculed him, when he found him putting pen to paper, remarking caustically that no newspaper or magazine would be interested in his work. And Sudhir's mom? She seemed to be the incarnation of Indian womanhood, Mother India herself, keeping her head covered with her sari's pallu, confining herself to the kitchen where she cooked wholesome meals for her husband and children, and not opening her mouth when the menfolk spoke. She was the sort of mother who would massage his head with oil on Sundays, and in whose lap he could place his head and cry. Conversely, his mom was a garrulous career woman who went to her dispensary and left the management of the home to servants. Let alone crying in her lap or on her shoulder, or being given an oil bath on public holidays, Siddharth couldn't recall being touched by her even once after he had ceased to be an infant.

34

Naturally, therefore, given half a chance to go to Belgaum again, barely a month later, Siddharth seized it by the collar. Circumstances this time were entirely in his favour. It was nearing Christmas, when colleges in Bombay closed for as long as ten days. Azad College may not have had a single Christian student on its rolls (the management was said to have RSS leanings), but it was an affiliated college and had to abide by university rules. And the rule was that colleges remained shut for two months in summer, a month during Diwali, and a week during Christmas. Given his nomadic lifestyle, this is what Siddharth loved about his profession. He resolved never to trade it for any other job, even though his father, from time to time, proposed that he switch to a better-paying job in the private sector. 'Rubbish,' he would swear to himself at such times. 'Has a mad dog bitten me or what?'

Again, the second half of December was the end of the semester for engineering students, when they wrote their exams and went on a fifteen-day break immediately afterwards. It meant that Sudhir would go with him to Belgaum, a thought that filled him with excitement. To cap it all, the climate in December everywhere in India was truly rejuvenating. For once, the sun that ubiquitously shone on the subcontinent all day wasn't as harsh. Thus, Siddharth enjoyed every moment, as Sudhir and he walked to the bus depot to reserve their tickets. They would travel by bus this time, for the buses went to Belgaum directly, while trains necessitated a change from broad gauge to metre gauge at Miraj Junction.

R. Raj Rao

Everything was set. They would leave on the 23rd of December and return on the 1st of January.

When they found themselves in the red-and-cream ST bus that was to take them to their destination, and eventually their destiny, he recalled the ST bus that the poet Arun Kolatkar had recently made famous in his poem *Jejuri*.

They reached Belgaum in the wee hours. However, Sudhir being present this time, they had no hassles getting home. A local, he knew how to deal with auto-drivers and suchlike. The driver tamely deposited them where he was told to and, impressively, didn't charge a single extra rupee. Seeing him take the reins in his hands for the first time since they'd met, Siddharth realised that it was here, in the town of his birth, that his yaar was in his element. He also discovered that Sudhir knew more than a few words of Kannada.

Dr Raikar hugged Siddharth when, waking up in the morning, he found him at the breakfast table with Sudhir, eating steaming hot upma and poha. 'Son, I'm so much happy to see you again,' he said and, then, without warning, fished out an old box camera from an almirah and clicked the two of them. Our wedding photograph, thought Siddharth. Aloud he said, 'This one is for keeps.'

Though Sudhir's father was happy to see Siddharth again, he realized with a twinge of regret that their guest's second visit was different from the first. He spent all his time with Sudhir, walking the length and breadth of the town as the latter showed him the haunts of his boyhood—his school, his college and various grounds where he had played cricket and football, desperate to be manly. Dr Raikar, on the other hand, saw Siddharth only at mealtimes. He tried to engage him in discussions on the Bhagavad Gita but, clearly, Siddharth's mind wasn't on it and he sought the earliest excuse to slip away.

Night came, and Sudhir's mother promptly laid two mattresses, with mosquito nets, in the first-floor room that allegedly was his. Siddharth surveyed their sleeping arrangements and noted with dismay that the good lady had separated the two bedrolls by a distance of more than three feet. There was no way, of course, in which he could register his protest, or demand that the mattresses be replaced by a flower-bedecked double bed.

It was Sudhir who took control of the situation again. Bolting the door from within, the moment his parents downstairs switched off the lights, he ruffled the sheets of his own bed to make it look slept in, before sneaking into Siddharth's, where they had a night of torrid fucking and sucking, kissing and pissing—they savoured each other's urine, taking Prime Minister Morarji Desai's prescription a step further. Siddharth managed to get the tip of his tongue deep into Sudhir's arsehole, which he licked clean, loving the smell. Sudhir, as he was being rimmed, asked his slave the question, 'Were you really a dog in your previous janam?'

The ritual went on for all the seven nights they were in Belgaum. For seven nights, they were in seventh heaven.

If jealousy was the word that best described Dr Raikar's state of mind, as the young man he admired dumped him in favour of his son, Siddharth too found some reason to be jealous. He was troubled by the closeness his yaar displayed, not towards his father or mother, but towards his sister Sneha. At home, they clung to each other constantly. They spoke a private lingo and laughed at jokes, of which Siddharth could never be a part. Once, left with little to do, Siddharth strolled into the kitchen to find Sneha applying mehendi to Sudhir's hands. She lovingly held his hand in her own and squeezed the chocolate-coloured liquid on to it from a shimmering red paper cone. In front of her was a book of patterns and she flipped through the pages with her left hand to choose the one that would suit her brother best. Though Siddharth seated himself next to them and pretended to enjoy what was going on, he was actually nonplussed. The mehendi went with

Sudhir's personality all right, but they weren't getting married yet, so why was he already indulging in this bridal activity? Didn't the physical closeness of brother and sister, as she painted his palms, amount to incest? Siddharth was reminded of a Ramanujan poem he taught at Azad College, in which the poet facetiously suggested that, since brothers and sisters had so much in common, they should be permitted to marry each other, instead of being betrothed to strangers with whom they had little in common.

35

Anarkali fell in love with Raj Kumar the moment she set eyes on him at a naming ceremony where she'd gone to dance. Raj Kumar was a distant relative of the hosts, mostly blue-collared mill workers in Bombay, with an ancestral home in Belgaum city. The matchmaking women in the gathering viewed Raj Kumar as a prospective bridegroom and sang paeans. What the ladies didn't know was that Raj Kumar was a mixture of masculinity and femininity, with the scales tipped in favour of the latter. Classmates teased him, calling him names. 'Chhakka,' they would viciously say. One or two even molested him in the school grounds. Unable to take it, Raj Kumar had left school. In time, Raj Kumar, as he loafed at bus stands and street corners, met others like himself. They called themselves kotis, all of them possessing hybrid sexual natures with a preference for those of their own gender. Though Raj Kumar lived at home and found a peon's job in the plaza, he felt most at ease hanging out with the kotis in the evening.

Raj Kumar's family had no inkling of his life with the kotis. By day he was an earning son, fulfilling his filial duties. By night, he sold his body to havildars, truck drivers and shopkeepers. The kotis mostly dressed like men, but on weekends they cross-dressed. They earned up to 300 bucks a day from sex work and massages, which they kept for themselves. After an evening's dhanda, they frequently repaired to a beer bar where they noisily laughed and frolicked, trying to entice all the men in the bar before getting home close to midnight.

Raj Kumar's wild ways with the kotis partially ended when Anarkali proposed to him after the naming ceremony, when the guests had left. Both of them needed an anchor in life, she argued, and they would do well to get together. While marriage would necessarily mean having a sex life together, they were both free to carry on their commercial sexual activities as before. That, after all, was a crucial source of livelihood.

Raj Kumar did not jump at Anarkali's offer but asked for time to think over the matter. Anarkali told him to take his time and gave him her address. What bothered Raj Kumar was that while he would be the man and Anarkali the wife, it was she who was taller and he shorter.

Still, Anarkali and Raj Kumar dated each other every Sunday night. They squatted on the grass in a public park where they chatted, gossiped, sang, played chess and discussed the latest Bollywood flick. Seeing them in the public park every week, a friendly passer-by remarked that they made a beautiful couple. Sometimes, the couple shopped in the plaza—the very plaza where Raj Kumar worked—but his finery so disguised him that there was no danger of his being recognized and seen with a hijra. They bought clothes, costume jewellery, slippers, perfumes and sweets, but never for themselves, always for each other. Such was their devotion.

The hijras in Anarkali's clan and the kotis in Raj Kumar's circle of friends rejoiced at their alliance. The joy was political as much as personal for, in committing themselves to each other, they were really turning their backs on a hostile society that saw them as freaks and exploited them without remorse. They did everything in their power to convince Raj Kumar to accept Anarkali's marriage proposal.

36

On the penultimate day of his stay in the Raikar home, just as Sudhir and he stepped into the house after a matinee show, Siddharth found his host frantically searching for something.

They'd gone to see *Shaan*, Ramesh Sippy's next offering after the record-breaking *Sholay*. Siddharth decided to show Sudhir the film when he found him humming the *Yamma yamma* number to himself (whistling it even) night and day. He settled for a matinee show because they were cheaper than regular shows by as much as 50 per cent. If *Sholay* saw Amitabh Bachchan madly in love with Dharmendra, in *Shaan* he was in love with Shashi Kapoor.

It was not just the doctor, but his wife and daughter too had joined in the search. He screamed at them for misplacing it (never before had Siddharth seen him lose his temper) but they did not retaliate, just quietly went about looking for it everywhere. Siddharth couldn't figure out what it was they were trying to retrieve, so he asked his yaar who told him it was a letter. A letter that the doctor wanted to show Siddharth because it concerned him, but now that he'd mislaid it his purpose was frustrated.

This made Siddharth anxious. He wondered who'd authored the letter and mailed it to Sudhir's father, of all people. Could it be his own folks who had somehow obtained Sudhir's address (they were good at espionage) and written to his father to give him a piece of their mind? Unlikely, for he had taken care not to leave the address anywhere in the flat. Or was it a letter from the editor of *Pathway to God*, rejecting his article on the Bhagavad Gita because it was phoney? That seemed more plausible. Dr Raikar had boasted he could get him in print and now felt slighted by the editor's decision. Yes, that was what it had to be.

The suspense ended when Sudhir's father summoned Siddharth to the dining table only to reveal that the letter was from 'a classmate of Sudhir's, by name of one Mr Ravi Humbe'.

Siddharth's immediate reaction was, 'Oh . . . him.'

Though the letter was now untraceable, continued the doctor, he remembered the contents clearly and would give his guest the gist of it. That he'd lost the letter meant, in truth, that he did not take it seriously, he added. But the letter, written in Marathi, accused Siddharth of playing with the future of the entire Belgaum gang, especially Sudhir, by taking their minds off their studies.

He's here in our hostel for most of the week, though he's supposed to have a lecturer's job in Bombay, it said. He conducts English language classes, but have we come here to study engineering or English? Above all, he's a bad influence on your son Sudhir, who's completely under his control and only does what the man allows him to do. I even have a dirty photo of the two of them, which I can't show you. At this rate, Sudhir will never pass his exams and will have to repeat the year. As such, he did badly in his internals. I request you, kaka, to write to Sudhir and warn him against the cunning of this man. He's using your son. Perhaps you should take a couple of days off from your dispensary and come to Pune to see for yourself. But don't let Sudhir know about this in advance. Make a surprise visit. But even if you can't come, please write him a stern letter asking him to keep away from this fellow. If this does not work, then you should write to the man himself, whose name is Siddharth, c/o our address, warning him not to visit our hostel again.

Dr Raikar, who hadn't looked Siddharth in the eye while narrating the contents of the letter, now made eye contact with him and saw that his face had fallen. He had frown-lines on his forehead.

The doctor burst into laughter. 'My dear son,' he said. 'Have no worry. I did not take Mr Ravi Humbe's letter seriously. If

R. Raj Rao

so, I would not have told you about it. I would have quietly made inquiries. I have full faith in you and am very happy that you are Sudhir's best friend. Now, I'll tell you about Mr Ravi Humbe's background. He is coming from a very poor family. His father is farm labourer in village close to Belgaum city. So Mr Ravi Humbe is getting jealous that why you are Sudhir's best friend only and not his best friend also? So he is writing letter. You please continue going to hostel whenever you wish, and continue Spoken English classes also. I am sure that in your company Sudhir will study more, not less. If Mr Ravi Humbe is not liking, he's free to leave hostel and find private room outside. But please don't worry. I have already forgotten letter, and if ever I am finding it, I shall tear it into pieces and throw them into fire. I promise you that, so you please don't worry.'

The doctor's speech relieved Siddharth somewhat, but he was still ill at ease. Dirty photo? That Neanderthal, Ravi Humbe, had to be liquidated. The question was: How?

He looked around the room and was startled to see Sudhir's mother at the door, furtively listening to what her husband said, one end of her sari's pallu stuffed into her mouth, as usual. She'd been there all along and he had not even known! There was a look in her eyes that seemed to say, Ravi Humbe is right. This man here is an outsider. Why is he interfering in our lives? Why are my son and husband taken in by his charm? I find him ugly. He has mesmerized my son and I see it as a bad omen. But what say in the matter do I have? Is a woman's opinion ever considered?

37

In Pune, Siddharth assigned Sudhir their next Bollywood song.

'Remember *Zanjeer*, released seven years ago? It was the film that changed Amitabh's fortunes. Had it not been for

Zanjeer he might have died unsung.' Siddharth went on to make an inventory of heroes with whom Amitabh Bachchan had been romantically paired by producers, directors and scriptwriters—Dharmendra, Rajesh Khanna, Shashi Kapoor, Vinod Khanna, Shatrughan Sinha and Rishi Kapoor. 'In *Zanjeer*, it's the redoubtable Pran, formerly a villain. The *Yaari hai iman* song that Pran sings to Amitabh is a love lyric. Amitabh looks so coy as the manly Pathan sings to him.'

They were about to translate the song when something struck Siddharth. 'You know, most of Amitabh's roles have been written by Salim-Javed, whom *Stardust* bitchily refers to as Shaw-Shakespeare. It's possible that Salim and Javed are projecting their own yearnings on screen, by pairing Amitabh off with other heroes. What I'm saying, is that Salim and Javed are gay lovers.' Sudhir laughed.

They racked their brains over the lyrics of the song, which took much longer to translate than the *Sholay* number. Two hours later they were done.

Yaari is my religion,
My yaar is my life.

I won't regret
Dying for the sake of yaari,
I'd sooner die than see my friend morose.
The fairground of happiness
Is where we are together.

Why does the flower of my garden look so sad?
Is he a victim of ill will?
Have no qualms, friend, let me into your heart.
Let me know the price of your smile.

Shall I bring you the moon and the stars?
Shall I bring you sights that gratify the senses?

I'm grateful you are my friend,
Your smile is my greatest treasure.

When my yaar smiles
My youthfulness returns.

38

Not one to heed warning signals, Siddharth made yet another trip to Belgaum in February. A total solar eclipse was to occur at Karwar, a three-hour bus ride from the town, and he brainwashed Sudhir into accompanying him. 'We'll be fools if we miss this once-in-a-lifetime spectacle,' he said. 'No matter what the reason.'

What did he know, then, of the impending total solar eclipse in his own life?

Sudhir went, his classes and project work notwithstanding. His father wasn't amused to see him during term (they had not informed him they were coming) but his honeymoon with Siddharth was not yet over. Not only did he give his son permission to go to Karwar, he also declared that he too would be joining them, causing Siddharth to swear. 'Kebab mein haddi,' he muttered under his breath. The ladies of the household expressed a desire to go as well and, for once, the patriarch agreed. He hired a Matador and soon they were off.

Once they hit the road, Siddharth stopped sulking and began to rather enjoy this family outing with his spouse and in-laws. They stopped on the highway to eat the idlis and chutney Sudhir's mother had especially prepared for the journey. These were washed down with tea from an Eagle flask. Sudhir was silent throughout the ride, except when he and Sneha giggled for no apparent reason. He was mortally afraid that Siddharth would out him with his indecent moves—fondling his crotch and balls when he thought no one was looking. The doctor—who, though seated next to the driver in front, kept turning around to give them a running commentary on what every village they passed through was famous for—hogged the limelight.

Eventually, they reached their destination, checked into a small hotel run by the brother of one of Dr Raikar's patients, and got ready for darkness at noon. That he knew someone who owned a hotel mattered, for it would have been a Herculean task to find accommodation otherwise, half the world having descended on Karwar.

The sky was overcast. Everyone was on the beach. Gradually, it grew dusky although it was early afternoon. And then it grew so dark that the birds began to fly back to their nests. Dogs howled. When the sun was completely eclipsed by the moon, a phenomenon known as the Diamond Ring was witnessed in the sky. It was a sight ten times more beautiful than the Kohinoor diamond. Siddharth whispered into Sudhir's ear, 'My love, this is the kind of cosmic ring I'll give you for our wedding.' Blushing, the latter turned around to make sure his folks hadn't heard.

The overcrowded beach had its share of hawkers too, who, instead of training their eyes on the skies above, resignedly went about selling their wares. It's useless casting pearls before swine, Siddharth thought when, to his chagrin, he saw the doctor patronizing one of the hawkers. He bought peanuts for the family—five paper cones of them—which he dutifully distributed. The distraction annoyed Siddharth who was busy with his camera, but he controlled his rage by popping peanuts into his mouth.

Then it was all over. And within half an hour of the sun being restored to its place of glory in the sky, Karwar was a deserted village. Everyone started their cars and left. The Raikars were among the last to leave because the driver of their Matador had disappeared. He surfaced an hour later, even as they fretted and, when the doctor sarcastically inquired whether the eclipse had affected his brain, he revealed that he had gone to another part of the beach to fish. The fish, it seems, committed a sort of hara-kiri as they voluntarily sprang on to the beach when the eclipse was at its height. People promptly put them into plastic bags and carried them home for a scrumptious dinner. The driver himself had acquired two large bhangdas which, he said, he intended to carry in the van—making the Raikars, especially Mrs Raikar, squirm.

'But fish is vegetable of sea,' said the driver, astonishing Siddharth with his wit. Maybe, he should stop driving and start writing articles for *Pathway to God*, he said to himself.

39

Anarkali and Raj Kumar solemnized their wedding in Karwar. Raj Kumar agreed, not because of the hijras and kotis, but because he was a singer. Anarkali with her dancing, and I with my singing, can team up to form a fine partnership, he told himself.

At the height of the total solar eclipse, precisely at the moment when the sky was enveloped by darkness and the Diamond Ring appeared, the offbeat couple garlanded each other before a portrait of the goddess Yellamma, and Raj Kumar put his own version of a diamond ring (made of cheap imitation jewels) on Anarkali's finger. 'That's all I can afford,' he said, in response to which Anarkali patted his cheeks and put her fingers to his lips. 'I promise to be yours for life,' she said.

All the other hijras and kotis applauded them. A fire was lit on the wind-blown beach, with firewood and oil, which the newlyweds circled seven times while coconuts were broken. Even mantras were recited. The chanting was the prerogative of neither the hijras nor the kotis, but the hermaphrodites, a handful of whom were part of Anarkali's clan. 'The hermaphrodites are the Brahmins among us,' Anarkali reasoned. 'None is as pure as them.'

Everyone popped pedas into their mouths. This was followed by a bada khana, a wedding lunch, comprising the most delectable non-vegetarian fare prepared by those among the hijras and the kotis who were culinary experts. The pell-mell on the beach as the eclipse ended did not bother anyone. They worked at their own leisurely pace, unfazed by the crowd of onlookers who, through with the total solar eclipse, now trained their cameras on them.

'Do remember to send us the photos you are clicking,' Anarkali yelled at the crowd, forgetting she was the bride. 'Remember, we're allowing you to photograph us for free. Where in India will you get to see a hijra-koti shaadi?'

Two shacks had been rented on the beach—one for the honeymooners, the other for everyone else. Raj Kumar engaged in active penetrative sex, remarking to Anarkali while they were entwined that it would prepare him for his real marriage, just around the corner. This hurt her so much she began to bawl.

But Raj Kumar wasn't joking. His putative family had no idea he was, at that moment, solemnizing wedding vows with a hijra. They had their own marriage plans for him and were showing his photograph to the parents of girls of their caste. Raj Kumar was doomed to live a schizophrenic life, comprising his parents, wife, children and job in the plaza by day, and Anarkali, sex work and the company of fellow kotis by night. And neither side would ever become aware of the existence of the other. This was what the total solar eclipse had prophesied for him.

In the late evening, several of the marriage party came by a windfall. They were ushered into suites of luxury hotels to massage scores of foreigners who'd gravitated to Karwar from nearby Goa. Charging their white clients six times the price they charged Indians for a maalish in a public park, they returned home with wads of currency notes.

40

Emboldened by the fact that the father had trashed Ravi Humbe's letter, and had given him carte blanche to visit Sudhir whenever he fancied, Siddharth now began to stay at the hostel with impunity for days at a stretch. He neglected his job at Azad College, remaining absent without applying for casual leave through the proper channels. In short, he bunked. Some call it French leave. The consequences didn't bother him. If the worst comes to the worst, I'll lose the job, he reasoned. Matters of the heart had grown to be far more pressing for him than a mere source of livelihood.

For his part, Ravi Humbe mobilized the Belgaum gang and founded a group that he malevolently called Siddharth Virudh Sanghatana (SVS). The group's one-point programme was to impose a blanket ban on Professor Siddharth, as they called him, at the Engineering College Hostel and rescue their bechara friend Sudhir from his clutches. As per their charter, Pune had two dangerous men to beware of: Bhagwan Rajneesh and Professor Siddharth. The latter's English class was to be discontinued forthwith, and he would be in dire straits if he was ever spotted anywhere near the rooms of the Belgaum boys. If he defied the ban, the SVS would contemplate reporting him to the police. Meetings were held every week in Ravi Humbe's room, where they discussed strategy. Some were in favour of printing pamphlets with Siddharth's photograph, cautioning all and sundry against his guiles. These would then be pasted on the walls of each hostel block, in the mess, and so on. There were others, however, who advised the group against putting anything in black and white, because the man could then sue them for defamation. There were also those who believed in violence and were ready to thrash the chap black and blue, if only their chief gave them the order.

Two hostellers who got word about the formation of the SVS and began to closely monitor its moves were, but of course, Gaurav and Vivek. According to them, what impelled Ravi Humbe was homophobia. 'He knows you are gay, and is gunning for you because he can't stand gay buggers,' said Gaurav.

Homophobia was on the top of their list of prejudices to be tackled, because that's what they were advised by their gay counterparts in Britain and the US, with whom they were in touch. They were quite willing to ambush the culprit, Ravi Humbe, as he returned from the mess or from coaching classes, and beat him up till he lay bleeding on the road. 'That's the way to deal with homophobia,' said Gaurav. 'Once their leader is eliminated, the others will put their tails between their legs and scram.'

It was now virtually impossible for Siddharth to stay in Sudhir's room. Someone or the other from the SVS kept a twenty-four-hour vigil and threatened their classmate with dire consequences if he played host to their enemy. Sudhir suggested to Siddharth that he move out of the hostel and look for a private room elsewhere. But it was hard to find a room during the middle of the term, engineering students having cornered every available inch of living space. If a room were available at this time of the year, the charges would be exorbitant. Some landlords offered him group accommodation on a 'cot basis', which Siddharth promptly turned down.

Finally, it was Gaurav and Vivek (again) who came to his rescue. They invited Siddharth to 'parasite' with them as long as he wanted. 'The warden hardly ever comes to the hostel,' they said. 'And if he suddenly pops up, we'll tell him you're

R. Raj Rao

our cousin who's visiting from the US. Just speak to him with a Yankee accent.'

Siddharth liked the argument and the arrangement—the only hitch being that, though in the same hostel, Sudhir and he would now be sleeping in separate rooms. Gaurav saw his downcast eyes and offered to put up Sudhir as well. However, Sudhir flatly refused to comply because (a) Gaurav and Vivek were la-di-da Bombayites who gave him an inferiority complex, (b) he didn't want them to see Siddharth going on top of him in bed, even if they were gay, and (c) members of the SVS would chop off his balls if he left his room to go and stay in C Block.

Gaurav and Vivek's room now housed even more gay literature and gay porn than when Siddharth had last visited them. Likewise, the walls had more pin-ups. The duo—especially Gaurav, the more garrulous of the two—constantly spoke of a revolution, a gay revolution, in the offing. He observed that whenever Gaurav spoke on the subject, he lit up. When Vivek asked him how many packs of cigarettes he smoked in a day, he tossed his brownish hair back and answered, 'Just ten.'

Mate, you'll die of lung cancer before your revolution happens, thought Siddharth. However, they had helped him score a point in his war with the SVS and he was grateful to them for that.

41

The constant taunting of his wife and the reference to the dirty photo made Dr Raikar return to Ravi Humbe's letter several times to read between the lines. He had found it and safely tucked it away in his almirah, as if it was a letter disclosing the whereabouts of Netaji Subhash Chandra Bose! According to Mrs Raikar, Siddharth was nothing but a glib talker, like the bogus sadhus she read about in the Diwali editions of Marathi magazines. What formed this impression was his self-proclaimed interest in the Bhagavad Gita, which was one of the two ways in which they saw him—the other, of course, being his role as an English teacher. But when his wife woke up screaming one night because she'd dreamt that Siddharth had kidnapped her only son and transformed him into a saffron-clad sanyasi, Dr Raikar felt it was time to travel to Pune and investigate.

Mrs Raikar lovingly packed puris and potatoes for him in a steel tiffin box, and she and Sneha saw him off at the door. He boarded the first available bus though it was packed to capacity. As a result, he had to stand in the aisle, precariously clutching the handlebar above his head, for a good two hours before the bus reached Kolhapur where several passengers alighted.

Six hours later, Dr Raikar was in Pune, a city he hadn't visited since his own college days. It seemed to him almost like a foreign country, with disciplined traffic, tree-lined pavements and, above all, dust-free roads. Hailing an auto-rickshaw, he reached the Engineering College Hostel.

Sudhir never suspected that his father was going to pay him a visit. Dr Raikar had made sure not to inform him in advance for, as Ravi Humbe had advised, he intended this to be a surprise visit—not unlike those made by health inspectors who swoop down on eating houses and revoke their licences for not being hygienic enough. He was away at the mess drinking his evening tea when Dr Raikar made his way to E Block after accosting scores of students to ask for directions.

On seeing his father squatting on the steps waiting for him, Sudhir was shocked. 'Baba, you? Is everything okay at home?' he asked in Marathi, trying his best to hide his displeasure. Then he picked up his father's suitcase and unlocked the door of his room, wondering where he would make his father's bed. Obviously, he would give his own bed

R. Raj Rao

to his father and sleep on the floor. Farouq would have no option but to put up with the nuisance for a day or two.

Taking advantage of the fact that, exhausted after the bus journey, his father lay down on the bed and closed his eyes, Sudhir slipped out of his room to make an STD call to Siddharth, who'd gone to Bombay for the weekend, and apprise him of the developments. 'Don't come here, even by mistake, till I call again,' he yelled into the phone.

As was his wont, Siddharth wanted answers to a host of questions. Why is he here? When will he leave? Does Ravi Humbe know? And so on. However, Sudhir cut him short, promising to phone later.

Afterwards, when his father woke up from the nap, he opened his suitcase and handed Sudhir the homemade ladoos and chivda his mother had sent. Farouq entered at this point and was happy to be offered the eatables. Not pleased that a parent would inhabit the room for the next three days, he, nonetheless, couldn't express his resentment or anguish for he had just consumed their victuals. Besides, only a month or so earlier, his own old man had come to Pune all the way from Basra and Sudhir hadn't batted an eyelid as they had incestuously slept on the same bed for a never-ending week.

The next day, virtually every student from Belgaum who was studying in the Engineering College (and some from other colleges too) came to pay obeisance to the revered Ayurvedic doctor. These included SVS members, who said in unison, 'The father of one of our friends is no less than our own father.' The doctor was truly impressed by their aphorism. However, they made it a point not to tell him anything about the SVS. 'It's a thing between us boys, and parents should be left out of it,' they decided, forgetting, or perhaps not possessing any knowledge of, the letter their chief had written to the man before whom they now respectfully stood, their arms behind their backs. Even Ravi Humbe, when he came to meet Dr Raikar, did not bring up the letter.

On his part, the doctor chose not to introduce it into the conversation either.

Yet, in his heart of hearts, Ravi Humbe was flattered—deeply flattered—because it was his letter that had motivated the doctor to come to the college and spy on his son's activities.

42

A day after Sudhir's father left for Belgaum, having given him a host of instructions on how to conduct himself, Siddharth arrived at C Block to find his room sealed. He knocked on his neighbour's door and was informed that the police had raided the room the previous day. Gaurav and Vivek had been taken into custody. The neighbour, a student from Nepal, handed Siddharth a note from his friends that read: *Please come to the police station as soon as possible to rescue us.*

He remembered something that he'd heard his mother say. When misfortunes come, they come together. Debating with himself about what was more important—meeting his yaar after nearly a week, or freeing his gay comrades from the police—he decided it was the latter and headed straight for the Shivajinagar police station. For once, he was letting personal interests take a back seat.

The sub-inspector in charge of the case, P.S.I. Kelkar, was suspicious of Siddharth from the moment he set eyes on him. In his scheme of things, the world was divided into two kinds of people—Maharashtrians and non-Maharashtrians. And, like the fellows whose release he'd come to secure, Siddharth too was a non-Maharashtrian pariah. How, then, was he to trust him? In the end, he capitulated only because Siddharth flashed his Azad College ID card, which introduced him as a professor of English. But Siddharth had to furnish a bail bond of 3,000 rupees, which was much more than a month's salary for him. And P.S.I. Kelkar gave them all (Siddharth included) a stern warning, and made them sign dozens of papers in triplicate before he ordered his constables to unlock the two chaps and let them go.

'If, ever again, I am finding dirty sexy magazines in your room,' he thundered, wagging a finger at them as he spoke, 'I am issuing non-bailable warrant against all you three persons, including your good self, Mr Professor. I am not caring even if you are bade baap ka beta.'

Phew, Siddharth exclaimed to himself as he parted with hard cash (hard-earned, too) and walked out of the police station with his comrades-in-arms.

Agitated though they were, Gaurav and Vivek were also proud of the fact that the police had got them. 'It means that the world is taking notice of our revolution,' Gaurav said, chewing gum and blowing a bubble. 'Look at the fucking Naxalites. Aren't they being continually chased by cops?'

'Indeed,' said Siddharth. 'But mate, you need to be out here to change the world, not behind bars. So, no harm in being discreet.'

Vivek, on the other hand, was interested in 'doing a post-mortem' of the entire episode. 'Obviously, some son of a bitch spilled the beans on us,' he said. 'We must find out who the chutiya is and rape him.'

This, Siddharth pointed out, wasn't going to be easy. Adopting their lingo, he said, 'You're on okay terms with everyone in C Block. So why would anyone want to take panga with you?'

To which Gaurav, once an avid Agatha Christie reader, replied, 'You never know who's a cat among the pigeons.'

'Talking of cats,' said Siddharth. 'I think I'm fairly certain who let the cat out of the bag.' He had the notorious SVS in mind. But no, he wasn't going to complicate matters by openly blaming them. Suppose it was someone else?

'If you're so sure, why don't you tell us? If it's any of your ghati pals from E Block, we'll strip them naked and parade them through the town, with each one's dick in his neighbour's arsehole.'

'Cool it, mate. It's useless doing anything that will ruin our own cause.'

They sat together, in solidarity, for a long time. When Siddharth looked at his wristwatch, he discovered it was well past midnight. His date with Sudhir, which always brought him to Pune, would have to wait till morning.

43

The rector of the hostel was on long leave when the police raid took place. This gave Gaurav and Vivek the impression that the college authorities were in the dark about the presence of cops on the premises.

'The matter will blow over, die down,' Gaurav told his room-mate who was worried that the college might summon them to give them a dressing-down.

However, their worst fears were confirmed when they received a curtly worded letter (in Marathi) asking them to vacate their room immediately. So they were being expelled from the hostel! They tried to take it as stoically as they could, yet they were terrified. Expulsion was a humiliating affair. The entire hostel would watch as they put their bags, mattresses, pots and pans into a tempo, and ignominiously left. Though they weren't criminals, they'd still be made to feel as if they were.

Some of their friends (not gay, but sympathetic) gathered in their room to console them.

'Thank your stars, you're only being thrown out of the hostel, not the college,' one of them said. 'Rustication is far worse than expulsion.'

'Why are you guys taking tension?' asked another local. 'Private rooms are much better than your crappy hostel.

Maybe you'll have to pay a little more, but it's worth it. At least you'll have your freedom. Anyway, you're welcome to stay in my flat till you find a room. We have a largish guest-room that the two of you can use, provided you don't stain our bed-sheets with cum, ha ha . . .'

Outraged though they were, Gaurav and Vivek had no option but to quit the hostel the next day. It was not as bad as they'd imagined. There were no onlookers when they left at midday, everyone being in class at that hour. Nor did they have to hire a tempo. Mr Cum-stains brought his father's Ambassador, which comfortably took in all their belongings. This enabled them to drive off inconspicuously.

Finding a room, too, proved to be less frustrating than they had thought. Hordes of Bombayites owned properties in Pune, as they soon discovered, which they kept locked till they found a suitable tenant. Gaurav and Vivek contacted an estate agent—a Marwari by the name of Agarwal who operated in the Shivajinagar area—and were shown a two-bedroom apartment that they liked. The owner was especially glad to let them rent it because, like himself, they were Bombayites, for whom he had a soft corner. He even reduced the rent by a few hundred bucks.

'One room will be our office,' said Gaurav, setting up the flat with Vivek's help, 'where we'll stock all our literature. I also have plans to start a newsletter.'

'Good idea,' replied Vivek, but also asked his pal where the money would come from.

44

Siddharth was in the soup. With Gaurav and Vivek thrown out of the hostel, and the SVS members unwilling to let him step into Room 131, he was left without a roof over his head.

Farouq came to his aid. Another Iraqi—his junior by a couple of years—stayed by himself on the first floor of E Block. Farouq decided that Siddharth would 'parasite' with him. 'He had better agree. I'm his senior, so I'm like his father or elder brother. I have the authority to order him about,' he told Siddharth when the latter asked, out of courtesy, if the guy would be disturbed by his presence in the room.

One had to grant it to the mustachioed and French-bearded Farouq—he volunteered to help without prying inquisitively into Siddharth's private life. Not once did he ask, for example, what the SVS was all about, or why Siddharth couldn't stay in their room like before. Again, he displayed no curiosity about what exactly had happened in C Block, why the police had come there. He was always around when Siddharth needed his help, but the help he offered never came with a price tag.

At the same time, he never imposed himself on others. Only a day before setting Siddharth up in his fellow Iraqi's room, Farouq had received bad news on the radio—Basra was being bombed again by Iranian aircraft. He'd been frantically trying to call home since then but, twenty-four hours later, still hadn't been able to get through. He was tense, but he did not show it.

45

Siddharth sneaked into Sudhir's room through the window. How long could he live without sex? Sudhir was glad that he was there. 'Farouq is not coming back till dinner time,' he whispered, bolting the door from inside. They hugged and smooched. Siddharth inspected the textbook Sudhir had been reading when he'd knocked. Maths as usual. A chapter called *Numerators and Denominators in Vulgar Fractions*.

Shutting the book and switching off the table lamp, he dragged his yaar to the bed. There, as they obscenely rolled on each other, Siddharth tickled Sudhir in the ribs and said, as the other giggled, 'My dear, I'll teach you all about vulgar fractions, where I'm the numerator and you the denominator and you the numerator and I the denominator and I the numerator and you the denominator and you the numerator and I . . .'

The game went on till both came in their underwear. The lesson in vulgar fractions was complete.

46

The summer of 1981 came and went. The Engineering College closed and reopened. And the results of the annual exams were pinned up on the noticeboard.

Students mobbed the noticeboard to get a glimpse of their roll numbers. Ravi Humbe was among the very first students to hear that the results had been declared. He scurried to the college. In his shirt pocket was a list of roll numbers, mostly belonging to his SVS friends. He seemed more curious about them than about himself.

But Ravi Humbe was severely handicapped by his height or, to be exact, by the lack of it. The six-footers from north India who studied in the college monopolized the noticeboard, and Ravi Humbe gasped for breath as the crowd of tagdas jostled him. He fell and was all but trampled upon. Extricating himself, he returned to his hostel. He would come back late in the afternoon, when the north Indian ghodas (for that was how he perceived them) were nowhere in the vicinity.

Which is what he did.

Now, Sudhir's number wasn't on the noticeboard. Ravi Humbe checked a dozen times to ensure he wasn't making a mistake. Doctor kaka's son had failed. He would have to repeat the year, for his number wasn't even in the ATKT list (a list of students who hadn't cleared all their papers, but were allowed to keep term in the second year). This meant that he had failed in three subjects at least. As for Ravi Humbe, who had forgotten to check his own result—he had passed in second class.

The news spread like an epidemic. Sudhir had flunked. The latter didn't even have to go to college to see the noticeboard because, by evening, the Belgaumites had gathered in his room to offer their condolences. Though no one uttered his inauspicious name, it was at the back of everyone's mind—the culprit, the chutiya responsible for their pal's failure and for bringing a bad name to their town, was Siddharth, the shani in Sudhir's life. It was he who had taken their friend's thoughts off studies for his own diversion and entertainment. He deserved to die. The SVS had achieved nothing. The man still roamed the streets unfettered.

Sudhir wasn't as perturbed about his results as his mates. When he received his mark-sheet the next day, he found that he had failed in not three, but four subjects. He wasn't sure if Siddharth really was the cause, or was only being made the scapegoat. He suddenly felt protective about his yaar, whom the whole world seemed to be gunning for.

47

It was Ravi Humbe who phoned and broke the news of Sudhir's failure to Dr Raikar, sparing Sudhir the bother. He was shattered. Ravi Humbe consoled him.

'You are knowing reason, no, Kaka, for Sudya's failure? Once it is eliminated, your son will again be able to concentrate on his studies and will pass exams next year.'

R. Raj Rao

But that wasn't all. Ravi Humbe wanted the Ayurvedic doctor to take a more militant stand vis-à-vis Siddharth. And what better way was there to achieve this than to send him clippings from *Sakal* and other local newspapers, about the C Block incident? Ravi Humbe painstakingly cut them out, put them in an envelope, wrote out the address and went to the post office. He did not forget to insert a covering note that cryptically said: *These guys are Siddharth's best friends. In fact, he's like them. What more proof do you want?*

Ravi Humbe's letter did not reach Dr Raikar for a fortnight. This was a blessing for, had it arrived on the heels of the news of Sudhir's failure, the weak-hearted doctor might have had a heart attack and succumbed. The two-week lull gave him time to soothe his nerves. By the time the postman delivered the letter, he was fortified. Still, the headlines of the news items, tasteless in the extreme, hit him like a thunderbolt.

'ENGINEERS OR HOMOS?' asked one of them. 'CLANDESTINE HOMOSEXUAL ORGIES IN ENGINEERING COLLEGE HOSTEL,' declared another. 'MEN DOING IT WITH MEN IN ENGINEERING COLLEGE HOSTEL,' announced a third.

Then came the text. The story of two boys, Gaurav and Vivek (the reporters had actually given their names), who were gay lovers (this, as if they were from Mars), had gay orgies in their hostel room and imported gay porn from America. Though reporters are supposed to refrain from judgement, these ones had actually taken it upon themselves to condemn the guys. They are a blot on society, said one. Another, called Suhas Hardikar, wanted to know what type of families they came from. A third opined that homosexuality was against Indian culture. All the reporters lauded the college authorities and the police for busting the racket. They were pleased that the black sheep had been expelled from the hostel. They ought to be paraded on donkeys through the streets of Pune,

Hardikar wrote. *Kesari*, founded by Bal Gangadhar Tilak, quoted a parent who said that he would have to think twice before letting his son stay in the Engineering College Hostel. And so on.

Dr Raikar felt faint on finishing. Mrs Raikar had to bring him a glass of glucose water. She wanted to know what it was that caused him so much stress. But he raised a hand in husbandly fashion to say, 'Not now.'

A string of questions stirred in his head. Yet, he felt helpless. He was here, in Belgaum city, and his wayward son in Pune, over 500 kilometres away. If they were face to face, he could lecture his son, man to man, slap him if he disobeyed, as he used to when Sudhir was a child. He could order his wife to punish the erring lad by denying him meals or, maybe, by going on a hunger strike himself.

He called Sneha, who was busy in the kitchen. And when she appeared before him a few minutes later, he asked her where she had died and told her to walk to the post office nearby and buy him a bunch of inland letters. 'My varan will burn,' she protested. He fielded that by calling his wife, Sudha, and commanding her to take over from the girl. Half an hour passed before Sneha returned from the post office with the inlands and the change.

In the interregnum, Dr Raikar paced the room, trying to compose a letter to his recalcitrant son. When the inlands arrived, he grabbed them from his daughter's hands and made straight for the dining table where he sat down to write.

My dearest son Sudhir, he wrote. Then he developed writer's block.

His wife appeared with a cup of steaming hot tea to revive his spirits. The tea would help, he thought, even though the cup was cracked. His false starts, however, impelled Dr Raikar to abandon the idea.

48

Siddharth sneaked into E block and knocked on Sudhir's door. Sudhir sprang to his feet, opened the door and, at once, threw his arms around Siddharth's neck and sobbed. Siddharth stroked his back. 'Everything will be fine, my love,' he said. Siddharth fished out a handkerchief (not the cleanest) from his hip pocket and gave it to Sudhir to dry his eyes. 'Crying is cathartic,' he said. 'But you mustn't cry too much. Failure is a stepping stone to success.'

Their eyes met. 'Was I really the cause?' Siddharth whispered into Sudhir's ear. Still looking into his eyes, Sudhir shook his head. No. Non-verbal communication was so poetic.

But Siddharth wanted a precise answer. 'Because I didn't study hard enough,' Sudhir replied. 'Whenever I opened my books, I saw your face in them.'

Siddharth laughed, growing a little in his pants. 'If that's the case, doesn't it make me responsible in a way?'

'No. Your face is so much nicer than what's written in the books.'

They smooched. Siddharth undressed Sudhir with typical urgency. The coast was clear. Farouq had gone to Bombay to spend the day with Ram. The SVS was probably in someone's room, outlining strategy. Their lovemaking over, Siddharth got back to business.

'I know what you must do,' he said.

'What?'

'Private tuition. Coaching classes.'

'Mister, do you think my father's going to pay for them?'

'No. Your mister will. I'm a responsible householder, isn't it?'

Sudhir was grateful to Siddharth. He gave him a plethora of sexual favours that evening, for his body was all he had to offer. They even forgot to have dinner. It was almost dawn before Siddharth unbolted the door, looked around for signs of danger and, wearing one of Farouq's *Jewel Thief* caps so he wouldn't be recognized, walked out of E Block on tiptoe to the barking, as usual, of dogs.

49

Dr Raikar popped yet another Sorbitrate. Ever since he'd received news of Sudhir's failure, his insomnia had worsened. The sleepless nights that he spent tossing about in bed, made him irascible. His wife bore the brunt of it, becoming his punching bag. Next came Sneha and, then, his patients, to whom he no longer appeared the benevolent healer of old. One of them, an Ayurvedic doctor himself, advised his friend to identify the root cause of his troubles and take it by the horns. 'That is the only way to find peace,' he said.

Another trip to Pune, then, seemed imminent. But this time Dr Raikar wouldn't drop in on Sudhir. Instead, he would sponge on Ravi Humbe. Espionage suddenly fascinated our man of herbal remedies. He recalled reading articles in glossies, published from Bombay and Delhi, that talked of detectives set by husbands on their wives, or by parents on their children. He wished he could hire the services of a detective and order him to shadow his son. That way, he would have the lowdown on what was going on in his life. But detectives were expensive and he was no business magnate based in Bombay, with an annual income running into lakhs. He would have to do his own jasoosi.

Three days later, he found himself in Pune, in Ravi Humbe's company. They were seated outside the principal's office, waiting to be summoned. A couple of other parents, fathers all, also wished to have an audience with the principal. More than an hour passed before their turn finally came and a peon ushered them in.

The principal, a balding, freckled man in a dark suit, was infuriated by the newspaper clippings that Dr Raikar had brought in a file. 'Are you here to rub salt in our wounds?' he thundered. 'We have expelled those two students from the hostel. If I had my way, I would dismiss them from the college too. But the rascals will then go to court. The college cannot afford to spend money on yet another lawsuit. We have enough admission-related cases on our hands already.'

Dr Raikar then told the principal about 'a certain parasite by the name of Mr Siddharth, best friend of Mr Vivek and Mr Gaurav, who illegally held coaching classes in Spoken English inside the hostel premises'.

The principal thumped his fist on the table. 'I have already made my position on parasites clear,' he began, as if in a lecture hall. 'My hostel wardens raid rooms well after midnight. What better time to catch the bloody rogues red-handed? We ask them to leave with their bags there and then, and warn them of severe penalty if ever they're found parasiting again. Not just that, the students in whose rooms the parasites are found immediately lose their hostel seats.' The principal looked at his wristwatch. 'I have an urgent meeting to attend. I must ask you to leave now.'

On hearing the word 'leave', Dr Raikar and Ravi Humbe stood up at once. The former perceived it as an insult—he was being thrown out of the principal's cabin. Even so, he shook his hand. Ravi Humbe, who had been silent all along, suddenly came to life as, for the first time since the interview had commenced, the principal looked at him directly and addressed him.

'Feed me with regular reports as to what goes on in the hostel,' he said.

'Yes sir, yes sir,' said Ravi Humbe, flattered by the importance given to him.

50

In the evening, Ravi Humbe took Dr Raikar out for dinner to a south Indian restaurant close to the hostel. The plush décor of the restaurant, complete with wallpaper and false ceiling, frightened the doctor for, though the invitation was Ravi Humbe's, it was obvious who would be paying.

'Isn't there another restaurant nearby?' he asked, pretending to be put off by the pink-and-blue lighting. The question offended Ravi Humbe, who thought of Dr Raikar as his father. 'Kaka, this hotel is very famous. Everyone who is coming to Pune is eating here,' he replied. Dr Raikar let the subject drop. If he fell short of cash, he would borrow. However, he didn't know from whom he could borrow in this strange city.

'Kaka,' Ravi Humbe nervously said, soon after he had placed the order for two thali meals without asking his guest what he wished to eat. He fiddled with the ornate menu card as he spoke.

'Yes?'

'Don't mind what I'm saying. But I think you should get Sudya married. He is ripe for marriage.'

The statement startled the doctor. 'No marriage for my children till they settle down,' he said matter-of-factly. 'I have already made it clear to them and to their mother also.'

'Aho, but Sudhir's case is different,' Ravi Humbe persisted. 'He needs sex. If he can't get it from a woman, he'll turn to men.'

The doctor was alarmed. 'I don't understand what you are saying,' he told his host, trying hard to suppress his vexation. 'Please come to the point straightaway.'

'I don't know how to tell you. But, one night, returning from a late show, we caught Sudhir and Siddharth red-handed. I wanted to write to you as soon as it happened, but I was too ashamed. I even took a photo of it. I can show it to you if you wish.'

This wasn't something that Ravi Humbe should have said to the doctor. It destroyed the doctor's appetite, or what was left of it, and he got up to wash his hands without finishing his food—chapatti, bhaji and all.

'Kaka, please don't tell Sudhir that I told you this,' he begged with folded hands. 'Or my life may be in danger.'

The doctor fished out a handkerchief from his trouser pocket and wiped away a tear. His only son had stabbed him in the back.

51

Back in Belgaum, he did not discuss Ravi Humbe's revelations with his wife.

Mrs Raikar observed that her husband had grown moody since returning from Pune and felt concerned, not just about him, but also about her son.

The husband himself became an inveterate letter writer. He took out the blue inland letters that Sneha had brought from the post office, and wrote. All his letters were addressed to Sudhir, who did not know that his father was no longer in the dark about his amorous activities. Sometimes, he received letters at the rate of one per day and suspected that his father was going crazy. The letters hardly stated anything new. They were tediously repetitive. Letter after letter contained the same advice. The same instructions. The same threats.

Break off with Siddharth forthwith. If he perseveres, complain to the hostel warden. Stay in the company of the Belgaum boys—they are your best friends. I feel ashamed that a man like Siddharth stayed in our house, ate off our plates, slept in our beds. He is worse than a harijan, worse than a leper. Your results have brought great shame to the family. Never before has anyone in our family failed. What advice did Krishna give to Arjuna in Srimad Bhagvatam? To do his duty. You must take your studies as your Battle of Kurukshetra and try to obtain victory. In your spare time you must read the *Jnaneshwari*, which is Sant Jnaneshwar's translation of Srimad Bhagvatam. Do not read Siddharth's articles in *Pathway to God*—they are evil. If he has given you a copy, burn it at once. I have informed the editor not to publish any more of his articles in the magazine. Siddharth is a crook who should be handed over to the police for penetrating your life. Keep a picture of the goddess Saraswati on your table and pray to her before opening your books.

52

To take Sudhir's mind off his failure, Siddharth gave him more Bollywood songs to translate.

'Let's attempt one from *Namak Haram*,' he said, 'where, after the cancer flick *Anand*, Amitabh was teamed with his bête noire, Rajesh Khanna, for the second and last time. A *Filmfare* reviewer spoke of the 'touch of homo' in *Namak Haram* and she wasn't off the mark. *Diye jalte hain, phool khilte hain, badi mushkil se magar duniya me dost milte hai.*

Lamps burn, flowers blossom,
Yet finding a friend in this world
Is no child's play.

When a man is separated from his yaar
His heart is in bad shape.
Memories pierce the heart.

Look, don't be vain about your youthfulness.
If a yaar asks for your life
Give it to him by all means.
Youth is transient,
The warmth of friendship
Is eternal.

Health and wealth all disappear in time.
The whole world becomes an enemy.
Only a friend offers
Lifelong companionship.

'But where does the phrase "child's play" occur in the original?' Sudhir protested, calling their work phoney.

To defend his choice of words, Siddharth got into the classroom mode. 'A translation can never be literal,' he explained. 'It must always be figurative, because the idioms of the source language do not exist in the target language, especially if one is Hindi and the other English.'

'Oh yes,' Sudhir said. 'Talking of idioms, I remember what you once told us. Writing "ido(ma)tic" on the blackboard, you said, an MA in English is the difference between idiomatic and idiotic English, ha ha.'

Their next song was from *Dostana*. 'Zeenie Baby, the heroine, is superfluous in the film,' Siddharth felt. 'The best songs are sung by Lambuji and the Bihari Babu to each other. They are full of pathos and bathos.' They began with a song, but after translating the first couplet—

My friend what's wrong
I hear you've turned unfaithful

—abandoned it for another. 'Heard the melodious *Salamat rahe dostana hamara*, with playback by Rafi and Kishore

Kumar?' Siddharth asked. 'What a duet it is! Beats those sung by Rafi with Lata, or Kishore with Asha. Like *Yeh dosti*, it's the theme song of our own relationship.'

> Even if the whole world turns into an enemy
> Let our friendship prosper.
> We swear by this friendship
> Not even death can separate us.

> If anyone asks us where we live
> We tell them
> We live in each other's hearts.
> That is the only address we have.

> May our friendship prosper.

53

Drenched to the bone, huddled under one umbrella, they looked like refugees from Mars. Rainwater dripped from their hair and streamed down their necks. They sneezed, their teeth chattered. Siddharth, Sudhir, Farouq (the umbrella being Farouq's who permanently carried it in his bag, as if Pune were London) and the wavy-haired Ram were on their way to Pune's walled city to meet a certain tuition-giving Maths professor, whom Ram knew through the brother of a friend of a friend. An odd quartet, each of whom was doing this for the other—Siddharth for Sudhir, Ram for Siddharth, Farouq for Ram.

The rain had caught them unawares. It had been unnervingly sunny when they left the hostel post-lunch, but soon the eastern sky had darkened and silver streaks of lightning, like Indira Gandhi's hair, embellished it. The lightning was followed by thunder, the thunder by heavy downpour. The rain started just as they got off the bus and began walking to the pundit's house. The piece of paper that bore the learned man's address, as well as a confusing map drawn by the friend's friend's brother, was soaked and all but torn. Still, Ram held it close to his face, wishing his glasses had wipers, and tried to read. He intercepted several raincoat-clad, umbrella-wielding passers-by to ask for the professor's house, till one long-haired fellow asked them to follow him without telling them he was the professor's son!

Professor Kulkarni welcomed them with a namaste. He had retired from the Engineering College four years ago, he explained, after seating them on steel folding chairs and serving them glasses of water in steel tumblers. He had, since, coached scores of students who ended up getting very high marks. He was confident that Sudhir would pass with flying colours.

When Ram asked, 'Sir, how much will your fees be?' Professor Kulkarni smiled and answered, 'I'll charge 500 rupees per month for each subject in which he has failed.' At this, Ram looked at Farouq who looked at Sudhir who looked at Siddharth, who nodded to say it was okay, he could afford it. They took turns shaking hands with the professor as they got up to leave.

So it was settled. Three times a week, Sudhir would cycle to Professor Kulkarni's house for private tuitions that would guarantee his success in the next exam. Siddharth would dole out the fees that would supplement the retired professor's meagre pension.

They climbed down the narrow stairs in single file. Siddharth, who brought up the rear, pinched Sudhir's bottom as they descended. Outside, the rain had stopped though it was still cloudy and the streets were waterlogged. The foursome broke up after a string of bye-byes and thank-yous, Ram and Farouq going one way, Siddharth and Sudhir another.

54

'I've come here to study, not to fuck,' Sudhir said to Siddharth, in the latter's room in E block (courtesy Farouq) where he had gone in his pyjamas, book in hand. The room was exactly above Sudhir's, and Siddharth toyed with the idea of drilling a hole in the floor to spy on his beloved.

'Sex is important,' replied Siddharth. He uttered these words whenever Sudhir started feeling guilty. He still couldn't cope with the idea of Brahmacharya coalescing into Grihast. Siddharth observed that this usually happened whenever he plied Sudhir with beer, as now. Unaccustomed to alcohol, Sudhir's system reacted badly.

'Maybe it's important for you, but it's not that important for me. Not before marriage.'

Sudhir's reference to marriage, and that too his own, made Siddharth guffaw. 'Hellooo,' he drawled, having had three beers himself. 'You are homosexual, remember? That's why I'm here. And you are going to get married?' He shook with laughter.

Sudhir thought he was the butt of the joke. 'You are no different from Ravi Humbe,' he said.

'Don't compare me with that arsehole, darling.'

'Why? You have a lot in common with him.'

'And you do not?'

'Of course, I do. We have Belgaum in common.'

This was a shot below the belt, straight in the balls. Sudhir could be nasty if he wanted.

'Okay, peace,' said Siddharth, making the sign with two fingers. He opened another bottle of London Pilsner with a rusty opener and filled his glass. The froth spilt over on to his desk, wetting his papers.

'How clumsy,' said Sudhir. 'Beer drinkers should also know how to pour it.' He picked up the bottle and demonstrated, pouring some of the stuff into his own glass, slowly and steadily, like the proverbial tortoise, the neck of the bottle going deep into the glass. There was virtually no froth. 'See, mister?' he proudly said. 'That's how you do it.'

It went on like that, the banter. Siddharth blacked out with a faint memory of Sudhir throwing up on the bed. He had no idea when Sudhir opened the door and slipped out.

Siddharth woke up with a headache and a hard-on, to furious knocking on his door. It was Gaurav. 'We're hatching a plan and need your help,' he panted.

55

The plan concerned Ravi Humbe, Kishore and Gajanan—who were to be ragged by them.

Not given to mischief, Siddharth was initially resistant, but acquiesced when he saw he was in the minority. However, he left the modalities to the other two and insisted on being a passive spectator. 'Ragging doesn't suit my personality,' he explained. 'I'm an introvert. Maybe it's because I've never ever lived in a hostel, but always at home as a day-scholar.'

On the appointed day, two days after they'd discussed it, Gaurav contrived to get the three Belgaumites to his flat, where they would be ambushed. He slipped a note under Ravi Humbe's door that said: *The Maths II internals paper has leaked out. If you want to copy, go to the address given below at 10 p.m. on Friday. Tell Kishore and Gajanan also.* The note bore the name of one Shriram Gaitonde, whom Gaurav knew to be a student of Metallurgy like the nerds they proposed to rag.

Ravi Humbe rose to the bait. He frenziedly pedalled, first to Gajanan's room, then to Kishore's (they weren't room partners now) and broke the news to them. Their hair stood on end—they were going to be conspirators in a crime.

As soon as the trio from Belgaum tremulously rang the doorbell at Gaurav's flat, they knew they had been taken for a ride. They were greeted with the words, 'Welcome, this is a ragging session. Do not offer resistance. If you cooperate and do as we tell you, you will be let off soon—and lightly. Otherwise, the session might turn sadistic.'

These words, sounding like a hijacker's to his hostages on board a flight, were spoken by Gaurav. As he was speaking, Ravi Humbe noticed Siddharth sitting on a chair in a dark corner, wearing a Hitchcock cap, smoking. He looked towards the front door to see if he could scream and scram, but it had already been padlocked. He hoped against hope that some SVS member would storm into the room and rescue him. The word 'sadistic' rang in his ears. Kishore and Gajanan seemed cooler than Ravi Humbe, who, it was clear to them, was the fellow their captors were after.

The three captives were made to shed every piece of clothing on their bodies including, naturally, their undies. Ravi Humbe was doubly embarrassed because the cheap white banyan he wore was full of holes.

Vivek switched off the tube-lights, leaving just a zero-watt red bulb on, which gave the room a sinister look.

Ravi Humbe's cock was a flaccid stump that induced laughter in the three Bombayites. Of the three nude men in the room, Kishore's equipment responded to stimuli with the greatest alacrity. Thus, he was made to penetrate a hunched, protesting Ravi Humbe, whom Gaurav and Vivek held in place. Siddharth continued to smoke.

Ravi Humbe yelled. Gaurav asked him to shut up, pointing out that it was natural for human beings to feel pain when their virginity was taken. What he was trying to imply was that Ravi Humbe was a woman, not a man, but it went over the latter's head, who worsened matters for himself by, suddenly and unexpectedly, asking for a Nirodh. This provoked more laughter in the Bombayites. Gaurav said, 'Why? Are you afraid you'll get pregnant?'

Kishore, on the other hand, seemed not to mind what went on (though Ravi Humbe wasn't a patch on his ultimate hero, Jackie Shroff). He came prematurely, with some of his semen trickling into Ravi Humbe's backside and the rest of it spilling on to the floor. As he cleaned up with a towel that Vivek flung at him, Gaurav gave orders to Gajanan to get ready. Gajanan had to cajole his cock before he could begin.

And so it went on. Gajanan followed by Vivek, Vivek by Gaurav, Gaurav by Siddharth, his desire to be a passive spectator notwithstanding. Five different men screwed Ravi Humbe within the space of an hour. He seemed to be nobody's type. No one enjoyed fucking him.

The Bombayites ordered the Belgaumites to dress and leave. As they pulled up their trousers and fastened their belts, Gaurav said, 'Now march out in single file. But before you go, listen carefully to what we have to say. If any of you makes a noise about what has happened, we'll get the mafia to eliminate you. Remember, we are Bombayites and we have links with the underworld. Heard of Vardarajan Mudaliar? Vardabhai? He's a good friend of ours.'

As soon as the Belgaumites left, Gaurav, Vivek and Siddharth high-fived and burst into laughter. 'Mission accomplished,' cried Gaurav.

56

Aware that it had acquired the reputation of being a spoilsport, the SVS unanimously decided in an emergency meeting—which its chief, Ravi Humbe, convened—that this time it wouldn't go to the principal, the police or the press. Instead, it would pay the three ringleaders back in the same coin. Tooth for tooth, eye for eye, Vardarajan Mudaliar ishtyle.

Three of its members would simultaneously carry out commando-like raids on Gaurav, Vivek and Siddharth, and sodomize them. Two of the shortlisted three were muscular six-footers with bulging biceps who went to the PMC gym every morning. Their names, appropriately, were Bhim and Shivaji, and both had learnt kushti under the tutelage of Raghuvir Maharaj, a Kolhapuri pehelvan. Ravi Humbe instructed them to screw the bhadvas in such a way that they got anal tears. The pehelvans were confident that they could carry it off.

When Siddharth opened the door thinking it was Sudhir, Bhim bared his teeth like an orang-utan, called him a halkat and harami and, wagging his finger, screeched, 'Don't make a noise or I'll eat you alive.' Afraid the others on the floor would hear and he would be outed, Siddharth hushed him, summoned him in and latched the door. Bhim's purpose was clear as water—he was Ravi Humbe's man, come for vendetta.

Since resistance would be counterproductive, Siddharth shrugged his shoulders and surrendered. However, civility wasn't a word in Bhim's vocabulary. He waspishly ripped Siddharth's clothes off, rendering his jeans and T-shirt useless. His uncut nails left scratch marks on Siddharth's skin. Siddharth sighed. This was going to be a sadomasochistic affair—he had better brace himself.

At Vivek and Gaurav's flat, the two chaps tried to put up a fight against the ruffians, but changed their minds on seeing that they meant business.

Their brief was to carry out the rape concurrently, even gang-rape the motherfuckers. But Kishore, the third chap, was shy and insisted on privacy. 'You do it first while I wait outside, and then you wait outside as I do it,' he said to

Shivaji in Marathi. Shivaji was reluctant to comply, but did not want to create a rift on matters of mere protocol.

When he was finished, Shivaji fretted in the parking lot of the building. He had doubtless inflicted pain on his victim, but he was in agony too—this was the first time he had had anal intercourse. He looked at his watch almost every other second and swore. Why was Kishore, that arsehole of a Belgaumite, taking so long to come down?

57

And Sudhir? He took to his tuitions with Professor Kulkarni so zealously that he was oblivious of the goings-on around him. Be like a blinkered horse, his father had written in one of his letters (which continued to arrive at a steady rate), and he took the advice quite literally. So much so that he did not even know when the Diwali vacations came, or when they gave way to the Christmas holidays. A boy who had been used to going home frequently sat glued to his books, burning the midnight oil.

Siddharth let him be, not distracting him with news of the adventures of the Bombayites and the Belgaumites. Nor did Ravi Humbe or the SVS think it necessary to spill the beans.

Again, there was a temporary lull in their amatory activities. 'I'm a brahmachari,' Sudhir declared. 'And the hostel is my gurukul.'

Aware that, when it came to Sudhir's dismal performance in the exams, all fingers pointed at him, Siddharth chose not to insist. When seized by the sexual urge, he frequented various public parks and loos in the city where men met—on which Gaurav and Vivek had a veritable directory, complete with maps. 'Got to do it because that prick of a boyfriend won't let me go near him,' Siddharth told his conscience at such times.

To Sudhir, the months sometimes passed like years, at other times like days. The seasons changed swiftly. December and January, when Pune's chilly climate is no different from that of Mediterranean Europe, directly led to February and March, when the city threatens to become hot like at the equator. Then came April and May, the city's worst months when it metamorphoses into a desert.

This is when universities, for some reason, decide to hold their annual exams and, now, Sudhir wiped the perspiration from his brow as he wrote his first paper, keeping an eye on his watch. The four backlog papers he had to clear were separated from each other by a gap of nearly a week. This gave him all the time in the world to prepare. Indeed, his preparation was so thorough that where earlier he would spend precious time during the paper pondering over what to write or how to solve a problem, and couldn't finish the paper, he now wrote non-stop, fatafat, like the Rajdhani. Professor Kulkarni's notes were of great help and, as Sudhir wrote his four papers, he recalled the rainy day when Siddharth, Farouq and Ram had taken him to the learned professor's house. Had it not been for them—and especially for Siddharth who shelled out the dough—would he have fared so well? By the time the papers were over, Sudhir was sure he would get a First Class.

He hugged and kissed Siddharth in his room, more out of gratitude than passion, and their happiness knew no bounds. They were interrupted, however, by a knock on the door. 'Telegram,' came the severe voice of the postman. When Sudhir, to whom it was addressed, signed and tore it open, he found it was from his father.

COME HOME IMMEDIATELY NOW THAT EXAMS OVER STOP

Quick at taking decisions, Siddharth told Sudhir, 'Can't stay without you any longer. I've been patient all these months, not disturbing you while you studied. But now the prospect of staying without you throughout the summer holidays will kill me. Know what? I'll go with you but stay in a lodge as long as you're there. We'll meet clandestinely every day. Your dad won't have a clue.'

Although he didn't say it in so many words, so as not to puff up his Majnu-Romeo-Farhad all rolled into one, Sudhir felt exactly the same way. His silence meant approval of the plan and Siddharth knew it. He got busy with his train timetables once again. 'Dar na, mohabbat kar le,' he hummed an old Hindi film song. 'Pyar kiya to darna kya.'

58

But the plan fell flat on its face. The Raikars discovered Siddharth's presence in their town within a day of his arrival. Word travels quickly in a place with a population of no more than five lakhs. With the connivance of the lodge-owner (again, a one-time patient of Dr Raikar), they set a trap for him.

Dr Raikar personally went to his room. 'Son, you have insulted me,' he began. 'I have already told you that my house is just like your house. Then why must you stay in lodge? I am wanting to see you in my house with your baggage in one hour.'

The lodge-owner, too, played his part. 'One marriage party has booked all rooms in lodge from tomorrow onwards,' he lied to Siddharth. 'So you will have to vacate.'

Sudhir hurriedly met Siddharth for a cup of coffee at Basava Tea House soon after his father left. The creases on his forehead indicated that all was not well.

'They have extracted a promise from me,' he informed Siddharth, gasping. 'That I will not see you for four years, till my studies are over.'

'And you gave it to them?' screamed Siddharth.

'I had no choice. I was one against so many.'

'Now, we'll be two,' Siddharth said determinedly.

He checked out of the lodge and, against Sudhir's wishes, trudged with his rucksack to the Raikar house. They took care, however, not to enter together. After Sudhir reached the house, Siddharth let fifteen minutes pass before he rang the doorbell.

The members of the Round Table Conference had already taken their places at the table. They consisted of Dr Raikar, his two burly brothers-in-law whom Siddharth would nickname 'carnivores', and another relative whom he'd never seen before. Dr Raikar was the first to speak.

'Son, we are not your enemies,' he came to the point directly. 'Nor are we heartless. But we would like you to end your friendship with Sudhir till his engineering course is complete.'

Siddharth panicked on hearing the word 'end'.

'Sir, I promise I will not . . .'

But the second uncle did not let him finish. 'I say, don't argue with us,' he butted in. 'Do as we say. We are your elders. Keep your friendship in abeyance for three or four years. That is all.'

Siddharth looked at Dr Raikar, seated at the head of the table, who appeared to be most reasonable of the lot. 'Kaka,' he said, letting the tears roll down his cheeks as he spoke. Never before had he addressed Dr Raikar as 'Kaka'. 'Please don't separate me from your son. I can't live without him for four hours, let alone four years. I love him as much as you do.'

At this, Dr Raikar began to sob too and said with folded hands, 'Son, I beg you. Please leave Sudhir. Have that much mercy on a poor father.'

The first uncle took over at this point. 'Are you a man?' he asked Siddharth in a high-pitched voice. 'Are you having any self-respect? Are you understanding what we are telling you? Do as we say or we will . . .' He raised a hand to indicate that they would beat him up.

'Please,' Siddharth brought himself to say, wheezing.

'Shut up,' thundered the third relative.

'You are not fit to be man,' uncle number one said again.

This uncle now addressed Sudhir, who was also seated at the table and made a part of the Round Table Conference, for the first time. Seated opposite Siddharth, he had been nudging him with his toes all along, as if to say, 'I am with you.'

'Now, Sudhir,' roared the uncle. 'Tell us, do you want to stay with your family, or go away with this creature here?'

'Go with him,' Sudhir audaciously answered. It would be the last time he expressed his views. The third relative almost involuntarily charged at him, stopping just short of strangling him.

'You, here,' the first uncle yelled at Siddharth. 'See how you have worked black magic on our child. I order you to leave at once, this very minute.' He snapped his fingers.

Siddharth continued to sob and noticed that Dr Raikar too was sobbing. Sudhir, on the other hand, remained composed. He did nothing to challenge his uncle, resigning himself to his fate.

All at once, the third relative rose, grabbed Siddharth's bag and threw it out of the front door. It landed on the street with a thud. Siddharth was stunned. He had never imagined things would go this far. But worse was still to come.

The first uncle, the heftiest of the lot, began to manhandle him even as he shrieked, 'Don't touch me, you swine.' But he was no match for the well-fed Maratha.

'Get out of our house, you chhakka, you homosexual, and never come anywhere near the place again if your life is dear to you,' he screamed at the top of his voice, as he held Siddharth by the shoulder and pushed him out of the house.

Siddharth landed on his knees but wasn't injured badly. He managed to stand up and look around. The Raikars had slammed the door shut in his face. Luckily, it was dark. Even so, the neighbours came out to view the tamasha. In their relatively staid surroundings, such drama wasn't a daily occurrence. They were going to be entertained to the fullest.

As Siddharth tried to come to grips with the situation, Sudhir's words echoed in his ears. 'Go with him.'

'Must rescue him,' he heard an inner voice say.

He picked his rucksack up and walked past the neighbours' houses. 'Madman,' some women giggled.

Just then, he heard footsteps behind him. He turned around and saw it was Lakshman, the cycle-shop owner who serviced Sudhir's cycle. Lakshman put a hand on Siddharth's shoulder.

'Friend, can I stay with you for a few days?' Siddharth asked him, blowing his nose into a handkerchief.

Lakshman blinked, and then nodded. 'No problem.'

59

It wasn't just in Siddharth's ears that Sudhir's defiant words 'Go with him' rang. They also echoed in the ears of the members of the Round Table Conference.

Beyond a shadow of doubt, they felt, Siddharth had occult powers by means of which he'd mesmerized their son. All that talk about the Bhagavad Gita and those articles he had written for *Pathway to God* were only a front. India, anyway, was famous for bogus god-men—half of them homosexuals like Siddharth.

Their first thought, therefore, went to Sri Sri Sant Pitambar Maharaj Baba who had an ashram in Khanapur, an hour's drive from Belgaum. Sri Sri Sant Pitambar Maharaj Baba specialized in exorcism. He used a combination of traditional and modern techniques, confining himself to havans and yagnas in the main, but also resorting to electro-shock therapy where necessary.

The foursome conned Sudhir into accompanying them on an outing in the third relative's newly acquired Premier Padmini Deluxe.

The drive lasted for over an hour. Even when the car pulled up in the flower-bedecked driveway of Sri Sri Sant Pitambar Maharaj Baba's ashram, Sudhir did not suspect a thing. His family was religious, so it was probably something to do with an upcoming pooja, he told himself. If he was sad about the ignominious way in which his yaar had been thrown out, he tried to camouflage it, though the grief sometimes showed on his face.

The baba—balding, paunchy, hairy—welcomed them and got to work without much ado. Dressed simply in a dhoti, he first placed two fingers on Sudhir's eyes and shut them as he chanted his mantra. Then he lit his sacred fire and began his yagna. Om this, om that. All along, he looked at Sudhir with bloodshot eyes, addressing, not the lad in front of him, but the vicious spirit that had lodged itself inside his soul. The ritual, during which Sudhir all but fell asleep, went on while his relatives allowed their thoughts to wander. Of the four, Sudhir's father alone tried to concentrate on what was going on. From time to time, he tried to imagine how the baba's ferocious chanting was causing Siddharth's evil influence to evaporate from his son's consciousness. Going, going, gone! The flames caused everyone to sweat profusely. The sweat, in turn, led to body odour. But they bore it patiently, convinced that it was the only thing that could save their child from ruin.

The baba ordered Sudhir to take off his shirt and lie down. A metal plate was placed on his chest. Fixed to the plate was a cream-coloured cord, at the other end of which was a 15-watt three-pin plug. The cold metal sent a shiver down Sudhir's spine. Without warning, the baba put the plug into a socket and switched on the button. A 440-volt current passed through Sudhir's body. At first he was silent, too dazed to react but, as the baba repeated the operation, shifting the metal plate from one end of his torso to another, the sheer agony of it brought tears to his eyes and made him howl. The pain was so excruciating that, even though he was barely conscious, Sudhir vowed to take revenge on the whole world. Each time the button was pressed, he wriggled like a fish in a fisherman's net. The torture seemed to go on interminably.

Then, the four men who accompanied him were asked to leave the room. Once they were out of sight, the baba closed the door, took Sudhir's pants off and examined his dick. 'Nooooo,' screamed Sudhir, as the baba stroked his penis. The hapless boy thought he would be given an electric shock on this part of his anatomy as well. Even castration would be less inhuman!

But the baba's intentions were entirely different. The electro-shock therapy was actually over. Now, this charlatan entertained himself with the very thing he sought to cure his victim of: perverted sex. But Sudhir, half dead, refused to respond. In all, he had received close to a dozen electric shocks.

His folks were summoned only after the baba, with the help of a servant, managed to get his clothes back on. 'Take him home now and let him rest all day,' he advised them, even as they respectfully genuflected before him. 'Bring him back for a repeat dose next Thursday. In a month, he will be a different person.'

R. Raj Rao

PART III
MAY 1982 TO MAY 1983

1

I wake up, not in the Vrindavan Gardens but in Lakshman's Cycle Shop.

I am surrounded by rows of decrepit cycles, discarded tyres, rusty air-pumps, broken spokes, swabs of cotton and cans of machine oil. I look at the squalor about me. There must have been a time when these cycles were brand new. When they sparkled and shone and waited in showrooms for people to pick them up. Today, they are in a state of disrepair. No one will take them—even for free.

There are other men in the derelict shop—workers who sleep here because they have nowhere else to go. Their homes are in villages far, far away. All of us sleep on bare mats generously stained with black grease. The presiding deity is grease. Then, there are the mosquitoes. They hover and hum and insert their syringes into our flesh, as if for a blood test. There are no fans here to keep them at bay. No mosquito nets or Odomos. To stop the wretched things from entering, the fellows here have rolled down the shutters. This makes the workshop a dungeon. Everyone sweats copiously and the air smells of dead rats. It's the smell of sweat mingling with that of grease. Somewhere, a cricket chirps noisily. It's just as well that the miserable 40-watt bulb is switched off, or else I might have had to witness more terrifying creatures of the night—rats, lizards and cockroaches.

The guys next to me are fast asleep. Nothing deters them. Such resilience—they can sleep blissfully in the most excruciating conditions. Some of them are shirtless and wear short shorts through which their equipment bulges. Their thighs are hairy. I am tempted to touch them, to run my hand over their calves or squeeze their nipples, but I restrain myself. As they toss and turn on their coir mats, they wake up momentarily to slap the mosquitoes off their necks and chests. Then they fall asleep again. Violent sobs shake me as I think of Su. I think no one can hear me, but am shocked when one of the sleeping men shouts gruffly from his bed, 'So ja re!'

The stone floor beneath me hurts. We use makeshift pillows—leather cushions, cycle seats, cardboard cartons. Mine is the best—an old moped seat that somehow found its way here. Yet my neck aches.

My sleep having broken in the dead of night, it's clear I'm not going to sleep again. I look at my wristwatch in a shaft of light that filters in through the window, but can't make out the position of the hour and the minute hands. Then I sit up and look again. It's 4 a.m. Just then, the cocks start crowing. It's dawn—a safe time for me to get up and go for a morning walk. But I continue to lie on my coir mat. I realise I can't leave until one of the chaps unlocks the iron shutter that separates us from the rest of mankind. Luckily, it's not long before that happens. The muscular men by my side are early risers.

I exit the cycle shop and walk around desultorily. This is risky business. I am in *their* territory, and yesterday I had brought the police here. It's imperative that no one recognizes me. But it's hard for me to disguise myself. At the most, I can wear a cap—which I do, but it isn't enough. Sunglasses might also help, but it's too early to put them on. The one thing that saves me is that most residents of the area are still asleep. The

R. Raj Rao

only people on the streets at this hour are newsboys and milk vendors. A few families, however, are awake and they sprinkle water outside their houses or adorn their entrances with rangoli.

One narrow lane leads to another and I keep walking. I don't have to go anywhere. My aim is to kill time and, also, to plan my next move. I've been told to leave town. The police and Su's family probably think I'm already on my way to Bombay. What if either party spots me?

I arrive at the neighbourhood tank. Because it's summer, young men are already in it, bathing. The guys are really young—adolescents, without facial hair. I stop to watch them sloshing about in the water. They are naked except for their briefs. One boy naughtily pulls down his friend's undies and grabs his cock and balls. The victim squeals. Since the lower half of his body is under water, he thinks no one can tell what he's up to. If only I had known how to swim, I would have undressed and joined the sun-tanned fellows in the water. I try hard to catch a glimpse of someone's dick, but the kids are smart. They take care not to emerge without their clothes.

The sight of the frolicking teenagers decides it for me. I will go to Peter's house.

2

Peter is Su's best friend, and they had studied in the same school. But Peter's house is far away. To get there, I have to board a bus and I'm not even sure of the bus routes. But I ask a few people and am on my way.

'Good morning,' Peter greets me as he opens the door. 'Long time no see.' He's dressed in a banyan and jeans. I enter the well-appointed drawing room, carpeted and with a prominent picture of Christ on the wall. Peter seats me on their three-piece sofa set. 'It's brand new,' he says. 'We got it only yesterday.' Peter's mother walks in, and he introduces me to her as one of Su's friends. The lady smiles cordially and brings me a cup of steaming hot tea.

Peter doesn't have a clue about what has happened. 'I didn't even know Sudhir was in town,' he says. I give him a synopsis of the events of the last two days—edited to suit me, of course. I don't tell him, for example, that I had dragged the police to their house. All I say is that his folks aren't letting him see me. Peter doesn't know the exact nature of our relationship, nor does he suspect. To him, as to the whole world, we're just close friends. Yaars. Men, after all, can only be close friends of other men.

He asks me what it is I would like him to do. 'Smuggle him out of the house under some pretext,' I reply, 'so that we can have a word with each other.'

Peter thinks that's easy. There are a hundred excuses he can give to Su's folks to get him out of the house for, say, half an hour. The family knows him well and are always courteous to him when he visits.

Peter puts on his shirt and we're off. When we reach our destination, he asks me to wait in a temple. I realize he's good at plotting. A temple, with its crush of devotees, is a nice place to camouflage oneself in without fear of being discovered. Peter sets out on his mission, while I stay back at the Sai Baba temple with the worshippers who enter in droves.

Everyone rings the huge brass bell in the courtyard upon stepping in. In addition, there are several smaller bells scattered all over the place. As a result, the air is rife with clanging. I plug my ears with my fingers to shut out the noise. The worshippers carry steel trays full of offerings for the humble saint of Shirdi. The trays contain garlands, coconuts, sweets, agarbattis and saffron powder. Many men, women and children apply saffron powder to their foreheads as well. The aarti has just begun and the devotees close their eyes and clap. Some of them sway their heads to the music. At one

R. Raj Rao

point, they all start spinning like tops. I'm caught unawares and feel foolish. By the time I start my gyrations, theirs have already stopped.

I retreat to a corner of the temple and pray. Sai Baba, please make Peter's mission a success. Please bring Su here, right into your abode, so that I can talk to him and touch him before I finally leave town. Is this too much to ask for? In return, I promise to get you a coconut.

Peter still hasn't come back and I grow anxious. What if he has decided to vamoose without informing me? Perhaps I should have set a time limit. I can't overtax Sai Baba's hospitality.

But Peter does, eventually, make an appearance. He's by himself, Su isn't with him. 'Sorry, boss,' he says. 'It was a failure.'

Turns out that Su's folks were okay as long as Peter sat in the house and chatted. But the moment he asked Su out (for a matinee movie, he told them, to give us maximum time), they smelt a rat. 'Who sent you here?' they demanded, shocking poor Peter. After that they harangued him, filled his ears with poison and told him things about me that he's too ashamed to report. So he did what any self-respecting man would—took his leave.

'In future, please keep me out of this,' he says with a hint of irritation in his voice. I apologize to him and we shake hands. Bells are still clanging as we get out of the temple and part ways.

So where do I go from here, with half the day still left? I re-enter the temple and strike up a conversation with a holy man. It's better than going back to Lakshman's Cycle Shop, my only shelter in this wretched town.

The holy man is scarcely in his twenties, but he has renounced the world like Gautama, the Buddha. He spends his time going from temple to temple, all over the country. He has already visited thousands of them. Sometimes he walks from one town to another. He shows me the soles of his feet, which are worn and chapped, like a land in drought.

I ask him how he controls his sexual urges. He explains that he does it by tying a heavy stone to his penis. The weight of the stone has to be just right, he elaborates. He smokes a chillum and gives me a drag.

3

Carnivores have a strong sense of smell. So do Su's uncles. The beasts have somehow got scent of the fact that I'm still around, buying time in Lakshman's cycle shop. They decide to give me chase. As in the case of quadrupeds, their odour precedes them. Long before I actually spot them coming, word has gotten round among Lakshman's boys, my bed-mates from last night, that they're on the way. There's commotion in the shop. The fellows are divided in their opinion as to what the best course of action would be. Some of them think I should scram, others want me to hide inside the shop, still others are of the view that I should face the predators—even attack them in self-defence.

'What the fuck!' they swear. 'Does the whole town belong to them? It's a free country. People have a right to go where they please.' Commendable logic, that, for guys who spend all their time mending corroding cycles.

The matter is put to the vote. 'Be quick,' someone shouts. 'They've already left their house.' I rack my brain to figure out how he knows. Su's house is a good ten-minute walk from here. So how can he be so sure? But it's settled. I must run away and return after an hour or two. There aren't enough hiding places inside the shop, its clutter notwithstanding.

I get out of the dungeon and look around. Having emerged from the dark, the afternoon sun makes me blink. I shield my eyes with my hands. I'm about to begin my marathon when I spot them. There they are, the two clowns, dressed in dazzling white kurtas and pyjamas. The colour of purity, to mask their impurity. Coming towards me at a slow, calculated pace, chewing paan. Paranoia seizes me. There's no way I can avoid being seen by them, for the crowds on the street are thin. I have visions of being devoured whole, like the men in Jim Corbett's books.

'Run,' Lakshman's boys command me, but my legs refuse to move. They're pinned to the ground. I quickly run through the inventory of excuses I have thought up for not leaving: Not feeling well. Train's in the evening. Have run out of cash and am looking for someone to borrow from. Can you lend me some? 'Do you need to be whipped like a horse to set you in motion?' one of the boys asks, and I reflect on the aptness of the simile.

By the time my legs unlock, it's too late. The men in white are so close now that it's impossible to escape. 'Hey you,' one of them says, unwilling to pollute his mouth with my name. 'Hey you,' cries the other. My footsteps quicken, finding an ally in my heartbeats. 'Hey you,' both of them shout in unison. I turn around and face them.

Lakshman's boys are having a hearty laugh at my expense. 'Stupid fellow. He deserves it for not acting fast,' they tell each other.

I get ready for battle.

4

When they talk to me I flinch. I'm revolted. I can't believe that the two men responsible for my predicament, both six-footers, are actually being reasonable.

'Mister, we wish to speak to you,' one of them begins. He's the dark-skinned one who looks like he bathes in tar. The other one is lighter, known for his large canines. 'Yes,' he concurs.

I keep mum. I'm like a cat cornered by wolves. It's imperative I stay still. Any movement on my part, and they'll pounce. But then I slowly move. 'Yes,' I manage to say.

'As I told you in the house, we are not your enemies,' says Canines. 'Nor are we heartless. But, I reiterate, keep your friendship in abeyance for four years. Till he finishes his studies.' I suddenly remember that he was once a lawyer. That explains his choice of words. In abeyance! Just as well he calls it friendship.

'Can I speak to him just once?' I ask, my eyes clouding up.

'No!' screams Canines. 'In abeyance!'

'Please,' I beg. The clouds break out in heavy rain.

'Don't you have any self-respect?' he thunders. 'Are you a man or a eunuch?'

I wipe my tears.

Tar baby steps in. 'Can I give you a piece of advice?' I don't give him permission, but he continues all the same. 'Look for orphan boys. Not boys from good families who have parents. They don't need you in their lives. God has given them fathers and mothers.'

Thanks, I say to myself. I'll go to a remand home first thing tomorrow.

Canines steps forward again, taking out a sealed letter from his shirt pocket. 'Here,' he says, handing it to me. 'He has sent you a letter.'

My heart is a joggers' park. I snatch the letter from him, transfixed by the handwriting—definitely Su's, even though it's a scrawl. It's a while before my dream is broken and I can bring myself to read:

My darlingest Siddharth,

May God keep you in peace. You did not do the right thing by going to the police station. You have brought shame upon my family. How will they ever be able to face the neighbours again? I told the inspector that my family was not to blame. That they had not locked me up in the house against my will.

My Romeo, I am convinced of your love. I know that none will ever match up to it. But you forget that my parents too love me. They have expectations. They do not want their son to be snatched away from them, from under their very eyes. In any case, the people of this world, how are they going to understand our love?

I've promised my parents that I won't see you till I graduate. That's about four years. After that, I promise you I am yours. My love will be as sweet, as delicious—even at that time. Remember Sapna and Vasu in Ek Duje Ke Liye? *Separation did not dilute their love. On the contrary it made it deeper.*

Don't bring any harm to yourself. You have got to live for me, for my sake. I will remember all that you have said to me, and will eagerly wait for the years to pass. But for now, it's goodbye. Please DO NOT try to contact me through letters or telephone calls.

Goodbye my yaar, my lover. I am yours.
Sudhir

After a letter like that, how can anyone not be overwhelmed? I squat on the floor and break into sobs, burying my face in my hands.

When the sobbing is over, I dry my eyes and get back on my feet. The carnivores have already left.

5

There's no option but to quit town.

I collect my belongings from Lakshman's Cycle Shop—a water bottle and a rucksack fraying at the edges. There are no ceremonies here. Houyhnhnm-like, Lakshman's boys are neither happy when anyone arrives, nor sad when anyone departs. It's all the same to them—it echoes the tide of life. 'Come whenever you wish,' one of them tells me as I bid him goodbye.

A radio plays at full blast in the shop, tormenting me with a song sung by Rafi, from the film *Dosti*, in which a young man tells another—

I'll love you
Morn to night
Still I'll never
Call out your name.

Both men are handicapped. One blind, the other lame. The song kills whatever residues of shame are left in me. As I walk to the railway station, I sob openly. It's twilight, but it's not as if people don't see me. Then I puke by the pavement. There wasn't much in my belly, but the last meal I had is now on display. And as if that wasn't enough, I finish off by unzipping and peeing on a portrait of Lord Hanuman. If the gods can't answer my prayers, they deserve to be peed on. Hanuman, after all, brought Sita to Ram, but not Su to me. He's homophobic.

Puking has made me feel better, but my head still swims as I negotiate the lanes and shortcuts that lead to the station. The man—nay, the boy—without whom life is unbearable, has just dumped me. And here I am, resigned to my lot, quietly accepting it as my fate. It's the passivity that gets me. In a few minutes, I'll be at the station waiting in a queue to buy a ticket that will take me out of town and farther away from Su. And I'm doing nothing to stop myself. I'm just walking.

A street performance distracts me. Joining the crowd of onlookers, I discover it is Begum Sahiba—dancing. She's a woman of many talents. Yesterday, it had been begging and whoring. Today it's a lavani-style dance that titillates spectators, serving as an appetizer. Her hair is done up in a bun and wrapped around it is a gajra made of jasmines. Even as her bare feet thump the ground, her hands reach for her skirt. She seems ever ready to lift her skirt. The other hijras are not with her. Instead, she's accompanied by a handful of

R. Raj Rao

young men who play the tabla and harmonium. One of them—the hero of the group, more muscular than the rest—sings in a shrill womanly voice, alternating between Hindi and Kannada songs. The crowd is ecstatic. It cheers the performers, urging them to go on nonstop. Begum Sahiba and party are showered with currency notes and small change that would outdo the earnings of a Bollywood extra.

The men in the troupe, I realize, are kotis. Effeminate, working-class men. Heavily made-up, with everything from rouge to kohl to lavender-coloured lipstick. Unlike Begum Sahiba, they're dressed in male attire, kurtas over pyjamas, or bush shirts over jeans. They wear their hair short. They also, presumably, retain their dicks, however malformed, whereas the hijras are castrated.

Do the kotis use the hjiras to procure men? That's plausible. When the show's over, the handsomest man in the assembly may proposition Begum Sahiba, but the others in the horny horde will have to make do with the kotis. Small wonder, then, that the bonding among them seems so fool-proof. Here are deviants who see the sense of hanging together, although devoid of education. We, of the middle classes, on the other hand, learned and all, myopically remain islands unto ourselves. (Except for a few noteworthy Bombay-wallahs I have had the good fortune of knowing.) Rebellion eludes us because we've been to college while, in truth, it should be the other way round. This, sadly, is one of the paradoxes of education. It makes us conformists.

6

Belgaum station. Scores of men, women and children on the platform, where the train to Miraj is due to arrive. They wait patiently as the train refuses to show up on time, even though the announcements inform passengers ad nauseam that it's running on schedule. Those by the edge of the platform lean over dangerously and crane their necks, trying to spot the engine's headlamp. But the train is nowhere in sight. Beggars and hawkers roam freely amid the medley of people.

An aging coolie grumbles because the family that has hired his services has kept him on hold. 'Is it our fault if the train is late?' they reason with him in Kannada, but he refuses to see reason. He hits his forehead with his palms. The family leaves him to his devices. As long as their work is done, of what consequence are the coolie's frustrations to them? But then the wife takes pity and offers him some of the yellow rice they are eating from open tiffin carriers. The porter, of course, knows his place. Knows better than to eat with upper-caste folk. Does he want to start all over again in the snakes-and-ladders game that is life? He raises his palm, the same one with which he had hit his forehead, to say no. Thank you.

Suddenly, everyone springs to life. The Kannadigas hastily shut their tiffin-carriers, their mouths still full of food. The coolie puts their VIP suitcase on his head, and picks up the smaller bags with both his hands.

As the train pulls in, the passengers on the platform survey the coaches as if they were soldiers at a Republic Day parade. The moment the train comes to a halt, everyone scrambles for the seats. I lose the tiffin-carrier family in the melee. They must have headed towards the front of the train, while I am stuck at the rear. I manage to find a seat in a compartment next to the brake van. Here, I have a new set of dishevelled passengers for company. They sit lifelessly on their seats, like corpses, giving the compartment the macabre look of those notorious Partition trains.

The only redeeming thing is that the train departs without much fuss. I realise with a twinge in my heart that I'm leaving Su's town. God knows if I'll ever be back here again. So long, I say quietly, as the brightly lit streets of the town come into view and I nostalgically recall the good times when we trod these streets.

Train sounds take over, as the train gathers speed quickly and goes along its forlorn course. It's a black night, dark as hair. The chant of the train is deafening and, yet, it seems to be conveying some esoteric message. What are its steel wheels saying to me as they trundle along? Forget him for now forget him for now.

I sit motionless, like my fellow travellers in the coach. The wind lashes my face. The train becomes my tranquillizer, lulling me to sleep when sleep is what I badly need. I can't remember when it was that I last slept well. The train is my lullaby. As long as it keeps running I will be okay. If only the train would never stop . . .

But, before long, the train reaches its destination and comes to a disconcerting halt. No, it will not go any further. The train's destination, however, isn't mine. Mine is faraway Bombay, while the train has terminated at Miraj Junction. The tracks, like our destinies, have gauges. I have to switch from metre to broad gauge if I am to get home. I join the alighting passengers in a procession across the footbridge, to the platform where the train to Bombay will arrive.

The scene at Belgaum station is played out again— coolies, beggars and all—but this time I refuse to observe anyone. My heart grows heavy, like a pair of jeans soaked in water. I meander towards the tea-stall and drink a cup of milky tea. The crowd on the platform seems to increase by the minute, for this is the train that will take people to Bombay—that city where dreams materialize and destinies take shape.

I resolve not to look at my wristwatch. Why should it concern me if the train is late? Late trains hassle those who have goals, whereas I revel in the purposelessness of life. Once, I was a lover and wished to excel at my job. But providence has taken that job away from me. Now, I'm idle and it doesn't matter where I am. I don't have to get anywhere. The college where I lecture reluctant students is closed for the summer holidays. I have parents, two parents, whose only son I am, who would like me to settle down and are concerned about my welfare. But I'm in no mood to see their faces. I'm better off here, on the platform with strangers.

I realize, as I pace the platform and gather bits of information from the coolies, that there isn't one train to Bombay, but two. The second train, apparently, will follow hard on the heels of the first. What if they collide, I ask myself. The morning newspapers will be full of pictures and numbers of those killed.

As these thoughts occupy me, the first train rolls in. If there are a lakh on the platform, there are two lakhs on the train. This train isn't for me and I let it go without any attempt to board. Strangely, missing the train makes me feel lighter. After all, Miraj Junction is closer to Belgaum, my Garden of Eden, than distant Bombay. However, there is still the second train to deal with, and I'm truly relieved to find it as choked with passengers as the first.

As the train leaves the station without me, I feel like Prince Gautama who, one dark night, escaped from his palace on his horse and headed towards freedom. I tear up my ticket into four neat bits, put the pieces on my palm and blow them away.

The platform suddenly looks deserted as I walk back to the tea-stall and drink more cups of sugary tea.

7

Negotiating the footbridge, I come out of the station. The air is unexpectedly cool. A light breeze caresses my skin. The streetlights are off, as usual, making the night seem murkier than it is. What little light filters on to the street comes from the houses that surround the station. They're cottages built by the British that now serve as the abode of railway personnel. Tongas stand in neat rows at the station's entrance, waiting for passengers. The tonga-wallahs call out to me. They mention the names of unfamiliar neighbourhoods and ask if I wish to be ferried there. I do not respond, just keep walking on.

Going past the railway cottages, I enter a street with a signboard saying Station Road. There is a cheap lodge a few furlongs away, where I decide to park for the night. The manager tries to fleece me, quoting a much higher price than a room here should normally cost. When I argue with him, he reduces the price by ten bucks. I open my purse in front of him to make sure I have the dough. He sends a guy with me to show me my room. He wears shorts and isn't a day over fifteen. I feel like fucking him. Maybe the fellow reads my thoughts, because he scrams as soon he unlocks the door and hands me my key.

The room has to be seen to be believed. It's rectangular, shaped exactly like the creaky, wooden single bed it houses. There's a small window by the bed, which is shut to keep out mosquitoes. The stingy manager has fitted just a zero-watt bulb in the room, adding to the air of misery. The peeling walls haven't been painted in decades, and I spot rat-shit on the floor. I lie on the bed, cum-stains notwithstanding, and gaze at the ceiling.

It's past midnight now, but sleep refuses to grace me. The best way to kill time is to shag. I turn on my belly to passively wank, and come in no time. I doze off soon after, but my sleep, light as tissue paper, breaks when an engine hoots. I suddenly become aware of the squealing of rats. They're probably right under my cot. I freeze. I dare not switch on the light to actually see the wily things at work. I reach for my rucksack which, luckily, is next to me on the bed, and dig into it for tranquillizers. Popping two into my mouth, I fish out a bottle of water and swallow the pills. Suppose I were to swallow the entire bottle at one go? Would it mean liberation from suffering?

The spurious tranquillizers fail me. I'm still awake, listening to train- and rat-sounds. I shag a second time, then a third. Always, it's the same fantasy—me screwing Begum Sahiba. I am dissipated by the crack of dawn.

8

First light and I check out of the creepy lodge, trek to the station and buy another ticket to Bombay aboard the Koyna Express. Unlike last night's trains, this one's empty. So empty that I have the whole coach to myself. I can pick and choose the seat I want. I occupy a window seat at the centre of the coach and place my rucksack next to me. Why isn't there a soul around, I wonder? Is it because it's early still, and the public hasn't woken up? Or because this train starts from here itself, from the small town of Miraj, unlike last night's expresses that originated in the big city of Kolhapur?

Kolhapur triggers a memory. Hadn't the carnivores said, a few days before the holocaust, that they would depute Su to attend a wedding in the city on behalf of the family? Could it be that the wedding was on now, and he was already there, all by himself? I could accost him then, ask him to explain his treachery. But didn't it amount to looking for a needle in a haystack? I have no idea in what part of town the wedding is taking place. And, yet, I do not wish to leave any stone unturned. If there's a possibility of finding him anywhere, it's my duty to explore it. I tear up my ticket a second time.

I get out of the station, make inquiries from passers-by and zoom off towards the ST stand. Dusty red buses go in and out of the depot continuously, so it isn't hard to find one heading to Kolhapur. In no time, I'm on my way again, straining every ligament in my body as the bus negotiates the jagged road. More so as I'm seated in the last row, with my head constantly hitting the roof. But there's more in store—the ride does funny things to my neighbour's stomach and he throws up, without warning, on my lap. The vomit looks like a coloured fountain as it springs from his mouth and paints me yellow. Luckily, he's my type and his vomit becomes my fetish.

Although my neighbour empties his bottle of water on me (maybe I should have asked him to clean me up with his pee), I arrive in Kolhapur with caked vomit on my clothes. I stand in the middle of the polluted ST stand to take stock of the situation. In what direction do I head off in pursuit of Su? Should I decide it by tossing a coin, as Veeru and Jai (barely disguised homos) do in *Sholay*? I make my way to the canteen for a bite and tea. Then I step out again and survey the scene afresh.

I must act.

9

I walk aimlessly through the lanes and by-lanes of the town. I don't know why I walk. As if I could find Su by just walking! But supposing I do? Suppose I bump into him, head-on, as I turn left or right and enter a side street? Or see him on the other side of a busy thoroughfare while I limp along with aching feet? Suppose?

I'll wave my arms frantically and call out to him at the top of my voice. 'Su . . . Su . . .' I'll scramble through traffic to seize him by the collar before he makes good his escape.

This, of course, is wishful thinking. Reality is very different. Although I'm on high alert, with all my radars pressed into service, he's nowhere in sight. How can he be? I don't even know when that damn wedding is supposed to take place. And even if it is today, who knows in what part of town? It's also likely that, post-Peter, the fucking carnivores have changed their mind for security reasons and decided not to send him to the wedding. Anything's possible, from their point of view. So the safest course would be to put him in purdah and keep him locked, the wedding be damned. There is no shortage of menfolk in that haveli to attend it.

In which case, what am I doing here, losing my bearings? I've strayed so far away from the city centre that, should I decide to give up and take the first available train or bus out of town, I would not know how. However, I'm made of sterner stuff. What has brought me here in the first place is my resolve not to leave a single stone unturned. Thus, I walk, as if on a sightseeing tour of Kolhapur, soaking up atmosphere, taking in everything—be it the dilapidated double-deckers tilting dangerously to one side, or the filth overflowing from the storm drains, or the noisy silencer-less three-wheeler autos spewing smoke. On the bright side, there are the sturdy Maratha men in white kurtas and pyjamas, their Gandhi caps giving them dignity. None of them is attractive and, yet, it's a treat to see them go past, their equipment dangling inside their pyjamas like bananas on a branch. I wish I could bite into a banana.

As usual, I have no choice but to stop some of these guys to ask for directions. Where's the station? Where's the bus stand? They're helpful, though arrogant. Clearly, I'm an intruder who has no business wandering purposelessly through their town. It was different in Belgaum, where my in-laws lived. But Kolhapur?

I reach the ST stand and locate a lodge just opposite the bus depot. Pravasi Lodge, it's appropriately called, and I check in, paying 60 rupees for a single room. The room is spacious and airy—much better than the one at Miraj—but I'm hardly here to wallow in its comforts. Depositing my rucksack on the bed, I lock up and leave.

10

I t's the fiftieth bus from Belgaum and he's not on it.
I have been here, at the ST stand, for the past four hours,
scouring bus after bus in a vain bid to track him down. This
isn't child's play. There are millions of buses, coming in from
a million different destinations, and I cannot afford to miss
even one of them. The State Transport Corporation, it seems,
runs buses to and from the state's remotest hamlets—with
names like Hathkangale and Pagalwadi—that are not listed
on any map. My modus operandi is to read the destination
board that the bus wears on its forehead like a bindi, even as
it enters the terminus and reverses into a platform. If it's from
Belgaum, I rush towards the entrance. I check each alighting
passenger, hoping against hope that one of them will be Su.
The sight of an arriving bus makes my heart leap because
every new bus has the potential to unite me with my obsession.
Then, as the bus empties out and he isn't among the
passengers, disappointment seizes me and the whole cycle
has to be repeated. The ST Corporation is to be thanked,
though, for running so many buses every minute that my
mind constantly fluctuates between extreme hope and extreme
despair. Still, this can't go on for long. It's intoxicating, this
sight of multitudes of people and multitudes of buses, but I
can't stay here all night.

For recreation, there's the canteen—complete with canteen
boys in shorts—where I have, by now, drunk a thousand cups
of tea. I can feel it going down my gullet even when I'm not
actually drinking it. I'm not sure that the stuff, prepared as it
is with jaggery, is good for my stomach, but I drink it because
it is cheap. It is to my system what fuel is to a car—without
it, I will stall. Who knows how much I've frittered away on
the tea? My wallet has suddenly ceased to jingle. If I don't
keep tabs, I may be left even without train fare. What will I

do then? Travel ticketless? Make the ST bus depot my permanent home?

The other thing I've grown terribly familiar with is the harsh, grating voice of the announcer. He goes on non-stop over the public address system, informing passengers of the status of incoming and outgoing buses. Clearly, he's in love with his voice. He loves his work and, over the years, has come to believe that he's no ordinary government employee doing just another nine-to-five job, but is Ameen Sayani compering *Binaca Geet Mala*. But his voice is so offensive that I want to stuff cotton into my ears, if only I knew where to find it.

My love, where are you?
Look at the trouble I've put myself through
Just to get a glimpse of you.

11

What a waste of hard-earned money! I pay the Pravasi Lodge guys a day's rent in advance, and now I decide to check out without spending the night there. Why, I've hardly stayed in the room. All I've used it for is to dump my rucksack. As if the rucksack were that precious. It contains no more than a few pairs of tattered jeans. No valuables, like a camera or a Walkman. But this crazy business of searching buses has worn me out, and now the sight of my room, of the bus terminus—of the whole city—is sickening. I want to go home.

The trains are crowded. There isn't a day when they're not, but I couldn't care less. If I don't get a reserved berth, a seat in the general compartment will do. And if not that, there's always the gangway where I can squat. Or the roof. The berths are full, but I manage a seat. I doze off in my seat, my single seat, as soon as the train gathers momentum. When my eyes open again, it's already dawn. There's a fellow by my side who must have boarded at some wayside station and has cheekily helped himself to part of my seat. I nudge him with my elbow till he's almost pushed off the seat and he gets up, giving me foul looks.

A big station is approaching. I have a nagging feeling that it's Pune, which I want to blot out from memory altogether. Pune and Su. Su and Pune. But I've slept enough, and sleep isn't going to oblige me at this hour, as station noises filter into the coach. 'Chai-coffee, chai-coffee,' I hear all around me. I buy a cup of tea but it fails to numb my senses. I'm overwhelmed by memories. Memories of Su and me, together in this very city—the city where we met, the city where he studies. Will he return to study here? Will he be my yaar again?

The train resumes its journey, now on its last leg. The driver must feel triumphant at bringing his train to its destination, while my affair hangs fire. I hate the mercenary city of Bombay but I have no option except to return to my parents' home.

Overjoyed by my arrival, my parents serve me breakfast and ask for all the news. From their faces, I can tell that they don't have a clue as to what has happened. His folks must be thanked for not calling my parents to give a blow-by-blow account of my indiscretions. Otherwise my parents and I may have come to blows.

Where do I go from here? What do I do with myself? I re-read *The Guide* and identify with the ditched Raju, which is edifying. Then I read the Bhagavad Gita for the nth time. I call up Anthony and Dhananjay and ask them over for dinner, forgetting the tiff we had at Khajuraho.

12

M otion. It soothes the mind. The rishis spoke of stillness as a means to cosmic peace. With me, it's diametrically opposite. A sedentary life compounds my misery, while movement fosters the illusion of tranquillity. It could be movement of any sort, even pacing the room. In my estimate, I have covered hundreds of kilometres—in my own microscopic room.

I go to VT station and buy a circular ticket. The summer holidays are still on, so I don't have to worry about taking leave. The circular ticket gives me the freedom to go where I please. I can zoom around the country, west to east, south to north. All for a few hundred rupees. I take off, telling my folks that I'm educating myself. A single journey can educate in a way that 20,000 books cannot. Besides, my parents know of my wanderlust. They think it's my hormones.

Where do I go? To all the holy places that adorn India. Madurai first, where, walking barefoot, I singe my feet in the Meenakshi temple. Like all religious places of the Hindus, footwear is banned here although the outside temperature is close to fifty degrees centigrade. From here, I go to Madras and board the Ganga-Kaveri Express (what a name!) to Varanasi, to take a holy dip in the putrid Ganges. I meet more sanyasis who tie stones to their dicks to control desire. It beats me how it works, but they refuse to explain, reading lust on my face. 'Aap ko aur kucch chahiye,' one of them smiles conspiratorially. He's beefcake, and I would love to destroy his vows of chastity, if only he'd allow me. But he directs me, instead, to Varanasi's opprobrious red-light district where I'm ambushed by a matronly whore. As she leads me to her brothel against my will, she guarantees me the Last Tango in Paris.

Breaking loose, I board a train headed for Haridwar. It is only the unreserved coaches that I step into, for the reserved ones have long waiting lists. They're also expensive. I squat on the floor with beggars and sadhus and smoke pot. As I peregrinate, memories of Su, weighing me down like a mass of lead, are temporarily obliterated. Trains, I discover, are my best antidote.

I swing on the Lakshman Jhoola at Rishikesh and inadvertently enter a temple with my slippers on. The priests are so infuriated they fling my footwear down from the temple's topmost tower. They land on the busy street and I run down the stairs to save them from being filched. Later, I find myself in Puri, in Dwarka, in Tirupati. It's good that there are so many trains and so many temples in India. My hair is long and matted, and so is my beard. It's around this time that I also begin to grow the nail on my little finger.

A whole month passes before my circular tour ends. I return to Bombay, then rush off to Pune, suddenly seized by panic.

13

Then, I am reunited with Su. On 13 July—unlucky number—precisely fifty-six days after I saw him last. It is around noon and I'm loitering at the Shivajinagar station doing god knows what. We collide head-on, like two cars, at the exact spot where the platform intersects with the foyer. We're at right angles so we don't see each other in advance, crashing into one another without warning. I am reminded of a sixties film, *Mere Mehboob*, where the hero and the heroine collide similarly on a university campus in north India. The heroine's books, which she is clutching tightly to her chest, fall to the ground. Suddenly, she's on all fours, picking them up, and the hero, too, apologetically gets on his knees to assist her. The books retrieved, they break into a song.

In our case, there's no such luck. Since there are no books that Su's holding to his chest (only a tattered shabnam bag), there's no question of their falling to the ground, or of my guiltily getting on my knees to salvage them, or of our bursting into a duet. It's a reunion full of anguish, the reunion of lovers turned enemies. It's a moment that neither of us could have anticipated. It catches us off guard—Su more than me who have only him, him, him in my thoughts, twenty-four hours a day. But in his case, it doesn't even give him the time, poor dear, to wear his mask.

Thus, for a split second, just a split second, I read the poetry, the earnestness in his eyes: I know you love me like Majnu loved Laila, I know you suffer, and solely because of me, but I am helpless against the forces of this world. What can I do? What?

Then he dons his armour. 'I'm sorry, I can't speak to you. I'm in a hurry. I have to go. Don't follow me. Don't!'

We make quite a sight on the throbbing street, with him quickening his steps and me in feverish pursuit, with fervent appeals to slow down, stop and listen to what I have to say. He's a fast walker. I realize, at that moment, that he's Pune Marathon material. Whereas I, despite my long legs, find it difficult to accelerate.

Still, victory is momentarily mine, and I manage to slip a hand into his and clasp it so tight he's unable to disengage. We're walking hand in hand now, as we've done a million times before. I'm the engine, he the carriage. I lead him into a nearby café and order two cups of tea. I'm willing to order every dish on the menu in order to prolong our stay, but he declines, saying he's had his meal and, of course, it's getting late. He's going to Chinchwad in suburban Pune, where his ghoulish uncle—nay, carnivore—works. I flinch at the mere mention of the rogue.

No sooner do we pay the bill and emerge from the café than I run out of luck. We're at yet another T-junction—the area seems full of them. A PMT bus pulls up by our side, barely a few feet away, as if the driver intends to mow us down. I'm irritated by the presence of the monster at such close proximity, especially as there's no bus stop nearby. Then I see the traffic lights ahead that have, doubtless, caused the bus to stop. As if this weren't enough, Su reads the destination board and finds that it's going to Chinchwad. He bounds in like a deer and flashes his Macleans smile. 'See you after four years,' he satanically says, as the bus begins to move. I'm dumbstruck. I stare at the bus till it is a tiny speck. I admonish myself for the rest of the day for botching up this chance of a lifetime.

Later that night, I write a letter to the General Manager of PMT Corporation, imploring him that bus conductors be strictly instructed not to let passengers board buses at traffic lights.

14

This failure is no different from failure in exams. And when one fails in an exam, one plans one's strategy so as not to fail a second time.

I first think of seeing Ravi Humbe, but dismiss the idea almost as quickly as it occurs to me. Ravi Humbe is nothing but an agent of the carnivores. Talking to him is bound to be counterproductive. Next thought—I will approach that closet gay, Kishore, and his bosom pal Gajanan. Maybe they'll provide useful leads. Besides, they're bound to be more accommodating than Ravi Humbe. After all, we accommodated them in our room in their hour of need. They shared a bed and took turns watching us sleep on the other bed. This fills me with hope. Something tells me they'll be compassionate. True, we also ragged them later, but that was really the handiwork of Gaurav and Vivek. I had no hand in it.

It is with some difficulty that I locate their hostel. These guys seem to change rooms like movie stars change shirts. I adopt the Indian way—ask this one and that one—till, finally, I achieve my goal.

But I don't come to the point straightaway. Instead, I first apologize for the ragging incident, saying that Gaurav and

Vivek had dragged me into it against my will. I then talk about a bash in Gaurav's room.

Kishore's face changes colour at the mention of Gaurav. As usual he's only in his undies. He feigns ignorance. 'Who Gaurav? What bash?' he mumbles and, then, fumbles.

Give me a break. Isn't it about time you acquired some guts and accepted yourself for what you are? This I don't say to him, however. My aim, all said and done, isn't to help Kishore or Gajanan come out of the bloody closet. It is to ferret out information about Su, and I must ensure I do not alienate these blokes in whose room I now stand (they haven't offered me a seat yet, the ill-mannered brutes). Or else, they might command me to leave, and the mission would be a dud.

'Don't you know?' they ask me point-blank, their eyes lighting up, as soon as I mention Su. 'It is common knowledge, the whole world knows.'

I grind my teeth in anger, wishing they would stop talking in riddles. But I quickly suppress my anger for they are my leads towards whom I must be civil, the civil engineers. 'I don't know anything,' I reply, shrugging my shoulders. Will you please be kind enough to tell me and end the suspense? This last, again, I say to myself and not aloud.

'Then listen,' says Kishore, while Gajanan idiotically nods. 'Your friend was taken by his family to a famous baba whose ashram is close to Belgaum city. He is so holy, even his shit smells good. There he was given electric shocks to get the bhoot out.'

'Bhoot?' I ask, incredulous, and feel asinine immediately afterwards, for the whole thing suddenly comes to me. His naive folks believed he was possessed, and that the evil spirits were transmitted to him through me. So they had taken him to a tantrik to exorcize him. I have never heard anything so nonsensical. I don't know whether to laugh or cry, but tears well up in my eyes as I imagine them administering those shocks to him. Like they had done to my granddad on his deathbed, in a bid to make his heart beat again. How he had wriggled and struggled, although pinned down to the four-poster by four burly ward boys.

'After the visit to the baba, he was no longer the same.' It's Gajanan who speaks, surprising me, for he is the quieter and less forthcoming of the two. 'All his friends found he had changed.'

'Yes,' Kishore concurs. 'He even refused to recognize me when I went to his place to ask for a book he had borrowed.'

Things begin to fall into place. Explanations emerge for his ludicrous behaviour at Shivajinagar station. Something certainly seemed amiss. 'Thanks for the news,' I say and abruptly move towards the door. 'Got to catch a train to Bombay.'

Neither guy asks me to stay, even for courtesy's sake. Why, they don't even stand up as I clumsily leave their room. I slyly look at Gajanan's dick, which still bulges to the left. Just then Kishore speaks, ending the denial he's in. 'If you were not a party to the ragging, why were you present in the room?'

I shrug, say, 'Sorry, brother,' and walk out.

15

I go to the Engineering College and hide by the railway tracks, close to the college back gate. I know that this is the gate Su uses to go home. Home? How can it be a home? It's only a drab hostel. Anyway, I wait. It's three o'clock in the afternoon. Classes are over and students begin to come out. Like him, they too use the back gate to go to their respective hostels. It's hazardous, so close to the tracks that any of them can be easily run over. What if one of us is run over, Su or I, I ask myself? Would that be a blessing in disguise? Would it put an end to everyone's misery?

Then, suddenly, I see him. Him, of the coquettish gait, walking all by himself. One two, one two. I let him pass then, keeping a steady distance between us, I do a Gaurav—I begin to follow him. He gets to the main road on the other side of the tracks and crosses it. I follow. He walks past the civil court. I follow. Now I quicken my pace, so that the distance between us reduces by half. I must strike before he enters his hostel. Soon, he's outside the gates of his hostel and I'm about to call out to him. But, to my surprise, he doesn't enter the hostel. Instead, he crosses another road and continues his trek. He's going towards Deccan Gym. A doubt crosses my mind. Has he found another guy whom he's going to see? Could it be a date? I follow. His swaying hips and dancing arse, seen from the rear, are always a turn-on.

At last I catch up with him and tap his shoulder. He recoils. There's a menacing look in his eye that terrifies me. I can swear it's something I've not seen before. I'm unnerved but I venture to speak. 'My dear, what's wrong?' I say tenderly. 'Why do you shun me?'

He grits his teeth. 'I've already told you,' he replies, almost sticking his index finger into my nose. 'Don't talk to me till I finish my course.'

'But this is unreasonable,' I protest. 'Four years is a long wait. You know I can't live without you for even a day.'

'Then go to Shivajinagar and lie down on one of the four tracks. Let a train run over you.'

This brings tears to my eyes, but I fight them back. How can someone I love from the depths of my heart be so vicious? 'Please . . . Don't do this to me,' I awkwardly mumble and break into fully-fledged sobs in the middle of the street.

He's flabbergasted. He notices a rusty blade lying on the sidewalk and bends down to pick it up. 'If you don't leave me at once, I'll attack you with this,' he screams.

I continue sobbing. Before I know it, the blade slashes my skin. He keeps his word and assaults me with it, making deep gashes on my hand. Paralysis strikes. I'm unable to withdraw my hand and simply run away. The blood comes to the cuts quickly. In no time, my smarting hand resembles a sheet of paper on which a child has mindlessly scribbled.

The sight of the blood causes a small crowd to gather. Their queries distract me. What happened? How? He uses the opportunity to slip away. I look everywhere, but he's gone. Vanished into thin air.

'Go to a nursing home and get your wounds dressed,' a good Samaritan advises me. 'Get an ATS injection,' adds another. The ATS is important, considering the blade was rusty. Or else I could die of tetanus. I pull away from the crowd, ashamed of the tamasha I have caused. As I walk, the pain in my hand increases. I notice a doctor's clinic, step in and await my turn.

The next day I'm back in action. Never say die. I loiter near the Engineering College Hostel. The moment I see him, I swoop.

Words first—I plead with him to take me back into his life. 'I promise to be a good boy and do exactly as you please,' I say with folded hands. 'No sex till your exams are over, till you get your degree. I promise to be a brahmachari.' Predictably, it doesn't work. He's still hostile. Luckily, there are no rusty blades here. I show him my bruised, bandaged hand, but this too fails to move him. So I resort to action. I bend down and touch his feet, as if he were Lord Shiva himself, from whom I want a boon. 'Please, don't dump me, I can't bear it,' I weep. He's disgusted. He steps back so that my fingers don't actually touch his toes. Then, all of a sudden, he begins to run. On your marks, get set, go! He runs so fast, before I know it, he's out of sight. I toy with the idea of giving chase, but it's pointless. As I've said before, I'm no sportsman. My body isn't as lithe as his.

I retreat to an Irani restaurant. Over cups of chai, I spend a whole hour writing him mushy, sentimental letters on ruled sheets of papers that I'm carrying in my bag. I allow my tears to smudge the ink in places. When I'm finished, I buy a stamped postal envelope from the paan-wallah outside, write Su's address on the envelope, seal it with my spit and put it into a nearby postbox.

But a whole week passes, and I have no way of knowing if he's got my letters. It's obvious that he's destroyed them, unread. Maybe that's what the tantrik instructed him to do. What a waste of paper, ink.

I take the last train to Bombay. Unlike before, I'm a nomad in this city, Pune, with no place to call my own. No roof over my head. My only consolation is my cheap season ticket which enables me to return to Bombay whenever I please, balls to my nagging parents. I can make sixty up-and-down journeys for the price of six. The Indian Railways be blessed.

Then, I hit upon another idea. Back in Pune, I buy him his favourite mithai, Mysore pak of all things, and take it to him. 'My love, this is for you,' I say tenderly. Failure again. He takes the box, wrapped in shimmering green paper, from my hand and chucks it into the gutter. His action stimulates my tear duct as usual. It's monsoon season for my eyes. I grab him by the shoulder. 'Don't you have any respect for my feelings?' I sob. He spits in my face. I can feel the warm saliva dribbling down my cheeks. I am at his door, which he slams shut on my face, lest fellow students, who have probably branded us as tamasha artistes par excellence, see us.

16

They say life is full of little ironies. Here is one of them: I get a job in Dinshaw College, one of Pune's savviest. It's only a leave vacancy that will cease to exist after a year, but some job in Love City is better than no job. Besides, it liberates me from the tyrannies of Azad College.

R. Raj Rao

I'm quite a sight as I enter the hallowed portals of the college dressed like a cricketer, in white shirt and trousers that I've got newly stitched as a metaphor for renouncing the world. My mode of transport is a rusty old bicycle that I hire from one of the college's senior lecturers at a monthly charge of fifty rupees. The students of the college, no trendsetters in discipline, find me outrageously comic. They give me a nickname, Laawaris, which is the title of another blockbuster, starring (yet again) Amitabh Bachchan. Maybe they see a resemblance between us, both of us being lanky. Or perhaps it's the story of the film they remember whenever they see me for, like the hero, the misery on my face makes me look orphaned. I hate the nickname, but accept it as my fate. What choice do I have anyway?

It's agonizing to be on the campus, not just because of the rowdy students but also because of the stinging memories— Su and I had come here together to look for a job for me. I frequently rush to the gents' loo to cry, and this makes one of the lady lecturers ask if I have diarrhoea. Her name is Rita and, like me, she has recently joined the college on a leave vacancy. Our leave vacancies are a story in themselves, for we substitute a husband-and-wife team that has gone to the US for the husband's treatment. Rita, whose subject is Commerce, fills in for the husband, while I replace the wife. Her vehicle, a Luna, is superior to mine. We become friends one morning when she overtakes me on Sangam Bridge, the bridge across the Mula river that joins the two parts of the city. Like the students of Dinshaw College, she finds my pedalling awkward. I arrive at the staffroom long after her, and she guffaws like a nanny goat when she sees me. Her laughter is infectious and I too begin to laugh. I'm laughing after months, and everyone notices. 'What's come over the guy?' I hear someone asking.

I tell Rita the story of my life, but resort to another substitution, like the husband-and-wife team we are substituting. I replace Su with a she, an invented girlfriend whom I was supposed to marry but who deserted me at the last minute because she found someone who drove a Mercedes. Rita buys the fiction and sympathizes with me. Maybe she's willing to stand in for the Unfaithful One who, according to her, is unworthy of my love. But she's afraid of saying so to my face because she isn't beautiful—short, with leucodermic patches on her face which she's getting treated. Her fluffy hair, though, reminds me of candyfloss and I tell her so. On her part, she hates the fringe on my forehead, which she thinks is for girls.

It's a tedious journey on bicycle to Dinshaw College and back. Every day, I cycle about five kilometres each way. This is something I am entirely unused to and I have swollen calves. Rita suggests that I rent a room on the other side of the river, close to the college—I'll save both energy and time. The distance and my clumsy cycling mean that I reach late on a couple of occasions and receive memos from the vice principal. As I read them, I think of the homely environment of Azad College. I suddenly realise that, for all its tomfoolery, I miss the college. Maybe I would have been better off there. But it's too late now. Too much water has flowed under the bridge.

However, I don't hire a room near Dinshaw College on purpose. Rents in this part of the town are no doubt high and, what's more, I'll be cut off from Su.

I thus take a private room in close proximity to the Engineering College Hostel. All the other boarders in the bungalow are Engineering College students. Somehow, I feel secure in their presence. I even begin eating in the mess attached to the hostel. Actually, outsiders are not allowed to sup there, but they make an exception in my case. They've seen me hanging out for too long to consider me alien. Joseph, the dwarfish man at the canteen who hands me my coupons, greets me cordially and says I'm a familiar face. He's Mangalorean and likes to speak English, finding a willing ally in me.

My room in Savli Bungalow, to the east of Shivajinagar station, is tiny. Its dimensions are a mere eight feet by four feet. I've never seen a student's room this small. What's worse, it has a tin roof that makes it a tandoor oven in the afternoons. It was initially a servant's room but the owner, Mr Dharmadhikari, does not have a servant. Hence, he lets it out, along with the other rooms in the bungalow, to Engineering College students. This, because the college is just a stone's throw away from the bungalow and the hostels can hardly accommodate everyone in need of shelter.

At first, Mr Dharmadhikari mistakes me for a student. When I tell him, somewhat self-righteously, that I'm a Dinshaw College lecturer, he raises his eyebrows in disbelief. 'You are looking like student only,' he says. Reluctantly, he gives me the room—the only one left—but asks me to pay more than what he charges the boys. 'You are earning, no?' he reasons. Then, to my horror, I discover that the room, worse than a dog's kennel, isn't going to be mine alone. I have a room partner with whom I must share it. I'm livid, but I pacify myself—I'll change to a better room in a couple of months. Mr Dharmadhikari gives me the key and leaves. 'I'll send you the pavti, the receipt, later,' he informs me, as he pockets the 750 rupees I give him as advance rent for three months.

Not only is the room small, it's shabby. The patchy walls haven't been painted in years. My bed, an iron folding cot, is against one wall, while my roomie's bed is against the other. There's no sign of him yet, although it's evening. I'm dying to check him out. I resolve to buy a tin of Apcolyte and paint the walls at my expense. There's no way I can live in this dungeon otherwise.

One glance at my room partner when he walks in— without knocking, late at night—and I realize he's not going to be my life partner. He's rotund. He isn't prepared to come home to find a trespasser fidgeting in his room and the irritation shows on his face. But Mr Dharmadhikari had forewarned him. 'You can't have such big room all to yourself. You will have to keep a room partner,' he must have said. So he now tries to come to terms with his fate.

'Welcome, sir,' he says, this last in deference to my professional status, although I'm just a few years older than him. 'My name is Ganapati. You may call me Ganesh.'

He extends his hand and I shake it. His palm is rough, with the skin having broken in places owing to the heat.

'My name is Siddharth,' I reply.

'Mr Dharmadhikari has told me all about you,' he continues. 'What a brilliant person you are, and so on.'

'Ha . . . Hardly,' I stammer. 'But thank you. That's very kind of you. And of Mr Dharmadhikari.'

Ganapati asks me if I've had dinner. I lie that I have—the truth being that I've lost my appetite. He boils two cups of water on a gas stove.

'I drink a lot of tea,' he lets me know. 'It helps me stay awake.'

His field is Electronics, a newly emerging discipline that has terrific potential. Only whiz kids are allowed to opt for Electronics.

We sip our tea. His next question is, 'Where are you from?'

'Bombay. And you?'

'Goa. Cuncolim, Goa. Have you been to Goa?'

'Yes, once. It's a fun place, isn't it?'

'For you. We Goans don't like to think of it that way. I mean hippies and all. Goa has its serious side too. Industries like Dempo. Life can't be a picnic 365 days a year.'

So Ganapati can think against the grain. Refreshing, after all those duffers I've hobnobbed with at the hostel.

'I think we're going to get on very well,' I tell him, and he agrees. We sit chatting late into the night, sipping gallons of tea. But when he undresses, I'm compelled to look away. The sight of his fleshy, un-muscular thighs revolts me. Like most hostellers far away from their moms, he's filthy. His undies stink, but what's really unbearable is the ghastly odour emanating from his socks and running shoes when he takes them off. Our badly ventilated torture chamber, with a lone window at the back, smells of a hundred skunks. I soak pieces of cotton in Tata's Eau de Cologne and stuff them into my nostrils. Ganapati notices and laughs. 'Tomorrow, I promise to wash my socks in Surf,' he says.

For all I know, Ganapati's straight as a foot rule. Yet I brainwash myself into believing he's my new yaar. I pretend we're a couple as we go to the mess together for meals and take long post-dinner strolls afterwards. The deception is comforting, for it alleviates, to some extent, my sense of rejection. But the thrill I derive most from it is making Su, my ex-lover, jealous. We bump into him almost every morning at the mess and he notices us together. I imagine him spending sleepless nights wondering who Ganapati is. Naturally, he doesn't know him—Ganapati being his junior by a year, and from a different stream. Also, he isn't from Belgaum, though Goa is close, and the Belgaum lot suffer from such an inferiority complex that they cannot bring themselves to make friends with anyone not from their backwater. But this is deception too, this business of obtaining a sadistic thrill by making him jealous. I return to my dungeon in Mr Dharmadhikari's bungalow each night with a headache.

As for Ganapati, he both knows and doesn't know what's going on in my life. Subconsciously, he knows I'm deeply in love with Su, Civil Engineering student, whom he sees at the mess where we eat. He senses that all the time I spend with him, Ganapati, providing intellectual company, is on the rebound—it will vanish the day my yaar returns. On a conscious level, however, he finds my obsession with another male strange. 'But he isn't a woman,' he frequently says to me during our post-dinner walks. We discuss everything under the sun. We discuss religion, Rajneesh, education, literature and prostitution.

I interject all our talk with references to Su and sometimes he loses his patience. 'What's a Dinshaw College lecturer doing with a fellow like that?' he remarks.

'Okay, let's give him a nickname,' he suggests. It comes to us easily, almost simultaneously. Devil's Disciple, we decide to call him, after the Bernard Shaw play we have both recently read—I, because I teach it, and he, simply because he found it lying in our room. We burst into laughter as we reflect on the aptness of the nickname, considering his affair with the tantriks. Then, on another impulse, we decide to abbreviate it to DD. So Su, Civil Engineer, is now DD to us whenever he comes up in conversation.

17

Farouq spots me on the street and calls out to me. He looks happier than usual, sporting a jazzy red T-shirt over faded blue jeans. The cap, the sunglasses and the cigar are still a part of his sartorial makeover.

'Care for a chai?' he asks me, shaking my hand, and I agree. 'Which hotel?' he asks and names an Irani and an Udipi joint in the vicinity. I settle for the Irani—I've had enough of the state of Karnataka. I imagine we're going to walk to the place, but Farouq has a surprise in store. He's just acquired a second-hand Yezdi, parked close to where we stand. We head towards the bike.

'Beautiful,' I say, as he pats the seat and asks me how I like the machine. He kick-starts it and we're off.

Farouq's company is comforting. Therefore, I indulge him, talk to him about his bike.

'How much did you buy it for?' I ask.

'Just 10,000 rupees,' he answers. His tone indicates he has conned the seller, an Indian Muslim by the name of Naushad, who could possibly have sold the damn thing for much more. 'Naushad now wants to buy it back from me,' he laughs. 'He has high hopes if he thinks that I'm going to part with it.'

We carry on like that for a few minutes. But I'm unable to sustain it and end the pretence. Abruptly, I change the topic. 'And how's your great room partner?' I cautiously ask.

Farouq lights a cigarette. Perhaps he wants to say, 'Oh, no, not again.' Instead, he says, 'He's wonderful. Seems very happy these days.'

'Does he spend his time studying?' Already Farouq is beginning to look bored. 'And whom does he hang out with these days?'

'Mostly Belgaum guys,' he replies. 'He doesn't have too many other friends. Not even a girlfriend.'

'A girlfriend, for god's sake,' I exclaim. 'And that too in the Engineering College?'

I'm suddenly caught off guard by Farouq who, for a change, asks me a question. 'What about you?'

'You mean do I have a girlfriend?'

'No. I mean, you don't come to the room nowadays. What happened to your English class?'

I fidget with the menu and a paper napkin before answering. My reply, doubtless, is unconvincing. 'Busy with my job. I've rented my own room. The boys were being disturbed by my visits.'

We keep talking. When we get up to leave, I realize, to my embarrassment, that our conversation had been monopolized by Su. As if this wasn't bad enough, I don't stop Farouq when he takes out his wallet to pay the bill.

A letter slips out of Farouq's wallet. Neither he nor I see it till he speeds off on his Yezdi. I have no choice but to shove the letter into my pocket and take it to my room, where it lies forgotten. In the dead of the night, however, as Ganapati sleeps, I remember the letter and jump out of bed to extract it from my shirt pocket. I unfold the letter and read it.

Even in my unruliest of fantasies, I could not have imagined the contents of the letter. I have to drink glass after glass of water to digest what's in front of me.

AMERICAN INTELLIGENCE CORPORATION
THE UNITED STATES OF AMERICA
February 1, 1980.

HIGHLY PRIVATE & CONFIDENTIAL
Dear Mr Farouq al Hosseini,
Re: Appointment Letter

The American Intelligence Corporation of the United States of America is pleased to confirm your appointment as Espionage Agent in Iraq, the country of your domicile, and India, where you study. You will be on our payroll on a monthly stipend of $2,500 (dollars two thousand five hundred), beginning today.

Apart from a general surveillance of military installations in Iraq and India, both countries with tremendous potential to someday go nuclear, you will also assist us in shortlisting soldiers, particularly those with a good track record of killing army personnel and civilians, on whom we may try out a new hormone weapon. The biological weapon has been developed by the US Air Force's Brown Laboratory in Ohio at an estimated cost of $5 million (dollars five million), and has been acquired by our client, The Pentagon, on whose behalf we act. Initially, i.e. at this stage, the hormone will be administered as an injection to selected soldiers. It has no side effects. In the long run, however, Brown Laboratory plans to manufacture a bomb that will contain a powerful aphrodisiac chemical.

We do not consider it fair to keep you in the dark as to how the hormone weapon works. Plainly said, it turns normal heterosexual men into homosexuals. As the US army is infested with homosexuals, the strategy is to cause recipients of the hormone to fall in love with American soldiers who anyway are every gay man's ultimate fantasy. Conversely, white American gay men are known to have a preference for brown or tanned skin. This would considerably weaken the enemy's resolve to wage war on America, which will be replaced by the opposite impulse to make love. The idea for the weapon, as you can thus see, first came from a bumper sticker that said 'Make Love Not War'.

When Brown Laboratory eventually produces its aphrodisiac bomb, the effects of the chemical will be much more widespread than at present. The Pentagon predicts large-scale homosexual behaviour to destroy discipline and morale in the armies of all countries that dare to challenge and oppose the interests of the United States. India, and especially Iraq, we're afraid, will be top-priority nations where the bomb will be dropped. Both countries, in the opinion of the Pentagon and the White House, have the reputation of being bullies in their respective regions—India in South Asia and Iraq in the Gulf.

Please get to work immediately and send us your list of soldiers as soon as possible. We shall then decide where and how to inject them.

Please confirm receipt of this letter and acceptance of your appointment by return of post.

Sincerely,
Steve Roberts,
Secretary, American Intelligence Corporation.

18

Ganapati is starved of 'congenial company'. Had it not been for me, he says, life would have been sheer drudgery. He is, therefore, ready to give anything to spend time with me, just to have a serious discussion. I play on his gullibility and suggest we take a trip. Motion, remember, relaxes the mind. And there are holy places near Pune I still haven't gone on a pilgrimage to. Like Jejuri, Alandi and Pandharpur. Tossing a coin, we settle for Pandharpur.

The tarpaulin-flapped, early-morning ST bus is exactly what we expect it to be—rickety. We sleep almost throughout the journey, opening our eyes only once when the bus takes a fifteen-minute halt at a wayside village so that the driver and conductor can take a leak. I remain seated in the bus, while Ganapati gets off to buy bananas. He returns a couple of minutes later, gasping for breath.

'What?' I ask, but he's too stunned to open his mouth. Instead, he drags me out of the bus and points to a female banana-seller sitting with her wares a few feet away. She's a village belle with a well-oiled bun and a nine-yard sari tightly wrapped around her butt.

'What about her?' I ask Ganapati but his tongue is still in chains. 'Will tell you when the bus moves,' he manages to pant.

No sooner does the driver start the engine than I nudge Ganapati. 'Tell me now,' I plead. Turns out that when he complained to the buxom banana-seller about the smallness of her fruit, her retort was that he should measure them against his own genitals to see which was bigger! 'Doesn't it amount to obscenely propositioning me?' he asks, as if raped. I purposely do not answer, not wanting to be drawn into heterosexual mumbo-jumbo. But a few minutes later I say, 'Maybe you should have taken her up on her offer.' Ganapati isn't amused. He doesn't possess a sense of humour. The low-caste woman's advances have violated his Brahmin sensibilities.

The bus roars on the highway. It's noisier than a Boeing 747. Not that it's going really fast—the roads simply do not permit it. It's just that its silencer hasn't been replaced for a quarter of a century.

When we finally reach Pandharpur, the first thing we see is mounds—nay, mountains—of saffron powder in the little shops that dot the pathway to the temple of Lord Vithoba. Good from a cinematic point of view.

We check into a cheap lodge, freshen up and go to the temple. The shopkeepers solicit us and are shocked to find us ignoring their pleas. In the end, we enter the temple without the customary thali full of offerings of coconuts, flowers, incense, sweets and, of course, red powder. The shopkeepers think we're heretics, an idea Ganapati loves because his trip in life is to break every rule in the book. But then, why did the kelewali's pass offend him? No answer, except that life is full of contradictions.

We emerge from the temple in less than ten minutes, doing a perfunctory namaskar to the deity. To travel all the way for hours and then to spend not even ten minutes with the Lord! But then, both Ganapati and I detest rituals. Religion to us is philosophy, spirituality, but certainly not ritual. 'Even the Buddha rebelled against it and founded his own order,' Ganapati says. Yet, ritual is the mainstay of the popular Pandharpur shrine, where it's impossible to find a quiet corner to sit and meditate.

In the evening, my ears cock up at the rattling sound of a malish-wallah's bottles. I'm instantly transported to my late teens when I would patronize the nocturnal malish-wallahs of south Bombay's Oval Maidan. Though dirty, they were the ultimate turn-on. The way they sat astride you and rubbed you all over, head to foot, genitals included, then turned you over and did the same to your rear. If you stiffened, they masturbated you for a small fee. They were also an excellent alibi, because if a cop suddenly appeared on the scene, emerging from the darkness like an apparition, you could always say you were only having an innocent massage, whereas the boy-prostitutes in the maidan offered no such ruse.

Ganapati snaps his fingers in front of my eyes to draw me out of my reverie. 'Sir, where are you lost?' he asks. Had he not been there, I would have taken the fucking malish-wallah into our room. But to do so in front of the nosy, inquisitive Ganapati is to, in an instant, let him know everything about me that he always wanted to know but was afraid to ask. So, although I summon the malish-wallah and check him out (quite a descendant of Shivaji!) and in the process kindle his hopes, in the end I'm forced to say nahin mangta, no thank you.

I'm stuck with Ganapati, the elephant god, and eat a vegetarian thali, while the poor malish-wallah goes away in search of greener pastures.

19

The pilgrimage to Pandharpur turns out to be inauspicious for me. Evidently, Lord Vithoba was offended by our lack of reverence. As soon as we return, I get news that my job at Dinshaw College has come to an end. The husband and wife, who had gone to America for treatment, have come back earlier than scheduled, not able to afford the cost of living there. And now both Rita and I have to take a bow and make way for them. We find comfort in each other's company in the staffroom, while the other professors are busy taking their classes. But Rita belongs to Pune, so at least she doesn't have to leave the city.

R. Raj Rao

As for me, how can I pay for my room in Mr Dharmadhikari's bungalow and grub in Joseph's mess without a job? The only course open to me is to pack my bags and return to Bombay where, despite differences with my folks, I can be assured of a roof over my head and two square meals daily. I mourn at the thought of having to leave this enchanting little city for good, a city that's synonymous for me with love and sex. But I've got to be practical. Besides, Su's no longer in my life. And with all the harm done to him by his folks and that evil tantrik, there's little chance of his returning.

In a way, I'm glad. Maybe I'm a mendicant at heart, like the ascetics of old. It's sort of comforting to close a chapter of one's life and move on without worrying too much about what the future has in store. The past and the future are, anyway, illusions. It's the present that brings bliss and peace of mind. At least, that's what the holy men say.

I walk to the railway station to book myself a seat to Bombay on the Deccan Queen. For the last time.

It's bye-bye to him, Su, my obsession for the past so many months. Bye-bye to all the good times we had. Bye-bye to Pune, this city that the Peshwas built, that brought us together and then separated us. Bye-bye to the Engineering College Hostel and to Room E 131 where we first met. Bye-bye to my English class and all the vernacs who studied under me. Bye-bye to Ravi Humbe and Gajanan and voyeuristic Kishore, born in the city of Belgaum. Bye-bye to Joseph and his mess that fed me and kept me alive. Bye-bye to Farouq the spy, because of whom I met Su, the love of my life. Bye-bye to his Yezdi, cap, goggles and cigars. May he succeed in finding as many soldiers as America can turn gay. Bye-bye to Gaurav and Vivek, bye-bye to all their gay brothers, bye-bye to the shady goings-on in Room C 83. Bye-bye to Rita and her Luna, with special thanks for the solace she offered. Bye-bye to Dinshaw College and its staff and students who called me Laawaris. Bye-bye to the husband and wife who first went to and then returned from the US ahead of schedule, rendering me jobless. But I bear them no ill will and I wish the husband a speedy recovery. Bye-bye to Mr Dharmadhikari and my room in his bungalow, bye-bye to the intellectual of intellectuals Ganapati and all our verbal duels, bye-bye to our pilgrimage to Pandharpur, bye-bye to Lord Vithoba, bye-bye to the banana-seller who propositioned Ganapati, asking him to place his banana against hers to see which was bigger. Bye-bye, bye-bye, bye-bye, one and all. I leave this city for good, having calamitously failed in love. To this city I shall never return, this much I know. Westwards I shall go or eastwards, but never again shall I set foot on the soil of Pune. Bye-bye.

PART IV

MAY 1983 TO
JANUARY 1985

1

I'm back on the train after a whole year. For a whole year, I have stayed away from the railway station, lest I'm tempted to return to the life I've relinquished. For a whole year, I have lived with my folks in their flat, hellishly suffering as I go about my new college job. Life has been mundane, worse than death this past one year, with little to look forward to.

But why this morbidity, as I sit in the train waiting for it to start? I ought to rejoice for it is the same train that took me to Su that first time, five and a half years ago. I was with my folks and their frolicking friends then. I'm alone now. Literally—I'm the only passenger in the coach.

Thoughts storm my mind. I push them out for, like the yogis, I prefer a state of thoughtlessness. But this isn't easy. The more I stave them off, the more they rush to me in a torrent. Perhaps, to be freed of thought, one has to live in a hermitage. Not in the sprawling city of Bombay where thoughts attack the mind at the rate of one per second.

The driver blows his horn and the train begins to move. It's a slow express that ambles along for quite some time before gathering speed. The chai-wallah appears.

Why am I on the train? Because Gaurav and Vivek, that revolutionary pair, haven't forgotten me. They have sent me a telegram that's a conundrum: YOUR PRESENCE URGENTLY REQUIRED. COME TO C BLOCK ON FIRST

AVAILABLE TRAIN. But why I do comply, when I'm cynical, sceptical? I take out the telegram from my shirt pocket and read it over and over again.

All of a sudden, the train has grown so crowded that it's impossible for me to make my way to the loo. The gangway is full of people, sitting, standing. The compartment, meant for ninety, currently accommodates more than 200. Why are we so restless as a nation, forever in need of movement? I abandon the idea of taking a leak and doze off with a book in my hand.

When my eyes open again, we're not far from my destination—good old Shivajinagar. My book has fallen to the ground. Some passengers have trampled on it and I look at them with murderous eyes, unsure who the culprit is. I pick up the book and kiss it. It's my way of asking for forgiveness. I strap my rucksack to my back and head towards the door.

Soon I'm climbing the stairs of the footbridge and crossing the busy intersections that lead to the Engineering College Hostel. Nothing has changed. The same traffic, the same people. My heart races. Skirting E Block on the east, I take an alternate route to C Block.

Suddenly, I freeze. I see a poster with Farouq's picture on it. An old photograph, minus the cap, goggles and cigar. It's stuck on the whitewashed compound wall that separates the Engineering College Hostel from the pavement outside. Printed above the photograph in bold is the word 'WANTED'. Below the photo there are words in Arabic, which I cannot read. My blood runs cold. Why did Farouq have to become an American spy? Only because his country conscripted young men into the army against their will? Or was it for the dollars? To me, Farouq can never be a villain. Few can live up to his ideals of friendship. We had promised him lifelong refuge in India, and now he's on the run and there's nothing we can do. We've reneged on our word, shame on us. Wherever he is, I hope Farouq's good. Jesus Christ, please keep him safe.

2

Gaurav and Vivek are both there, waiting for me. We hug. How did they know I would be arriving on the Deccan Express?

'Intuition,' says Gaurav.

'Telepathy,' says Vivek.

'But first things first. How come you're back at the hostel?' I inquire.

'Things have a way of blowing over, dying down,' answers Gaurav. 'Both the principal and the rector changed. We reapplied for the hostel and got it. The clerks who allotted it to us hardly know our history. That is how government departments in this country work. They're in a state of perpetual anarchy.'

'And your activities? Have they slowed down?'

'No way! Or you wouldn't be here. We continue with gay abandon, ha ha. Your E Block friends have lost interest in us. In any case, most of them are such duds they find it difficult to pass their exams. All their energies are now focused on this goal, everything else in their lives has taken a back seat.'

'That's wonderful,' I manage to say.

'Yeah,' agrees Vivek, chewing gum. He looks hotter than before, with a military-type haircut and gabardine shorts. I train my eyes on his loins.

Gaurav asks me if I need a wash or some food and, when I say I'm fine, he breaks the news.

'The reason we called you here is because your yaar approached us.'

I choke on the water I'm drinking, and break into a sweat. 'What . . . Su . . . You?' I'm too stunned for speech.

'Yes,' he continues. 'He came here a couple of days ago to ask if you'd be willing to let bygones be bygones. Bury the hatchet.'

I can't believe my ears. There's bound to be a catch somewhere. Both Gaurav and Vivek keep mum. They have said their piece and are waiting for my reply.

'Of course, I'll let bygones be bygones,' I stammer.

'Brilliant!' remarks Gaurav. 'We were sure you wouldn't stand on false pride. I mean, it's true he treated you odiously. But it wasn't his fault. It was because of what his folks did—electric shocks and so on. He told us so himself.'

'I know,' I mutter. 'But please give me the dope. What exactly brought him to you?'

Vivek lights a cigarette and speaks. 'Oh, he's just lonely. He feels desolate and remembers the good times you guys had together.'

I'm flattered. Mushily, I think—My love, I promise to keep you happy till your dying day.

Gaurav speaks. 'In fact, we counselled him and told him it was in his best interests to make up with you.'

'Thanks,' I say to Gaurav and find my eyes welling up.

'Where are you parked for the night?'

'Oh . . . I haven't thought about that. I'll check into a lodge.'

'You don't have to. We have a spare mattress. You can stay in our room if you don't mind sleeping on the floor.'

3

After a sleepless night, morning at last. But it isn't till after breakfast that Vivek goes to fetch Su. Gaurav keeps me company in the room, pretending not to notice my fidgetiness. He reads a textbook and pushes the morning newspaper in my direction. I give it a cursory look. Half an hour passes, but there's no sign of Vivek.

Just then, there's a knock on the door and my heart leaps. Vivek arrives. With Su in tow.

R. Raj Rao

'Hello, Su,' I say to break the ice, but he remains silent. There's a faint hint of a smile on his face.

Gaurav raises a hand to intervene. 'Na,' he says to me. 'You can't talk to him directly yet. We're mediators in this now. So everything must go through us.'

How despotic, I tell myself, as I give Su the once-over. But Gaurav means business. He fishes out a moth-eaten, pink sari from somewhere—god knows how it got there—and ties it from one end of the room to the other to serve as a partition. Su and I are now on either side of the sari, hidden from each other's view. Vivek cannot stop laughing, but Gaurav is undeterred. 'Be serious and grow up,' he chides his mate. None of us knows what he has in mind as he fumbles with the knots. What if Dr Raikar walks into the room this very minute? What would he make of the scene, with his son on one side of the sari and me on the other? Like Vivek, I find the idea hilarious.

Now, there's actually a knock on the door.

Gaurav goes to the door. 'What a nuisance,' he grumbles. One of his straight classmates is at the door. 'I'm tied down with something very urgent right now,' he informs the chap, making sure he doesn't see the sari. 'Come back later.'

The guy leaves and Gaurav bolts the door. He gets back to work, now setting up a cassette player to record the proceedings of this historic reunion for posterity! His attention to detail makes the rest of us yawn.

Gaurav senses our boredom and claps his hands. 'Okay guys, I'm done. Shall we begin?'

4

Gaurav lights a candle and puts a question to Su. It's similar to the question his folks had asked him that fateful night. 'Do you want to go away with this man here?'

Gaurav sounds like a Christian priest asking the bride if she wishes to marry the bridegroom. 'I do,' the bride must coyly say, before the wedding is solemnized. But he, my heart-throb, doesn't utter those auspicious words. Three times Gaurav repeats his question, three times my yaar does not reply. Then, he says from the other side of the sari, 'On one condition.' I fix my eyes on Vivek's bemused expression.

'On one condition?' screams Gaurav, upset that things are not going right. 'What? What?'

Finger on lips. Then, 'I will become a woman.'

Vivek looks at me open-mouthed, as if about to suck my dick. Gaurav tries not to lose his cool.

'Why?' he manages to ask.

'So that we can get married.'

The logic is so foolproof that the rest of us are stricken by paralysis of the tongue. Two men cannot get married, but a man and woman can. So what's the harm if one of them changes his sex?

'Is that all?' asks Gaurav after much introspection, as if all Su wants is new underwear.

'No,' he replies, bewildering us further. 'We must migrate to another country where no one knows us. There, we'll begin our lives afresh.'

Gaurav heaves a sigh of relief. He cannot be blamed for expecting worse, say, Su insisting on bearing his own babies. No sex-change operation in the world could do that.

'Hey, be practical mate!' Vivek suddenly butts in. 'Sex-reassignment surgery is expensive. Damn bloody expensive! Where do you think the lolly will come from? And then you want to migrate? To the West, I presume. Who's going to foot the bill? Our princey?'

Su is mute. His obstinacy puts me off. Why hadn't I met Vivek instead of him that December morning five and a half years ago? Life would have been smooth as butter.

I look at Gaurav, our resourceful team-leader, and find him to be sympathetic to Su's extravagant demands. 'Money's not such a big deal,' he declares. 'We have friends in many cities abroad who'd be more than willing to chip in. Even the migration bit can be sorted out.'

'Then what's the delay?' Vivek asks, sarcastically.

'What I wish to know from Sudhir here is whether he's absolutely certain.'

'Yes,' Su burbles from the other side.

'Very well,' says Gaurav. 'Now let us ask our friend Siddharth what he has to say about the whole thing. All said and done, it's he who'll be spending the rest of his life with you in a faraway country.'

Three pairs of eyes are on me all at once. I'm expected to open my gob and speak. I present my considered opinion.

'Frankly, I think it's phoney to chop off one's cock and balls, especially when they are as beautiful as Su's, and replace them with a cunt. And then affix a pair of breasts, like postage stamps. Come on, I'm a goddamn homo, not a breeder like the rest of civilization. If a cunt was what I wanted, I would go for the real thing, not for a fake. An uncle of mine in Rajahmundry—heard of it?—once asked if I fancied the cunt of the home minister's daughter. He would make her my ardhangini, he promised.'

My words render everyone speechless. From the other side of the sari, I can hear Su breathing hard. Vivek bites his nails, trying to digest what I've said. Gaurav is worried that things are going wrong again. Failure would probably affect the funding he hopes to get from support groups abroad.

When the silence, like hymen, is finally broken, it's Gaurav who does the deflowering. 'Let's compromise,' he says optimistically. 'Both you guys are right in your own way. If Sudhir feels like a chick trapped in a male body, he has a right to release himself. What say, Siddharth?'

'Yeah,' I reluctantly consent. Refusal to do so might take me back to square one. For some reason, I am aroused and my cock is now at right angles to my thighs.

'However,' continues Gaurav, walking over to the other side of the sari to address Su. His fondness for the word reminds me of a Marathi lecturer in Azad College who had peculiar way of pronouncing it—Ha-weaver. 'However, Siddharth has a point as well.' He places a hand on Su's shoulder. 'What Siddharth is really concerned about is that he may not be drawn to you minus your male sexual organs, even though you're passive in the sex act. His fears are justified. You must understand that, after you become a woman, you'll be a different person altogether, with a different identity. What's the guarantee that the man with whom you are in a relationship now will continue to have the same feelings for you? Besides, a guy like Siddharth isn't just homosexual. He's also homo-political, if you know what I mean. By changing your gender, you're compelling him to defect to the other side—the side of his opponents. In other words, you are thrusting heterosexuality on him. Compulsory heterosexuality.'

The razor-blade nature of his argument impresses me. This man Gaurav indeed has it in him to change the world. What's he doing studying Metallurgical Engineering? But Su is too self-obsessed to make head or tail of what Gaurav is saying. He remains silent.

Then something strikes Vivek and he's dying to get it out of his system. 'By the way,' he addresses Su from my side of the partition, snapping his fingers. 'Do you know any doctor who does sex-reassignment surgery? I believe there are very, very few in India.'

'That is not my problem,' Su replies. 'If he cannot find a doctor, he doesn't get me.'

Just as I'm cursing myself for the rigmarole I'm in, Gaurav allays Vivek's fears that—thanks to Su—are now my fears as well. 'Of course, there are doctors who do it,' he enlightens us. 'In Bombay, in Delhi, everywhere. The best one, as far as I know, is the doc who operated on Faroukh Rustom. Faroukh was an art critic and celebrity who's now called Farah Rustom. I recently attended a talk by Farah at the House of Soviet Culture in Bombay. She spoke on Rachmaninoff. Believe me, she looks every bit a woman, complete with long hair and waxed legs.'

5

Now Su lapses into a soliloquy. All of us fade into the background and the spotlight is on him. Never before has he spoken so much—that too at one go.

'All my life,' he begins, without provocation, 'I have been doing what others wanted me to do. I wanted to study Arts. But my father pooh-poohed the idea and forced me to do Engineering. I hated it, but I did not know how to say so. So I came to a place where I never wanted to be. The subjects did not interest me at all. I did my best, but still couldn't pass my exams at the first attempt. At the hostel, I met Siddharth one afternoon. He knocked at my door and started making love to me without asking if I enjoyed it or not. Some months later, he came to the hostel again and I tried to avoid him. But finally, I too got hooked. I started to miss him badly. We kept on having sex. Many times, while having sex, I would think of my father. What would he say if he knew what I was doing here in Pune, far away from home? I did not want Siddharth to meet my father. But, again, he followed me to Belgaum during the holidays. At first, my father was good to him. But after some time he realized that Siddharth had penetrated my life deeply. He felt the only reason I failed my exams was because Siddharth wasted my time.

'One of my own classmates, whom I trusted, betrayed me by writing to my father and telling him all that happened in the hostel. I hate Ravi Humbe for making my life a mess. I don't even feel like taking his name. We are from the same town. We came to Pune in the same bus. What did Ravi Humbe get by becoming my father's chamcha? To make me forget Siddharth, my father and my uncles took me to a tantrik who gave me electric shocks. They were so painful. How could my own people be so cruel? Even my beloved mother and sister did not stop them. The shocks temporarily affected my brain. I thought I was going mad. When Siddharth insisted on chasing me, even after all that had happened, I grew desperate. I slashed his hands with a rusty blade that I found on the pavement. I should have known better but, at that time, I did not know what I was doing.

'How strange it is! None of these men in my life—be it my father or Siddharth or Ravi Humbe—even once asked me what I wanted. All of them took me for granted and manipulated me according to their will.

'But actually, I'm thankful to Siddharth. He opened my eyes. I have always felt like a girl, not a boy. As a child, I longed to wear my mother's saris. My sexual attraction is towards boys, not girls. But if Siddharth hadn't seduced me, maybe I would never have known this. I would have allowed my parents to marry me off and make our lives, both mine and my wife's, unhappy. Now, I have made up my mind to do as I please. It's my life, not anyone else's. If a spring is suppressed, it regains its original shape with khunnas. It's the same with me. I have decided to be my natural self. For that, however, I have to change my sex. If I feel like a lady from the inside, what's the use of being a man on the outside? If I'm a man and am caught having sex with another man, people will call me chhakka or a homo—both words of abuse. Why should I allow people to abuse me? But if I am a woman, they'll accept my relationship with a man. Because it's a relationship that society understands. So, in a way, I'm doing it not just for myself, but also for society. I'm not even scared of the pain. In surgery, they use anaesthesia. Then how could I feel the pain? Certainly, it would be less painful than those electric shocks my family gave me. I'm really quite excited about the whole thing. I'm waiting for my old self to die and my new self to be born. If Siddharth is unwilling to stand by me, he's free to leave. I'll find someone else to love me. There's no shortage of men in India.

'And if he misses the man in me, he can still fuck me in the backside.'

6

A month later, as I sit in the staffroom of K.K. College in downtown Bombay, reading a book, I'm shocked to see Gaurav. A peon brings him along, and says, 'Sir, apko koi milne aaya hai.'

I greet Gaurav and offer him a chair. My discomfiture is obvious. The staffroom is full of professors and students with whom I perpetually socialize. Gaurav, now associated in my mind with sex change operations and gay marriages, is hardly the person I want to meet here.

But Gaurav, who has just had both his ears pierced, is animated. 'Came to Bombay to see my folks,' he says, his mouth full of chewing gum, as usual. 'So I thought I'd call on you to give you the good news.'

The phrase alarms me. Gaurav's good news is bound to be bad news for me if blurted out here, in the K.K. College staffroom. For one, it would out me to my colleagues and students who, unlike the simpletons of Azad College, are from sophisticated neighbourhoods such as Marine Drive and Malabar Hill. Some of them are film stars' kids.

'Not here, Gaurav,' I whisper, dampening his spirits a little. 'Can we discuss this later, say, in the evening?'

But Gaurav is a busy man who's rushing off to Pune as soon as he's finished with me. I am compelled to cut my next class and accompany him to a nearby café, where there's enough privacy. When we're comfortably seated in a corner of the air-conditioned restaurant, Gaurav says, 'The airmail letters I wrote and the international calls I made have finally borne fruit. We've managed to collect a thousand US dollars and five hundred British pounds by way of contributions from well-wishers, which more than takes care of the doctor's fees. Dr Doctor, who operated on Faroukh Rustom, is even willing to accept the dough in foreign currency. He has Swiss bank accounts, you know—he's that much of a big shot. He said he'd be happy to perform the surgery at Emerald Hall Clinic in Pune and is going to get back to me shortly with possible dates.'

I'm moved by Gaurav's perseverance. I mean, who are we to him? And yet he labours so much for us? In a flash, I'm transported to the rainy day Ram and Farouq had laboured for us, risking pneumonia to find Su a professor who would teach him Maths. Their efforts had paid off. As, doubtless, Gaurav's will too. But finding a Maths professor is not the same as looking for a doctor who could transform you from a man to a woman. I still find the idea preposterous. Where's the certainty that I will be turned on by Su in his female avatar? And supposing I'm not, how can we live together for the rest of our lives? Even if he allows me to fuck him from the back? To make matters worse, the stubborn mule wants to emigrate. Do I really wish to live in a Western country? Who knows what life's really like out there? Whatever it's like, it's bound to be very different from the life here, at which I freak out. East or West, India is the best. In India, the streets are full of people whom one can patao, while in the West everyone's in their cars. In India, I'm too much in the sun, in the manner of Hamlet, whereas in the West the sun is in short supply. Bombayite that I am, the cold gives me gooseflesh. How would I survive the vicious winters when the temperatures fall below zero degrees centigrade? I have half a mind to wriggle out of the whole thing and run away, like Raju in *The Guide*, who tries to flee when holiness is thrust upon him.

7

D r Doctor keeps his word and calls up Gaurav to give him an appointment. The countdown begins.

Ten, nine, eight.

Gaurav visits various chemists to buy the drugs that Dr Doctor has prescribed.

Seven, six, five, four.

Su has started growing his hair. His folks haven't a clue as to what he's about to do. Or they would castrate the doctor who would dare to emasculate their progeny. Dr Doctor, of course, is shrewd. He makes Su sign a letter in which he declares that his consent to the surgery has been willingly given. The doctor can't have Su sue him later for tampering with his genitals. But shouldn't he secure my consent too, as a husband?

Three, two, one. Zero.

Gaurav, Vivek and I accompany Su to the operation theatre of Emerald Hall Clinic. We reassure him. All will be well. Have faith in the Almighty. But he seems extraordinarily composed, in no need of our encouraging words. The spasms he will suffer don't scare him one bit. To him, anaesthesia is a wonder drug. 'You are very brave,' I whisper into his ear as the nurses lead him to the operation theatre and impolitely slam the glass door in our faces.

The surgery takes a whole day. Gaurav and Vivek leave, but I remain seated in the visitors' lobby, trying to imagine them mutilating my yaar. Wish I could've had a dekko at his cock one last time—to say goodbye, to stroke it, to kiss it. I imagine them implanting silicone in his hairless chest. Henceforth, I can have a free drink of milk whenever I'm thirsty, I joke to myself. And what about his slit-and-clit? Do they work on it as a tailor works on buttonholes? Some of these thoughts occur to me in a waking state, others in sleep for, intermittently, I doze off on the long sofa—again with a book in my hands.

After one such sleeping bout, I find that Gaurav and Vivek are back. I look out the window. It was broad daylight when we had come here, now it has grown dark.

'The surgery was successful,' Gaurav informs me. 'Dr Doctor came out of the operation theatre a few minutes ago to give us the good news. You were asleep, so we didn't wake you.'

Presently, Dr Doctor emerges from the operation theatre again. Ignoring me, he addresses Gaurav. 'The operation is over,' he explains, 'but the entire process of changing your friend from a man to a woman will take about six months. During these six months, he'll be on electrolysis and we shall also give him hormone therapy. It can be a trying time for him because he'll look neither man nor woman.'

Dr Doctor steps out of the visitors' lobby, then, as an afterthought, returns. 'Oh, and I forgot to mention the painkillers,' he says. 'When the effect of the anaesthesia wears off, your friend will be in pain for a while. I'll scribble out the names of a few painkillers. Please give him those whenever the pain becomes excruciating.'

Gaurav follows the good doctor to his cabin to get the prescription. There is something he has forgotten to ask the doctor and I try to gesticulate to him, but he fails to notice me. When he returns, ten minutes or so later, I tell him, 'You forgot to ask how long he'll be kept in the hospital. When do they discharge him?'

'Oh,' says Gaurav and runs back to Dr Doctor's cabin.

'A week,' he pants, when he reappears. 'A week to ten days.'

I let Gaurav catch his breath. Then I ask him if we can go into the operation theatre to see Su. Somehow, the prospect of setting eyes on him—her—scares me. Gaurav runs back to Dr Doctor's cabin a second time, to inquire. He has grown pally with the doctor and doesn't mind seeing him any number of times. Undoubtedly, he sees him as useful to his movement.

While he's away, I turn my attention to Vivek who has been superfluous to the whole enterprise. Why are your corduroys always so tight? I want to ask him. Instead, we talk about section 377 of the Indian Penal Code, which describes sexual intercourse between two men as 'unnatural' and 'carnal.'

'It's known as the anti-sodomy law,' Vivek comments, trying to sound learned. 'But, now, you needn't worry. The law won't see you guys as criminal, for both of you aren't of the same sex.'

Thanks for rubbing it in, I want to tell Vivek. I shake his hand under some pretext and let my hand stay in his—which is how Gaurav finds us when he returns a couple of minutes later.

'You may go in, pronto!' he exclaims and, even before he finishes, I disengage my hand from Vivek's and nervously head towards Su's ward. I push the swing door open and step in cautiously. Su's eyes are closed but his wiggling toes indicate he has regained consciousness. Disturbed by the noise I make, he opens his eyes and smiles. I put my hands in his. 'Does it hurt?' I ask, to which he nods. I remove the sheet with which he is covered and feel his breasts. Then I look for the ultimate confirmation. His cock and balls have indeed gone and, in their place, is a vagina.

As I examine him, trying in vain to run my finger along the aperture, the door opens again and Gaurav and Vivek enter. 'You're not supposed to touch any of the implants yet,' Gaurav warns me, as if he were the doctor himself. 'They may come off.' Handing over Dr Doctor's prescription to me, he commands me to go out and get the painkillers. 'He's fine now, but soon he'll be in pain.'

For a whole week, I spend much time with Su in the nursing home. Except for occasional spasms of pain, which bring tears to his eyes and make him howl, he's fine. I am sole witness to the process he goes through to become a fully-fledged woman. I'm entirely in the dark as to how expensive the electrolysis and hormone therapy are, nor do I know what Dr Doctor has charged. Gaurav takes care of that, footing all the bills with the money he has received from abroad. My job is simply to be there (like a ward boy) to nurse Su into his new life.

I write a letter to my parents announcing that I'm leaving home to become a hippie, so they shouldn't look for me. To K.K. College, I don't even bother to formally tender my resignation. Prolonged absence amounts to dereliction of duty which qualifies me for dismissal, anyway. As for Su, he doesn't wish to write to his folks at all. 'That's my past life,' he declares, 'and has nothing to do with my present.'

When Su is discharged from the hospital, we move into a flat—the very flat in which Gaurav and Vivek had stayed when they were expelled from the hostel. Somehow, this flat has acquired the reputation of being occupied by queers. The neighbours do not suspect that Su is a guy. They think he's a tomboyish woman. Furthermore, they take it for granted that we're man and wife, and ask me in Marathi, when I bump into them on the staircase, if we're newly-weds—navra-baiko.

'Yes, we tied the knot just a month ago,' I say.

'Please call on us if you need anything,' the chairman of the society, Mr Chaudhury, very kindly says to me. Other neighbours regularly send us platefuls of upma, poha, shira and puran-poli on Sundays and festive days.

Su is happy. 'It's a dream come true for me,' he says, licking me all over. For regular sexual intercourse, however, we have to wait for six whole months.

8

It's one thing to be seen with Su in our housing society, and quite another to walk with him on the streets. I'm not quite ready and have an anxious time when he insists on going to Lakshmi Road—that teeming, throbbing thoroughfare with rows and rows of sari shops—to acquire a new wardrobe.

'I can't continue to wear shirts and pants,' he reasons. 'I've got to switch over to ladies' garments soon.'

People cast glances at us as we walk past them. Some pass lewd remarks that we are forced to take in our stride. To the booing, cat-calling public, Su probably comes across, in his present state, as a hijra or a prostitute from the city's red-light district. Su, however, is unperturbed. He calmly steps in and out of an assortment of shops, picking out saris, blouses, salwar kameezes, brassieres, even a frock! My role is no more than that of a hanger-on though, to be fair, he does consult me on matters of design and colour, as Indian wives invariably do their husbands.

I can't help looking at the salesmen who attend to us, some of whom snigger as he haggles over the price in the high-pitched voice he's trying to cultivate. 'Madam, our item is cheap and best,' they tell him in English. They are Marathi-speaking locals and so is he but, as things stand, they can't imagine someone who looks as weird as him to be a Maharashtrian.

In the end, Su's saddled with a bill of several thousand rupees. But he doesn't look to me for payment. Instead, he vainly opens his newly acquired red handbag (with real gold embroidery) and pays up. I don't even have to ask from where the dough has come. Obviously, it's the Americans who seem to derive a spectacular thrill from robbing us of our manhood.

The next day, Su shocks me further by making a bonfire of his old clothes. 'No boy's clothes for me anymore,' he winks, donning his frock. The flames all but set our flat on fire, almost compelling me to dial 102 and call for the fire brigade! Somehow, the pile of smouldering clothes and the ashen smell that emanates from it remind me of the freedom struggle when satyagrahis burned perfectly good shirts, pants and three-piece suits imported from London. Su is as determined as Mahatma Gandhi. There's no stopping him from doing anything that seizes his fancy.

Moving about the house, one day in his frock, the next day in a Punjabi dress—saving the saris and blouses for more formal occasions—Su asks me to give him a new name.

'Among us Maharashtrians, wives are given a new name by their husbands after marriage,' he lets me know, as if I'm an ignoramus. 'So what name can you suggest? Suman? Sumati? Sunita?'

'I'm against women changing their names,' I retort, 'because I'm a feminist. I wouldn't even like women to take on their husbands' surnames after marriage, let alone change their first names.'

Nevertheless, we go through a whole list of female names beginning with Su. These include Sunaina, Sunanda, Suhasini and Subulaksmi. Finally, we settle for Sumati—both Suhasini and Subulaksmi narrowly losing out because they are needlessly musical. Of course, the choice is really his, I being against the whole thing from the start. 'I would like to be known as Mrs Sumati Naidu,' he declares.

'Okay, memsahib,' I consent, and am suddenly overcome by another fear—am I being transformed into the proverbial henpecked hubby who dances to his wife's tune? Who gives in to her every whim and fancy?

Now Sudhir may have become Sumati, but I'm accustomed to calling him Su and the name he's adopted makes it possible for me to do so still. With some luck, therefore, I shall never once have to bring the absurd name Sumati to my lips. The real problem is with pronouns. I simply can't think of him as a she. Su knows this and confronts me one muggy afternoon.

'In your mind, you refer to me as "he" even now, no?' he accusingly asks. I confess I do, and explain in self-defence that it'll take me a while to get used to thinking of him as "she". But Su will have none of it. 'This very minute, you must come with me to the Sai Baba temple and take a vow,' he says.

'What sort of vow?'

'That never again, even in your thoughts or when you have a dialogue with yourself in the WC, will you think of me as "he". That person is dead and there's no point in seducing his ghost.'

This is thought control of a kind that even George Orwell could not have anticipated! And the year is 1984! However, in order not to make it an issue, I comply. I accompany Su to the local Sai Baba temple, coconut in hand, and take the desired pledge.

'Dear lord, from this day—nay, from this very minute—I promise never to think of the person standing by my side, with whom I'm in love, either as Sudhir or as "he". Always, always, it shall be Sumati and it shall be "she". If ever I forget, please give me a rap on the head. Amen.'

Outside, there are little shops selling bangles and other ladies' paraphernalia like fancy bindis. We spend close to an hour examining their wares, but leave empty-handed.

9

Six months pass. Su's electrolysis and hormone therapy begin to bear fruit. What little facial and bodily hair she once had is now all but gone. Her breasts look real. Even her voice has become feminine. Shriller and with more treble (and more terrible) than that of the two famous women I can think of—Usha Uthup and Luku Sanyal. One an accomplished singer, the other a TV star. Her beauty spot looks ravishing.

We're at the passport office with one Mr Shaikh—a travel agent who's struggling to get us our passports. The officers in charge are convinced we're forgers trying to travel on fake passports. I don't blame them. While Su's birth certificate and other documents declare her to be male, the person actually before them is a female.

'Sir, Mrs Sumati Naidu was formerly Mr Sudhir Raikar,' I try to explain to them in vain. 'Now, she has had a sex-change operation and become a woman. Believe me, she is the same person. One and the same.'

But the officers are adamant. 'Why?' one of them has the audacity to ask. 'Why she has become lady?' Another says, 'Go and bring an affidavit to that effect from a first class magistrate, and then we will issue the passport.'

Mr Shaikh takes the officers to one side and tries to bribe them. But it boomerangs. In corrupt India, the officers dealing with us are shining examples of honesty and dedication. Fit to head the ACB!

'Do you want us to hand you over to police?' they threaten him.

I'm so exhausted by the whole thing that I saunter off to the loo. The footrests in the Indian-style toilet remind me of my friend, the Azad College Marathi lecturer. A poet too, he once read out a poem to me:

The padukas in the loo
To which god do they belong?

As if this wasn't sacrilege enough, the man had gone on to deconstruct the word 'paduka'. Padu ka? May I fart? Perhaps the poem would be an appropriate birthday gift for the brainless passport officers who refuse to see reason.

The first class judicial magistrate they send us to is no

R. Raj Rao

better. 'How can you claim she was a gentleman when she's looking every bit like a lady?' he asks us with a lecherous smile. I want to know who gave him his law degree and why it shouldn't be revoked. But we leave the nincompoop alone.

Mr Shaikh has an idea worth pursuing. 'Suppose we get a certificate from Dr Doctor himself?' he asks. 'Or better still, can Dr Doctor be brought to the magistrate's office in person?'

For this, of course, we have to butter up Gaurav. He alone is on backslapping terms with the doctor. Gaurav obliges—my bottle of Scotch proving to be quite unnecessary—and so does Dr Doctor, who certifies on his letterhead, in one of those to-whom-it-may-concern type letters, that Su was a male on whom he had performed sex-reassignment surgery.

A couple of days later, armed with the letter, we march back to the magistrate. Su has become something of a liability, what with her insistence on make-up and click-clacking high-heeled sandals that make us needlessly conspicuous. Some think she is a Bollywood extra. 'Mohamaya,' they call out—familiar, apparently, with the names of extras too. Mr Shaikh is embarrassed but puts on a façade of professionalism. He's in business for financial gain and must be willing to serve every type of client. Even he, with all his experience, is unprepared for the magistrate's response to Dr Doctor's letter.

'But what is proof that he is government-recognized doctor?' he asks, returning our certificate. 'Bring me attested copy of his MBBS or equivalent degree and then I will consider.'

Frustrated, but trying not to lose our cool, we rush back to Gaurav who rushes back to the doctor. Dr Doctor wishes to know the names of both the first class magistrate and the passport officials who are making us run from pillar to post. We don't readily have their names, but Mr Shaikh (his resourcefulness be praised!) procures them on our behalf, initials and all. Dr Doctor then calls up a minister of state upon whom he had once operated (not a sex-change operation, he assures us) and asks for a favour. In no time, our passports are delivered to our doorstep. Even the police verification is waived.

I open Su's passport and am shocked to find both 'Male' and 'Female' struck off and replaced by 'Other'. All the same, we're glad to have the documents in our hands—our first symbols of liberation, of the new life in store for us. Our passports, literally, to freedom and happiness.

We celebrate with a dinner attended by Gaurav, Vivek and Mr Shaikh. Dr Doctor, naturally, is also on our guest list, but is too busy—and too big—to accept our invitation. Mr Shaikh, devout Muslim though he is, gets obscenely drunk. Gaurav takes us all to his room where he strips Mr Shaikh naked, the man offering no resistance whatsoever. *He* is big in another way. Afterwards, the five of us have an orgy reminiscent of the party we once had in this very room. Mr Shaikh, I notice jealously, squeezes Su's breast and penetrates her vaginally. His circumcision makes it easy. What's worse, Su does not restrain him. On the contrary, she appears fulfilled.

But I too have my compensation—Vivek. It's probably the last time I shall be with a man.

10

The next day, in spite of our hangover, we travel to the US consulate in Bombay to apply for our visas to the Land of Plenty. There's no chance of bumping into my folks, whose flat is a good five miles away. Yet, I'm apprehensive. What if they or any of their cronies see us? I don't want them to set eyes on Su in her present state. They might abduct one or both of us and pour ice-cold water on our immigration plans. Even as we alight from the taxi, I furtively look around for signs of trouble.

Su, however, is calm. 'Aho, this is Bombay with a population of eight million,' she reminds me. 'So work out the possibility of coming face to face with your mummy-daddy.'

Her engineering studies, I think to myself, were not entirely in vain. At least she understands the concept of probability. Nor is she widely off the mark. The crowds in Bombay are so dense that, even if my folks were to suddenly materialize out of thin air, we could always merge into the mob to seek cover. Still, for the sake of argument, I refute Su. 'It's easy for you to say so,' I tease her, 'because this is my hometown, not yours. If we were in Belgaum, I bet you'd be equally scared of being spotted by your folks.'

Su has an answer for this as well. Her operation has made her argumentative, though this wasn't one of the side effects listed by Dr Doctor. 'That's because Belgaum, unlike Bombay, is a teeny-weeny town. Everyone knows everyone else.'

I leave the subject alone and turn my attention to the scene inside the consulate, which, in spite of its plush interiors, orange carpets and a giant portrait of President Reagan, resembles the waiting hall of VT station, with rows and rows of plastic chairs. Whole families, with babies in tow and frequently accompanied by decrepit old grandmothers and grandfathers with one foot in the grave, wait to be interviewed by the Americans. I am told many of them had spent the previous night sleeping on the pavement outside the consulate, just to be in queue. I had not known that so many people from different corners of the country disliked India so much that they wanted to board the first plane that would get them out of it.

'What's left in India?' a suited-booted gentleman with rimless spectacles, seated next to me, asks in clipped accents. 'India is shit. Indian cars, the Fiat and the Ambassador, are a joke. The States is the place to be, the happening place where all the action is. Heard of the American dream? Know what it means? That anyone who's got what it takes can make it. Can we say the same about India? Nehruvian socialism is a hoax.'

So much for patriotism. For the martyrdom of those who had won us freedom.

However, when it's the gentleman's turn to be interviewed by the chief visa officer—a surly African-American—he's refused a visa. He looks downcast and slips away, too humiliated to disclose the reasons for his failure.

I begin to get anxious. Unlike the others, we have no surety bonds and share certificates to prove we weren't going to America to milk it. All I have is my bank passbook with a shameful three-figure balance. What if our application is rejected? Will Dr Doctor give us permanent shelter in his home? Most hopefuls who are turned away have failed to prove that they do not wish to stay in America for good. The chief visa officer and his colleagues suspect that, their proof of wealth notwithstanding, they use higher education, or work, or tourism, or whatever reason they have stated in the application, as mere excuses for gaining entry into the world's richest country, from where they never intend to return. This would be okay with the officers, provided the fellows in question were European and white, but not if they were wogs from a third-world country without enough to eat. It's like allowing slum-dwellers to enter our upmarket flats and inhabit them for life. Who in his right mind would permit that?

Our names are called out and our heartbeats quicken. But after we have finished introducing ourselves and narrating our strange tale, Ms Alison Brown, the lady officer who has been assigned to us, is suddenly very affable. Unlike the Indian officials in the passport office, Su's ambiguous identity does not baffle her. Nor does my warped sexuality. 'We know what you must go through,' she benignly says. 'And our country, the United States of America, will be very pleased to give you refuge. We shall admit you to the States on very special grounds—asylum. Asylum is generally given to people who perceive a threat to their lives in their own country. And I'm quite convinced that, for the two of you, life in India would be no bed of roses. You may stay in the US as long as you wish.'

With these reassuring words, Ms Brown smiles and stamps our passports. It's the rosiest smile I've ever seen. Thank God she and not the chief visa officer interviewed us.

On coming out of the consulate into the warm Bombay sun, we're mobbed by the people in the queue. They can tell from our faces that we are successful. 'Kya puccha? Aapne kya answer diya?' they ask us in Hindi.

Brushing them aside, I hug Su and decide to give her another tour of the metro by local train and BEST bus. The last time we had taken such a trip, during Su's first visit to the city, had been in very different circumstances. Who knew, then, that a day like this would also dawn in our lives?

'Bombay is the poor man's New York,' I tell her, as the crowds jostle us. 'So you had better get thoroughly acquainted with the fake before you encounter the real.'

Each time we step into a jam-packed train, Su's bottom is pinched. To the repressed commuter, she's Mohamaya, the Bollywood extra, the poor man's Helen, complete with violet rouge and indigo lipstick. 'Madam ko ladies mein bhejo,' an elderly Parsi at Borivali station advises me.

'This won't happen in New York,' I whisper into Su's ears. But she's occupied with other thoughts.

'What did the lady at the consulate say?' she asks, looking worried. 'That she was giving us asylum. Does it mean she thinks we're crazy? Only madcaps are sent to the lunatic asylum.'

11

In Bandra, a hijra goes past. I retrace my steps to check out the familiar face. Begum Sahiba!

'Hello, Begum Sahiba,' I insolently say. 'Aren't you from Belgaum?'

A fataka clap comes my way. 'I am from Belgaum but my name is Anarkali,' she retorts. 'And you?'

I tell her all about ourselves, introducing her to Su who looks like her twin. Begum Sahiba immediately puts one of her silver bangles on Su's wrist and presses her knuckles to the sides of her head in blessing.

'Keep it on always and it will protect you from the evil eye,' she says to Su.

A young koti joins us and she tells us he's her hubby, Raj Kumar. I realize he's the winsome guy who had sung in a shrill voice at Belgaum station, while Begum Sahiba danced.

We sit in a restaurant where I order falooda with ice cream for all of us.

'What brings you to Bombay?' I ask Begum Sahiba.

'Oh, business. There's a limit to what we can earn in a small town like Belgaum. So we make periodic trips to big cities like Bombay.'

When we tell Begum Sahiba we're off to America for good, she blinks. 'What's wrong with our own desh?' she asks. 'Why must you cross the seven seas?' Then, figuring it out, she says, 'Ah! It's because you are educated. See what education does? It makes you ashamed to live in your own country, on your own terms. You have to run away. Look at us hijras. We live as we please and no one tells us a thing. To hell with the world!'

Begum Sahiba addresses Su. 'What's the difference between you and me?' she asks. 'I'm a hijra, and you are someone from high society who's had a sex-change operation, paying thousands. In truth, however, we're no different.

I ask Begum Sahiba about Raj Kumar.

'I'm his first wife,' she says. 'But no one outside the clan recognizes our marriage. He has another wife to whom his family got him legally married. The funny thing is that she does not know about me.'

Su wonders whom Raj Kumar loves more, Begum Sahiba or his official wife?

'Of course, Anarkali,' comes Raj Kumar's prompt answer. 'I got married to Lakshmi, my legal wife, only to keep up appearances. Now society thinks I'm a respectably married man with two children. Their opinion is important to me. I cannot be bindaas like Anarkali. To be ostracized by society is unthinkable to us kotis. We can't live a gay lifestyle either, like you westernized types. You may say that we want to have the best of both worlds.'

12

Shortly afterwards, we find ourselves at Sahar International Airport. We're in the Air India queue, waiting to check in our baggage and collect our boarding passes. The flight, a Boeing 747 Jumbo, isn't till much later, in the dead of night, but airport procedures require us to be here aeons before time. Already, the queue is a mile long, and we recognise some of the people we had met at the consulate while they waited for their visas.

'You too?' a Gujarati businessman with a leather briefcase and an upturned nose asks me, laughing.

'I too,' I reply.

'Madam is Mrs?' he continues inquisitively, pointing to Su. He laughs for no apparent reason, as if he has inhaled laughing gas.

'No, girlfriend.'

I turn to Vivek who's here to see us off. 'Gaurav's on his way,' he informs me. 'Should be here any minute.'

'Well, thanks for everything,' I say, squeezing his hand till he shrieks. 'Had it not been for the two of you, we'd never be here. What luck I met you guys at the Engineering College Hostel. I still remember the day Gaurav first followed me, and I quickened my pace just to get rid of him.'

'It's your destiny,' shrugs Vivek in his minimalist manner. 'We're only instruments.'

Su's ears cock up at the word 'instrument'. More proof that the engineer in her is still alive. What about your instrument? I want to ask her spitefully. I used to be so fond of it. However, I check myself as we're in a public place.

Gaurav arrives in a highly agitated state. 'Bad news,' he pants. 'They've ganged up, all of them, and are on their way here with the cops to stop you from catching your flight.'

'Who?' I yell.

'Everyone. Your folks, their friends, Sumati's dad, Ravi Humbe, SVS members—even Ram for Christ's sake!'

'How do you know?'

'Don't ask. I have my sources.'

'So what do we do?'

'Pray that the queue moves fast. Once you have your boarding passes, you can proceed to your departure gate where only bona fide passengers are allowed. No one can reach you there.'

But the queue inches forward at a snail's pace. After all it's janata, economy class. The business class queue is short, but we won't be entertained there. Why don't they have separate 'asylum' queues, I wonder, just as they have asylum visas? Seized by panic, I keep casting backward glances to see if our tormentors have arrived. Su presses my hand to reassure me.

Gaurav tries to ease our tension by giving us last-minute instructions. 'Wear your seat belts as soon as you've taken your seats,' he says. 'Don't remove them till the flight takes off and seat-belt signs are switched off.'

I'm livid. We may be travelling by plane for the first time in our lives, but he doesn't have to make us look like villagers from Buti Bori! I mean, what will our fellow passengers in the queue, like the Gujju with the upturned nose, think?

Then he reiterates something he has told us a dozen times already. 'Our friends Brian and David will come to receive you at JFK Airport. As you know, they're a couple. They'll drive you to your apartment and help you start your new life. Not to worry, everything is under control.'

The suspense is nail-biting. Assuming Gaurav's news about our folks is correct, will they get us or won't they? I pray that the traffic to the airport is heavy and they're stuck in a nerve-wracking jam. The queue has moved a few paces forward, no doubt, but not enough.

Su, as always, is less frantic and less frenetic than me. 'I don't think what Gaurav says is true,' she whispers into my ear. 'How on earth would your parents or mine come to know all of this?'

'You may be right,' I whisper back. 'But we can't take any chances. You don't want our plans to go awry at the last minute, do you?'

I keep looking at my watch and wiping the perspiration off the nape of my neck. It's useless. The queue moves so slowly it seems unlikely that the last passengers in it will catch their flight. If there's no sign of our enemies yet, we have only Providence to thank.

Then, like a Borivali-slow, we reach the counter all at once and are treated extra-courteously by the lady and gentleman on duty, on account of our refugee visas. At last, Su's gender is no longer an issue.

'Would you like aisle or window seats?' asks the lady.

'Smoking or non-smoking seats?' asks the gentleman.

'Give us anything,' I say, 'but please make it snappy. It's a life-or-death question for us.'

'We understand,' says the gentleman as he hands us our baggage tags and wishes us an enjoyable flight.

We quickly hug Gaurav and Vivek. All of us have tears in our eyes. Perhaps this is the last time the two of us will see the two of them.

'Be on your way,' says Gaurav, looking around to see if the party of heteros has arrived. 'And write to us as soon as you reach.'

We get our passports stamped at the immigration desk and scram towards Gate Number 20 from where our Jumbo is to depart. Here, we spend another uncertain hour before our flight is announced and we actually step into the plane.

But even as we take our seats and fiddle with our seat belts, I'm uneasy. I want the flight to take off this very minute for I've lost my faith in humankind. Dr Raikar, Ravi Humbe and my own folks are perfectly capable of lying on the tarmac in front of our plane, saying, 'Over our dead bodies.' This might leave the airline with no option but to deplane us. Yet, instead of being airborne, the Missing Links show us a film on what we must do in case the plane lands in water!

Finally, the engines start and, after taxiing on the runway for a bit, the airplane takes off. The brightly illuminated city of Bombay beneath seems rocked by a phenomenal earthquake. Both Su and I have a funny feeling in our ears but we do not know that we can ask for earplugs. I close my eyes. When they open again, God knows how many seconds later, I look out the window. The lights have disappeared and we're flying over the Arabian Sea. I kiss Su on the lips, to which she does not object.

'Do what you want now,' she says. 'We're no longer in India.'

'The first time I met your father,' I remind her, 'he said he would like you to go to America one day. And now we're actually going there.'

The stewardesses bring us delicious continental snacks and a choice of alcoholic beverages. As we munch and sip, our names are announced on the intercom. We flush. The captain addresses us. 'Please come to the cockpit at once,' he says in a nasal voice. We turn pale. All eyes are on us as we leave our seats (and our eats) and walk down the aisle, first through economy and then through business class, to reach the cockpit, fearing the worst.

'Good evening,' the Captain greets us and I realize he has

a cold. 'There's a call for you from control tower on my wireless set here. Only in emergencies is this allowed, I tell you. Speak up to make yourselves heard.'

The captain hands me his headphones. There's a disturbance in the line but the voice, unmistakably, is my father's. 'Hello, son,' he begins. 'Just want to say that you are our children, no matter what. We will always love you. We've come to know everything but it makes no difference to us. Enjoy your stay in America and come back soon.'

'Dad, we're emigrating,' I manage to say. 'There's no question of coming back. But yes, we'll keep in touch. And thanks for your concern.'

But my father is adamant. 'What will you do in America, idiot? Here you have a college job. Your wife can stay at home as our daughter-in-law, our bahu, and help with the household chores. Your mother and I, after all, are getting old.'

'That's sweet of you, Dad,' I say. No one has ever before called Su my wife—it sounds scandalous!

Dr Raikar is the next to speak. I give Su the headphones, but it's me the gentleman wants.

'Son, your father is right. All of us love you. We want you to be happy, even if we disagree with your views. I apologize for throwing you out of my house. Sudhir is now yours. Please look after him in America, but come back to your motherland. If you had been an Ayurvedic doctor, I would have given you my practice. I think you should resume your college job in Bombay when you return.'

'Uncle, Sudhir is no longer a he,' I say, amazed at my guts. 'He's a she, and her new name is Sumati. Sumati gets offended if we refer to her in the masculine gender.'

'Yes, yes, I know. But as I said, you are our children and this comes first.'

'So kind of you,' I say and pass on the headphones to Su. Father and daughter speak interminably in Marathi. When they're done, it's the turn of the ladies, my mother first.

'Look after yourselves,' she sobs into the control-tower phone. 'Don't compromise on food. I know my career may not have permitted me to be an ideal mother. But I promise to make amends.'

'Thanks, Mom, I appreciate. Rest assured I love you.'

Su's mother and Sneha take over, and there's large-scale weeping on both sides, flustering the captain. He gives Su sidelong glances but she doesn't get the hint. In the end, he has to put his foot down and grab the receiver from her hands.

'I'm sorry, I can't let you speak on the wireless anymore,' he says. 'It'll endanger the lives of 300 passengers.'

Su blows her nose into a paper napkin. We walk back to our seats.

As we pass through business class, I stop in my tracks. There's a passenger by the window whom we know. He is seated by himself—the seat next to him is vacant. He still sports his *Jewel Thief* cap and goggles, even on the flight.

'Hi Farouq,' I say. 'Recognize me? What are you doing here?'

As I talk to him, Su slips away and heads straight for our seats. She obviously doesn't want Farouq to see her in her new avatar. Not that Farouq will recognize her. But if he does, we'll have to provide him with lengthy explanations. Where do we begin? If we're outlaws, so is he, considering he's an American spy.

Initially, Farouq pretends not to recognize me. 'Excuse me,' he says. 'I don't think I know you. You are probably mistaking me for someone else.' Then he puts an end to the farce himself. 'Was only pulling your leg,' he laughs and pats the seat next to him. 'Sit down.'

'But I don't have a business class ticket,' I protest.

'Never mind,' he chuckles. 'A few minutes won't do you any harm. You're not going to be sitting here all the way to America . . . So, give me all the dope. How's your yaar?'

R. Raj Rao

'Oh, I'm done with him,' I lie. 'I'm off to America to teach at Yale.'

'Wow!'

'How about you?'

'I too have chucked my course at the Engineering College. I now work full-time for the American Intelligence Corporation.'

'I know,' I mumble and immediately regret my faux pas.

'What?' Farouq asks, astonished.

How can I tell him that I had ripped open one of his confidential letters and read it? 'No . . . Nothing,' I stammer. 'What I meant was that I know you quit the Engineering College. Ram told me.' I want to say to his face: So you are an Iraqi spy! But I cannot bring myself to utter those impolite words. Instead, I ask him, 'What takes you to America right now?'

'Espionage,' he replies, but volunteers no further information. As if I don't know what his assignment is—to collect hormone weapons that will turn Iraqi soldiers homosexual!

As we are thus engaged, Farouq scares me by pulling out a syringe from his jacket pocket and pretending to inject me.

'What's this?' I scream.

'Insulin,' he laughs. 'Didn't you know I was diabetic? Are you as well?'

We go on like this for a while. In the end, Farouq owns up to the nature of his work by telling me everything himself. Then, he shocks me with his parting words: 'We are going to make more people in the world like you.' This means he had known about me all along!

The air hostess requests me to return to my seat. I say goodbye to Farouq and abruptly leave. I walk back to my seat in economy class. The food and drink are still on our trays. Passengers loiter in the aisles, waiting for the toilets to be free.

I tell Su all about Farouq. Then we discuss our cockpit telephone call.

'What a fairy-tale ending to our story,' I whisper into Su's ear, still dazed. 'Who says Bollywood isn't for real?'

Bollywood reminds Su of something she had forgotten—her cabin baggage has sheaves of film songs that we must translate on the flight.